A *NEW YORK TIMES* NOTABLE BOOK OF THE YEAR

"One of the season's best escapes . . . Leonard's prose and his hero keep as cool as a mug of beer under the trees."

Washington Post Book World

"Explosive . . . Elmore Leonard [has] a strong style and infallible ear. . . . *Cat Chaser* demonstrates the quality that has given him such a wide following. . . . It really moves."

New York Times Book Review

"The reigning master of hard-action crime fiction . . . Few fiction writers match the artful ability of Elmore Leonard, first to persuade you to read his next sentence, then to draw you into reading his next chapter, and finally to seduce you into reading his entire book."

Cincinnati Enquirer

"The coolest, hottest writer in America."
Chicago Tribune

"Elmore Leonard is an awfully good writer of the sneaky sort; he's so good, you don't notice what he's up to."

Donald E. Westlake

"He turns out first-rate thrillers . . . crime books that sketch the dark side of the dollar, a world where street-crazies plot, scams rise and fall . . . Leonard has simply set loose the most frightening psychopaths in the pages of literature. . . . By any standard, 'Dutch' Leonard is a rare find."

Bergen Record

"America's finest, funniest low-life novelist . . . gives his readers everything they would expect: a sense of place and milieu, lively characters, drop-dead dirty talk, situations you can't describe in a family newspaper . . . and poetic justice flecked by the unfairness of life."

Boston Globe

"Elmore Leonard is the master of the oddball. His stories are quirky and his characters are definitely not the people who live next door (unless you live in a very strange neighborhood). . . . His prose is heaven-sent."

Milwaukee Journal-Sentinel

"The best writer of crime fiction alive."
Newsweek

Books by Elmore Leonard

And in Hardcover

When the Women Come Out to Dance

ELMORE LEONARD

CAT CHASER

HarperTorch
An Imprint of HarperCollinsPublishers

This is a work of fiction. Names, characters, places, and incidents are products of the author's imagination or are used fictitiously and are not to be construed as real. Any resemblance to actual events, locales, organizations, or persons, living or dead, is entirely coincidental.

HARPERTORCH
An Imprint of HarperCollins*Publishers*
10 East 53rd Street
New York, New York 10022-5299

Copyright © 1982 by Elmore Leonard
Back cover author photo © Linda Solomon
Excerpt from *Tishomingo Blues* copyright © 2002 by Elmore Leonard, Inc.
ISBN: 0-06-051222-9

First HarperTorch paperback printing: February 2003
First William Morrow trade paperback printing: November 1998
First William Morrow hardcover printing: June 1982

HarperCollins ®, HarperTorch™, and ♥™ are trademarks of Harper-Collins Publishers Inc.

Printed in the United States of America

Visit HarperTorch on the World Wide Web at www.harpercollins.com

10 9 8 7 6 5 4 3 2 1

For Katy Leonard

_____

1

MORAN'S FIRST IMPRESSION of Nolen Tyner: He looked like a high risk, the kind of guy who falls asleep smoking in bed. No luggage except for a six-pack of beer on the counter and the *Miami Herald* folded under his arm.

He reminded Moran of a show-business personality going to seed. Long two-tone hair thinning fast, what was left of a blond pompadour receding from a sunburned peeling forehead. Moran could see dark roots that matched his dark, neatly trimmed mustache. The khaki shirt was neat too, freshly laundered, faded, the cuffs of the sleeves turned up once, shirttails hanging out, aviator sunglasses hooked to one of the flap pockets. Onetime dude over the hill at forty. Maybe half in the bag. Dreamy eyes looked up from the registration card to the calendar on the wall behind Moran, then half-closed, squinting.

"Is it October already?"

It was almost November.

He filled in another line of information about himself, looked up and stared directly at Moran, deadpan.

"This is the Coconut Palms Resort Apartments. Is that correct?"

"That's correct," Moran said, just as dry.

Nolen Tyner's gaze shifted to the inside window of the office that looked out toward the Atlantic Ocean, past the oval-shaped pool and empty lounge chairs. His sleepy eyes returned to Moran.

"Then why don't I see any palm trees?"

"Some bugs ate 'em," Moran said. "I had to have six trees removed."

"It doesn't bother you," Nolen Tyner said, "you call this place the Coconut *Palms* there isn't a single palm tree out there? Isn't that false advertising?"

"The high rise on the south side of us, nine stories, is called the Nautilus," Moran said, "but I don't think it's a submarine. The one on the other side, it's ten stories, is the Aurora. Tell me if you think it looks like a radiant glow in the upper atmosphere. That'll be thirty dollars. You're in Number Five, right next to the office."

Nolen Tyner continued to stare at Moran. He nodded. "Okay. How about if I sit out by the pool and drink my beer and I don't take a room? How much is that?"

"That's also thirty dollars," Moran said. "For the ambience and the music."

"I don't hear any music."

"I haven't turned it on yet," Moran said. "I'll tell you what though. You can take your six-pack up the road, you might find something more to your liking. Maybe even less expensive."

Nolen Tyner was looking at Moran's beard, his white T-shirt and cutoff jeans. "You work here or own the place?"

"Both," Moran said. "My desk clerk'd stand here and chat with you all afternoon, but he's off today."

"Being courteous to people who come in off the street," Nolen Tyner said, smiling a little, "I imagine that can be a pain in the ass at times, huh?"

"It can if you let it," Moran said.

Moran looked at the reservation card.

Nolen Tyner, 201 Alhambra Circle, Coral Gables, Fla. 33134. Make of car: '76 Porsche. No license number.

Written in an arty back-leaning style, half-printed. Give him an "A" for neatness but an "F" for lying about his home address, since 201 Alhambra Circle was a big glass building, the Ponce de Leon Plaza, where his former wife's lawyer had his offices. It wasn't more than a mile from where Moran had lived during the seven years of the marriage.

If Nolen Tyner did live in Coral Gables or had an office there and he liked to sit outside in the afternoon and drink beer, why didn't he go to Bayfront Park? Why come all the way up to Pompano, an hour's drive, pay thirty bucks for a room and then sit outside? Which the guy was doing now. Lying in a lounge chair on the afternoon shadyside of the pool. Holding a can of beer on his chest, moving it almost in slow motion when he'd take a sip. Wearing his sporty safari shirt, but also wearing, Moran noticed, very unsporty black socks with his open-toed sandals. If he wasn't meeting a woman here—and after about an hour and three cans of beer it didn't look like it—then he was either hiding or looking for action.

But if he was hiding he'd stay inside. Wouldn't he?

And if he was looking for action and had heard something about the Coconut Palms' SECRETARY SPECIALS—advertised twice a year in big-city papers up north—it was possible he'd come with the idea of picking up some poor secretary who was here by herself, bored out of her mind. Except that October was a very lean month for secretaries compared to February and March. And the guy had not said anything clever or hinted around about looking for girls.

So maybe he was looking for somebody in particular. And if that was the case, without checking the guest chart Moran knew who it would be. Not the secretaries from Dayton in Number Three. Not the ones from Fort Wayne in Four. Or the elderly couple who wanted Seven so they could keep an eye on their Buick parked on the street. No, it would have to be the afternoon lovers in Number One, the lower oceanfront apartment.

They had been meeting here every afternoon except the weekend for the past eight days: the young Cuban-looking guy who wore rings and chains, gold-rimmed sunglasses up in a nest of thick hair, and the stylish woman who was about ten years older than the guy and probably married to a Cuban businessman in Miami. The guy had signed in *Mario Prado* and Moran, taking in the guy's glistening hairdo, said, "Haven't I seen you on TV?" Mario Prado said yeah, he did guest shots on Tony Marvin's show; he was playing cocktail piano at the Sheraton in Palm Beach; his manner so bored, relaxed, Moran was afraid the guy might collapse, melt into a puddle of grease. Mario took Number One oceanfront for a month, paid fifteen hundred cash in advance, without Moran asking for it, and the mystery woman appeared a short time later.

Mario Prado waited on the street, sunglasses over his eyes now, until the gray Mercedes pulled up. He took a case of champagne out of the trunk. After that they arrived separately each afternoon between one and two and usually left about five, not much later. Neither of them ever spent the night.

One time, a few days ago, the woman arrived on schedule, but the piano player failed to show. Moran watched her come out of Number One to stand by the low cement wall that separated the yard from the beach, the woman in a white sundress and heels, her dark hair shining in the sunlight, tied back with a violet scarf. She had her arms folded and seemed impatient, though she didn't move much. Moran went out in his T-shirt and cutoffs to get a look at her.

He said, "Mrs. Prado, how're you today?"

She appeared to be in her late thirties, about Moran's age, stylishly thin, holding a languid model pose now, wrist bent on her hip, as she studied Moran from behind big round violet-tinted sunglasses.

"That's not my name," the woman said, with an edge but only the hint of an accent.

"It's the name your husband signed," Moran said.

"My *hus*band?" the woman said. "You think that's my *hus*band?"

"Well, whoever you are, we're glad to have you," Moran said. "You like me to put some music on? We've got outside speakers."

"I like you to beat it and leave me alone," the woman said and turned to look at the ocean. She had a nice profile, thin, straight nose, her hair pulled back tight to show round white earrings.

"Well, enjoy your stay," Moran said and got out of there. He couldn't imagine her being much fun. Maybe that was why they brought all the champagne, get her loosened up. Lula, Moran's part-time maid, would come out of Number One in the morning with a plastic bag of trash and give him a report. " 'Nother dead soldier and the brandy's near touching bottom. Should see how they tear up a bed." Moran never went into occupied rooms out of curiosity, to see how people lived or what they'd brought with them; he respected their privacy. But he did consider sticking his head into Number One, some quiet evening after the lovers had gone. Inspect the setting on the off chance it might reveal something about them. Still, it had to be a purely sexual relationship, and if that was the case then what would he be looking for, pecker tracks? He could think of a lot more important things to do— if he put his mind to it.

The day following the brief meeting with the woman the piano player came into the office, his pink shirt open to show his chains and said to Moran, "I understand you try to make the moves on the lady with me. I'll tell you something, man, what's good for you. Stay away from her. You understand?"

At this point the piano player and the woman had used up only about two hundred of the fifteen-hundred-dollar advance. The numbers registered in Moran the innkeeper's mind as he considered grabbing the piano player by his pink shirt and throwing him out on the street, and the numbers gave him pause. It wouldn't hurt to be polite, would it?

Moran said, "I'm sorry if I gave Mrs. Prado the wrong impression. I didn't much more'n say hi to her."

"You ask her if she want to dance with you."

"No, I'm not a dancer," Moran said. "I asked if she wanted me to turn some music on." He grinned in his brownish beard. "I suppose a lady as attractive as your wife has guys hitting on her all the time. I can see where she'd become, well, defensive." Which was not an easy thing for Moran to say. Now if the piano player would accept this and leave . . .

But he didn't. Mario Prado spread his ringed and lacquered fingers on the counter like it was a keyboard, like he was going to play Moran a tune, and said, "I hear you go near her again you going to be in deep shit, man. You got it?"

Moran said to him, no longer grinning, "Mario, there's a certain amount of shit you have to put up with in this business, but you just went over the limit. You want, I'll give you the rest of your money back. But if I do I'll probably pick you up and throw you in the swimming pool, and with all those fucking chains you got on you'll probably sink to the bottom and drown. But it's up to you. You want your money back?"

The piano player squinted his dark eyes and got hard drawn lines around his nostrils. This, Moran assumed, was to indicate nerves of ice banking the Latin fire inside. Moran wondered if the guy practiced it.

The piano player said, "Just wait, man. Just wait."

That was a few days ago and Moran was still waiting for the Cuban's revenge—the guy and the woman in the apartment right now doing whatever they did. While Mr. Nolen Tyner reclined in a lounge chair on the shady side of the pool, beer can upright on his chest, as though he might be sighting the beer can between the V of his out-turned sandals, aiming his attention directly at oceanfront Number One. Keeping an eye on the Latin lovers who, Moran had decided, deserved one another.

Wait a minute. Or was Nolen Tyner watching out for them, protecting them? Hired by the piano player.

Christ, he could be keeping an eye on *you*, Moran thought. It gave him a strange feeling. It reinforced the premonition he'd been aware of for a couple of weeks now, that he was about to walk into something that would change his life.

Except that it wasn't time for Moran's life to take another turn. He was thirty-eight, not due for a change until forty-two. He believed in seven-year cycles because he couldn't ignore the fact that every seven years something happened and his life would take a turn in a new direction. Only one of his turns was anticipated, planned; the rest just seemed to happen, though with a warning, a feeling he'd get. Like now.

When he was seven years old he reached the age of reason and became responsible for his actions. He was told this in second grade, in catechism.

When he was fourteen a big eighteen-year-old Armenian girl who weighed about thirty pounds more than he did took him to bed one summer afternoon; she smelled funny, but it was something, what he learned the human body liked.

When he was eighteen he misplaced the reason he had acquired at seven and joined the Marines, Moran said to get out of being drafted, to have a choice in the matter, but really looking for action. Which he found.

When he was twenty-one, back on the cycle and through with his tour, he left the Marines and his hometown, Detroit, Michigan, and went to work for a cement company as a finisher, to make a lot of money. This was in Miami, Florida.

When he was twenty-eight Moran married a girl by the name of Noel Sutton and became rich. He went to work for Noel's dad as a condominium developer, wore a suit, bought a big house in Coral Gables and joined Leucadendra Country Club, never for any length of time at ease in Coral Gables high society. He couldn't figure out how those people could take themselves and what they did so seriously and still act bored. Nobody ever jumped up and said, "I'm rich and, Christ, is it great!" Moran knew it was not his kind of life.

And when he was thirty-five Noel, then thirty, divorced him. She said, "Do you think you can get by just being a hunk all your life? Well, you're wrong, you're already losing it." Answering her own question, which was a habit of Noel's. Moran told her answering her own questions was a character defect. That and trying to change him and always being pissed off at him about something. For not wearing the outfits she bought him with little animals and polo players on them. For not staying on his side of the court when they played mixed doubles and she never moved. For "constantly" bugging her about leaving her clothes on the floor, which he'd mentioned maybe a couple times and given up. For drinking beer out of the can. For not having his Marine Corps tattoo removed. For growing a beard. A lot of little picky things like that. He did shave off the beard, stared at his solemn reflection in the mirror—he looked like he was recovering from an operation—and immediately began growing another one. Henry Thoreau had said, "Beware of all enterprises that require new clothes." Moran believed those words ought to be cut in stone.

The divorce was not a bad turn in the cycle. Moran had never been able to say his wife's name out loud without feeling self-conscious or thinking of Christmas. So that was a relief, not having to say her name. Also, not having to look bright and aggressive when he was with her dad. Or look at beachfront property and picture high-rise condominiums blocking the view.

He had certainly been attracted to Noel, a petite little thing with closely cropped dark hair and a haughty ass: she seemed to be always at attention, her back arched, her perfect breasts and pert can sticking out proudly; but he wasn't sure now if it was love or horniness that had led him to marriage. In the divorce settlement Noel got the house in Coral Gables and a place her dad had given them in Key West and Moran got their investment property, a twelve-unit resort motel in Pompano Beach, the Coconut Palms without the palm trees.

Sort of a U-shaped compound, white with aqua

trim. Two levels of efficiencies along the street side of the property. A wing of four one-bedroom apartments, two on each level, that extended out toward the beach. The apartment wing was parallel to a white stucco one-bedroom Florida bungalow that also faced the beach. And the oval swimming pool was in between, in the middle of the compound.

Moran moved into the bungalow and found he liked living on the beach and being an innkeeper, once he'd hired a clerk-accountant and a part-time maid. He liked meeting the different people. He liked being in the sun most of the day, doing odd jobs, fishing for yellowtail and snapper once a week. Renting the efficiencies for fifty a day in season and the apartments for seventy-five Moran grossed around eighty thousand a year. Taxes, utilities, upkeep and salaries ran thirty-five to forty, so Moran wasn't exactly socking it away. Still, it was a nice life and he was in no hurry to change it.

Then why did he feel it was about to take another turn on him?

He was planning a trip next week: fly down to Santo Domingo in the Dominican Republic, a vacationland Moran had invaded with the Third Battalion, Sixth Marines in 1965 when a revolution broke out and Johnson sent in Marines and Airborne to safeguard American lives and while you're at it run out the Communists. "I'm not going to have another Cuba in the Caribbean," the president said. In his thirty-day war Cpl. George S. Moran, Bravo Company, Third Platoon, a First Squad fire-team leader, shot a sniper, was wounded, taken prisoner by the rebels, got a Purple Heart and met a Dominican girl he would never forget. He wanted to walk those streets again without sniper fire coming in and see what he remembered. He might even look up the girl who had once tried to kill him. See if she was still around.

Maybe it was the anticipation of the trip that Moran mistook for a premonition of something about to happen.

But maybe it was something else. Something winging in at him out of the blue.

2

THE FOLLOWING AFTERNOON at the municipal tennis courts, Moran worked his tail off to win two hard sets, hanging in there against a kid with a vicious serve and a red headband who'd try to stare him down whenever Moran called a close shot out of bounds. Moran was only in doubt about his calls a couple of times. He dinked the kid to death with left-handed backspin junk, sliding the kid around on the clay, until the kid threw his racket at the fence and dug out a ten-dollar bill folded to the size of a stamp. Moran said to him, "You're all right, kid. Keep at it." He had always wanted to call somebody "kid" and today was the first time.

When he got back to the Coconut Palms there was Nolen Tyner out by the pool with a six-pack.

Jerry Shea, sitting at the office desk with a pile of bills, was whistling as he made entries in the ledger. Moran never knew the songs Jerry whistled. He asked him today, what's the name of that? And Jerry said, "This Year's Crop of Kisses." Jerry was

a retired insurance salesman, sixty-seven, who
cocked his golf cap to one side, slapped his broken
blood vessels with Old Spice and went after lonely
widows who'd invite him up to their condominiums for dinner, happy to cook for somebody again,
have some fun. Moran pictured withered moth-
eaten flanks, or else globs of cellulite getting in the
way. Jerry said there was more active poon around
than you could shake a stick at. With the fat ones,
you rolled them in flour and looked for the wet spot.

Moran said, sitting down, taking off his tennis
shoes and socks, "That guy out there drinking
beer—"

"Mr. Nolen Tyner," Jerry said. "Works for Marshall Sisco Investigations, Incorporated, Miami.
Actually their office is in Coral Gables."

"He told you that?"

"Ask a person what they do, they generally tell
you," Jerry said. "Especially since I recognized the
address. We used to use Marshall Sisco on insurance investigations from time to time; it's a good
outfit. Nolen says he's been with them a year, but I
think he's part-time help. Before that played dinner
theaters up and down the coast and says he's been
in movies. He was an actor."

"I think he still is," Moran said. "He checked in
yesterday about two and left at six, didn't use the
room."

"Well, when he come in today," Jerry said, "he took it for a week. Number Five. I asked him was he taking some time off and he says well, you could say that. Sort of combining business with pleasure."

Moran got up and turned to the window to look at Nolen lounging in the shade. The two secretaries from Fort Wayne had their recliners on the cement walk out by the wall, aimed at the sun that soon would be hidden behind the condo next-door, the Aurora. Moran's gaze moved from their pink corrugated thighs to Number One.

"How about the lovers?"

"They're in there." Jerry swiveled around from the desk. "The woman got here first for a change. Then, when the piano player come, Nolen Tyner got up and went over to say something to him. They talked a few minutes, the piano player goes on inside Number One, then comes out again and has another talk with Mr. Tyner."

"Arguing?"

"I don't believe so. A lot of nodding, both of 'em, getting along fine. Then the piano player goes back inside and Mr. Tyner returns to his beer."

"This is a nice quiet place," Moran said. "I don't want some husband coming here with a gun."

"Maybe they're friends," Jerry said. "Or she's a rich woman and Nolen Tyner's her bodyguard;

why he thinks it's pretty good duty, combining, as he says, business with pleasure."

"Maybe," Moran said. "But I better find out."

He didn't want to talk to the guy in his sweaty whites, barefoot; it wasn't his natural image. It reminded him of the country club, standing around in whites in polite conversation, waiters coming out with trays of tall drinks. Moran followed the walk to his bungalow, passing behind the figure reclined in the lounge chair, waved to the two 40-year-old secretaries from Fort Wayne and went inside. He drank a beer while he showered and changed into jeans, a T-shirt and dry tennis shoes, old ones that were worn through and he slipped on without socks. He got a fresh beer from the refrigerator, then on second thought another one and took them, one in each hand, out to the Marshall Sisco investigator lying in the shade.

"You must like the place you sign up for a week."

Nolen Tyner opened his eyes behind the aviator sunglasses, startled, about to rise, then relaxing again as he saw Moran extending the beer.

"Cold one for you," Moran said. "Yours must be pretty warm by now." Four empty cans stood upright on the ground next to the lounge chair with two full ones still in the cardboard casing.

"That's very kind of you," Nolen said. He jerked the backrest of the chair up a notch and reached for the can of beer that was beaded with drops of ice water. His sleeve rode up to reveal a bluish tattoo on his right forearm, a two-inch eagle with its wings raised.

While on Moran's left forearm, also extended, was his faded blue Marine Corps insignia.

They looked at each other. Nolen said, "From the halls of Montezuma, huh?" Smiling, popping open the can of beer.

"And I take it you were airborne," Moran said. "Not by any chance the Eighty-second?"

"That's the one."

"Second or Third Brigade maybe?"

"Third. You're leading up to something, aren't you?"

"As a matter of fact," Moran said. "I wonder if you were in Santo Domingo sixteen years ago. Sitting on the bank of the Ozama River by any chance?"

"Sitting high on the east bank, up on the grain elevators," Nolen said, smiling some more. "You don't mean to tell me you were there?"

Moran pulled a recliner over with his foot and sat down, straddling the leg rest, now eye to eye with Nolan. "You had a weapons squad up there, didn't you? Up on the silos, or whatever they were. With a one-oh-six recoiless rifle?"

"We had a bunch of 'em up there."

"And one day you're using your one-oh-six trying to hit a sniper, firing across the river at this *one* guy. He was in a building the corner of Isabella Catolica and Luperon."

Nolen raised his eyebrows. "Marines weren't ever that close to the river. Were they?"

"I got excited," Moran said. "The heat of the chase."

"You mean you fucked up," Nolen said. "Got suckered."

"The dinger would fire a round, then disappear," Moran said. "You never knew where you'd get shot at from next."

"I remember snipers," Nolen said. "Yeah, and I remember the troopers talking about they took this guy out. Little fucker with an M-one."

"It was a medium-size fucker with an M-fourteen," Moran said. "It was *me* they got. We're chasing the dinger, I run upstairs, he's gone. I look out the window and a fifty-caliber racer round nearly took my head off."

Nolen was nodding again. "Fired from the spotting rifle."

"I *know* what it was fired from," Moran said. "Followed by screaming one-oh-six. I had a mitt I could've stuck my hand up and caught it."

"Didn't kill you, huh?"

"It took out the back end of the third floor and

the stairs. I got hit here, below my flack jacket and down my leg. Fifteen pieces of iron they dug out and gave me a Heart," Moran said. "So you were Airborne. What'd I bring you a beer for?"

"You felt something, a kinship," Nolen said, "one grunt sniffing another. I'll tell you what. Even if it wasn't me I'll buy you a drink later on. Make it up to you."

"I'm going down there next week," Moran said.

"Where?"

"Santo Domingo."

"Jesus Christ, what for?"

"Walk my perimeter, see if it looks the same. Stay at the Embajador—we were bivouacked right there. Maybe look up some people. There doesn't seem to be anything going on; now it's El Salvador."

"If there's any place down there we can go in and fuck things up," Nolen said, "Reagan and Haig'll find it, don't worry."

"You been back to the D.R. since?"

"I ate that chow just one time and got Trujillo's Revenge," Nolen said. "I partied with *one* girl, *one* and took home a dose. I take a vacation, man, I go to Las Vegas where everything's sanitary."

They took a sip of their beers. Looking at Moran Nolen Tyner said, "Well, well . . ."

"I'm not gonna say it's a small world," Moran said, easing back in the recliner to get comfortable, crossing his sneakers, the strings hanging loose.

"You want to know how small it is," Nolen said, looking across the pool. "You got a couple Dominicans right in that end apartment. The piano player and the broad, the lovers. Though my sheet says the piano player might be Puerto Rican."

"I thought they might be Cuban," Moran said, "all the Cubans in Miami. "Your sheet—what do you mean by your sheet?"

"The IDs of people I got under surveillance. The broad, for example. She's married to a guy by the name of Andres de Boya. Miami big bucks, I mean big."

"Wait a minute," Moran said. "The woman in there?"

"They got a house on Biscayne Bay looks like that Polynesian restaurant in Lauderdale, the Mai Kai, only bigger."

Moran agreed, nodding. "That's right. But the woman isn't Mrs. de Boya."

Nolen gave him a funny look, guarded. "How would you know?"

"Mrs. Andres de Boya's from the same place I was originally," Moran said. "Detroit. And she's no more Dominican than I am. She's a very nice-looking woman. In fact she's . . . well, she's a nice person."

Nolen was looking at the holes in the toes of Moran's sneakers, the left one larger than the right. He didn't seem too sure about Moran.

"Maybe it's a different de Boya, a relative."

"How many Andres de Boyas are there?" Moran said. "He was in Trujillo's government, something like twenty years ago, right up to the time Trujillo got shot on the way to see his girlfriend."

"Twenty-seven times they hit him," Nolen said. "A prick like that, I guess you have to be sure."

Moran was patient. "De Boya came to Miami—I imagine with a few million he'd scored. He was a general in charge of something or other . . ."

"Something or other—try head of the secret police," Nolen said, "the Cascos Blancos, the white helmets. You're a poor Dominican you see a guy wearing a liner painted white you run for the fucking hills."

"I thought he owned sugar mills," Moran said.

"That's how he got rich. Trujillo used to pass out sugar mills for good behavior. Three days after the old dictator's killed, de Boya's on his yacht bound for Miami. With all the U.S. dollars he could get his hands on." Nolen was looking at Moran's sneakers again; his gaze thoughtful, still somewhat skeptical as it raised to Moran's beach-bum bearded face.

"How do you know him?"

"Leucadendra Country Club. I played golf with him a few times. Actually it was twice," Moran said, "in the same foursome. That was enough."

"Too rich for your blood, uh, the bets? Little Nassau?"

"No, the guy cheats," Moran said. "You believe it? Guy that's worth, easy, forty fifty million, he cheats on a hundred-dollar round of golf and all the clucks, the guys that play with him, know it. I couldn't believe it. They not only pay up they go, 'Gee, Mr. de Boya,' give him all this shit what a great game he plays."

Nolen said, "Yeah?" Still a little hesitant. "What about you? You pay him?"

"No, as a matter of fact I didn't," Moran said. "My father-in-law at the time, I thought he was gonna have a stroke. 'You out of your mind? You know who that is, for Christ's sake?' I said, 'Yeah, a guy that cheats. Fuck him.' My father-in-law goes, 'A hundred bucks, Christ, I'll give you the hundred.' I tried to explain to him that wasn't the point, but my father-in-law was nervous because de Boya was putting money in his condominium developments and I worked for him, my father-in-law. So he was afraid it would look like he was siding with me, not making me come across. I told him that was too bad, I wasn't gonna pay any tinhorn hacks his way out of the rough like he's cutting weeds, three-putts the hole and says he took a five. Bullshit."

"You belong to Leucadendra?" Nolen's tone of skepticism was giving way to mild surprise.

"Not anymore," Moran said. "De Boya tried to get me blackballed. He not only didn't like the way

I played golf, he hinted around I was trying to hit on his wife."

"Were you?"

"No. I told you, she's a very nice person. Her name was Mary Delaney, worked for de Boya's lawyer before they got married."

"Change her luck and marry a spic, uh, with fifty million. Shit, I'd marry him too."

"Be careful," Moran said.

Nolen grinned. "Got a little soft spot there? I won't say another word."

"De Boya didn't get me blackballed," Moran said, "but it didn't help my standing at the club any. Then when my wife divorced me for not playing the game, her dad helped give me a shove and there went the club membership. Which was fine, I never liked golf that much anyway."

"So you were married to bucks, too."

Moran shrugged. "It might've worked, it didn't, that's all. The last time I saw de Boya—he came by here about six eight months ago like nothing had happened, like he hardly knew me, and offered to buy the place, build a condominium."

"What'd you tell him?"

"I turned him down. I got real estate people calling here every week. They're trying to build a solid wall of condos from Key West to Jacksonville."

"I won't ask you the last time you saw his wife." Nolen grinned to show he was kidding around.

Moran didn't grin. He said, "Good. We leave her out of this." He said, "I understand you had a talk with the piano player today."

"You got eyes even when you're not here," Nolen said. "Yeah, actually I felt sorry for him. I told him I had him under surveillance with a woman he wasn't supposed to be with. Then, before he started to sweat I told him he was perfectly safe, I wasn't gonna turn him in. Even though I was taking a terrible risk."

"You made him understand," Moran said, "the risk ought to be worth something."

"Like fifty a day. Why not."

"And you don't even give 'em clean towels," Moran said. "What do you do when you're not hanging out?"

"I rest," Nolen said. "I got rid of my goals, decided to take it one day at a time. Don't overdo it, never drink more than a case of beer or a fifth of booze in any given day. Unless there's a party."

"I've always admired restraint," Moran said. "Not overreaching your capabilities."

"There you are," Nolen said. "I was an actor for twenty years. Well, ten years professionally. Some film work in New York, mostly dinner theater down here. You're trying to act, the audience's sitting there trying not to break wind out loud. They want to leave, go home, but not any more'n I do. I played either the lead guy's buddy or the broad's brother. You know, just a straight asshole type of guy, wrings his hands a lot, opens his eyes real wide: 'Gee, Scott, I don't know if I'd do *that*.' Doesn't ever know what the fuck's going on. I start playing the guy as a drunk, give the part a little dimension. Or I'd play it, give it just a hint the guy's homosexual. But the asshole directors on that dinner circuit, to get any respect from them you had to be Forrest Tucker . . . Doug McClure. You know what I mean? That type."

"I imagine it's tough," Moran said, "when you think of all the Doug McClures out there." He saw Nolen eyeing the two Fort Wayne secretaries, their chairs backed up to the low cement wall, the highrise shade now up to their knees.

"I'm at a motel in Golden Shores," Nolen said, looking at Moran again. "It's not bad, three bills a month, it's fairly clean. The thing is, I'd like very much to give you the business—"

"I think you are," Moran said.

"But even your off-season rate, thirty bucks a day, and you know, come on, that's not only steep it's unrealistic. Maybe not for transients, no. But what I'm offering you is the assurance of a permanent tenant."

"How permanent?"

"What have you got? With the lovers and the secretaries you got about four units out of twelve rented, am I right? And it's like that I bet eight nine months of the year. Okay. For a fair rate you'll have guaranteed occupancy of Number Five the year 'round. I'll even help you out keeping the place up. Skim the pool, cut the grass—"

"We don't have any grass."

"Feed the chickens—I don't know what you do around there. You tell *me*."

"Six hundred," Moran said.

Nolen said, "George, six hundred, I can get a furnished two-bedroom apartment for six hundred."

"Maybe over at the Seminole Indian Reservation. Not on the beach you can't."

"How about three? For old time's sake, the Dominican Republic," Nolen said. "I'll entertain the secretaries, teach 'em how to sit up and roll over. Listen, I'll even sign a year's lease."

And leave in the dead of night, Moran thought. But what would he be out? He liked Nolen. He didn't trust him especially, but he didn't have to. Moran said, "Okay, but no smoking in bed. You promise?"

Saturday Nolen Tyner moved into Number Five with everything he owned. Two old suitcases and several cardboard boxes loaded with magazines, letters, glossy photographs of himself in different outfits and poses, a hair dryer. A liquor case that held bottles of scotch, vodka and rum, most of them nearly empty. A lot of clothes, soiled-looking, out-of-style shirts, trousers and sport coats doubled up over bent hangers. A big Northern tissue box of sporty shoes, tan ones and white perforated ones that caught Jerry's eye and Nolen told him he could have any pair he wanted if they fit. The man's life was in cardboard boxes he carried from one motel to another.

Jerry left with his shoes and Nolen poured Moran and himself a scotch to mark the occasion.

He said, "You're right, that Dominican broad is not de Boya's wife."

"You find out who she is?" Moran sat at the Formica table with his drink.

"She's de Boya's sister. I see the address, Bal Harbor," Nolen said, "I guess I assumed they're separated and she moved out. So this morning I ask Marshall, 'Why'd you tell me it's the guy's wife?' He goes, 'I didn't tell you that. I told you her name's Anita and who the client is, that's all. You musta decided she's his wife.' Marshall's one of those guys, he's never wrong. He gives me the information on the back of an envelope."

"His sister," Moran said. "I didn't know he had one."

"Anita's forty-two, divorced for the third time." Nolen poured himself a little more scotch. "She starts fooling around de Boya calls Marshall. 'Anita is doing it again with somebody.' De Boya protecting the family name. 'Find out who she is fucking and let me know.' This's been going on for years. One time he follows her all over Miami, she keeps giving him the slip. Marshall's sitting in his car in front of a place over on Collins Avenue, a store where he *knows* she went in. He looks in his rearview mirror, Christ, here she comes up behind him in her Mercedes, slams into the ass-end of Marshall's car, backs up, doesn't give a shit her grille's all smashed in, and gives him the finger as she drives past. Gives him the old finger. . . . Another time, Anita starts out she's balling this jai-alai star in Dania. Right in the middle of the investigation, Marshall's moving in, getting the goods, she switches over to a bongo player with some reggae band doing a gig on the Beach. This broad, she's got gold fixtures in her bathroom, I mean *gold*, man, and she's fucking this guy wears a wool cap pulled down over his dreadlocks out in the sand. They don't even get a *room*."

"Love is funny," Moran said.

Sunday night Moran saw lights on in Number One and checked with Jerry. Jerry said it was the Latin lovers, they'd paid for the place they could come anytime they wanted, couldn't they? Moran was always patient with Jerry; he said yeah, but why at night all of a sudden when up till now they'd only come afternoons from one to five? Jerry said, don't ask me; those Cubans, you never know what they're up to. Moran checked with Nolen and Nolen said the piano player was off Sunday and Monday. Moran said well, maybe they were seeing what it was like at night, like regular folks. He wouldn't worry about it.

3

MORAN WAS WATCHING Monday Night Football on television, Detroit Lions and the Chicago Bears fighting it out for the obscurity award, Moran trying to decide if he'd rather be a wide receiver or a free safety . . . whether he should have another beer and fry a steak or go to Vesuvio's on Federal Highway for spaghetti marinara and eat the crisp breadsticks with hard butter, Jesus, and have a bottle of red with it, the house salad . . . or get the chicken cacciatore and slock the bread around in the gravy . . . The phone rang.

Moran got up out of his chair and walked barefoot across the vinyl tile floor. It felt sticky and he thought again of carpeting the living room, redecorating the place and getting rid of the dumb furniture that was here when he moved in: the jungle floral print, black and pink and green, curved bamboo arms on the chairs and sofa. He could hear the wind outside, that overpowering ocean pounding in out of the night. Sometimes it made him feel daring to live on the edge of it, fifty yards away watching a professional football game in color. The phone was on the end of the high counter that separated the kitchenette from the rest of the room. He said, "Coconut Palms. . . ." and expected to hear the voice of a secretary calling from up North somewhere.

Jerry said, "George, could you come in the office a minute, help me out here?" Then a silence, waiting.

It was Jerry's voice but it didn't sound like him. His tone was quiet, cold sober and that wasn't Jerry's sound after six in the evening, even when he was doing the books.

Moran said, "What's wrong?"

Jerry said, "There's a party here looking for somebody. I don't know they're registered or not."

There was an innocence in this voice that was not Jerry. Jerry knew everything.

Moran said, "Hang on, I'll be right there."

Outside he felt the wind through his T-shirt and looked for stars. There weren't any. Tomorrow it would continue to blow and the secretaries would moan about the weather. Their apartments were dark, only the amber porch lights on. Number One showed light behind draperies drawn closed. It surprised Moran. The second night in a row for the lovers. Here all night—they'd left sometime this morning and were back at it. Couple of alligators.

Moran couldn't picture them saying romantic things to one another. He imagined the woman scowling, impatient with the piano player, telling him what to do as the poor guy tried to service her. Moran walked past the warm underwater glow of the swimming pool and approached the office. Through the window he could see Jerry behind the registration desk that was like a narrow counter, Jerry shaking his head, saying something past the two men who were leaning on the counter close to him, not meeting their gaze, nervous, evasive, not like Jerry.

Both of the men wore lightweight jackets with open sport shirts, the collars folded out flat. One dark, with thick hair and Latin features, a mustache that curved down around the corners of his mouth. The other older, pink-skinned, heavyset going to fat; he wore dark-framed glasses and pushed them up on the bridge of a pug Irish nose as the door opened and he turned from the desk.

Moran's first-glance impression: Miami Police.

Jerry was tense, frowning. He said, "George, do we have a guest name of Prado staying with us?" He had a stack of reservation cards in his hand. "I don't recall that name. Less they checked in on my day off."

"Let me see," Moran said, coming around the counter now, playing the game with Jerry for whatever reason he was doing it, but knowing one thing

for sure, before they said a word: They weren't police. Jerry and the police were buddies. Moran took
the guest cards and started going through them.
They were old ones, from last season.

The Latino younger guy was staring at Moran,
weighing him and apparently not impressed. He
said, "Come on, what is this?"

Moran said, "What was the name, Bravo?"

"*Prado.*" The younger one reached across the
counter, held his arm extended and snapped his
fingers.

"Give me those. Come on, let see what you got."

Jerry said, "I told him, George, they're private
property. I'm not supposed to show 'em."

The heavyset Irish-looking guy put his hand on
the younger one's outstretched arm. The arm went
down to the counter and the heavyset one pushed
up his glasses again. He said, "George, we're not
getting anywhere fast here, are we? Looking
through cards—what've you got, maybe two units
rented, three? You got five cars outside counting
mine." He turned to the windows that looked out
on the courtyard and the illuminated pool. "You
got lights on in one unit I can see. Maybe they're in
there watching the ball game, which I wish I was
home watching right now myself. But I know this
fella we're looking for doesn't care too much about
the NFL or who goes to the Super Bowl next Janu-
ary, so he's probably doing something else in there.

We can go down and knock on the door. We can knock on every door you got here, but I don't want to disturb any your guests might be sleeping. Cause a commotion, give the place a bad name. That's where I stand. What I want to know, George, is where you stand, why you're being uncooperative."

Moran didn't say anything. He was trying to think of the phone number of the Pompano Beach Police.

"He owe you rent money?"

Moran still didn't say anything.

"That's a pretty easy question, George. You don't have to scratch your head on that one, do you?"

The Latino one said, "Come on, George, cut the shit. What room is he in?"

The heavyset one turned to look at the Latino. He said, "Corky, go on outside, okay? Go on, I'll take care of it."

The Latino took his time, reluctant, but went outside toward the pool.

The door closed and the heavyset Irish-looking guy said, "Fucking spic. Somebody told 'em they have hot blood, they have to live up to it. Don't worry about Corky, I'll put him on a leash I have to."

"Or I can call the cops," Moran said.

The heavyset man sighed. He dug into his rumpled size-44 jacket, brought out a business card and laid it on the counter. "Jiggs Scully. I used to be a cop myself. City of New York, borough of Manhattan, George. I bet I can talk to 'em better'n you can."

Moran picked up the card. "Business Consultant . . ."

"That's correct," Scully said, "I'm a consultant. See the address? New World Tower, Biscayne Boulevard. I advise people on business matters, act as a go-between, bring people together that want to make deals . . . things like that. You want to know any more, come by my office we'll have a coffee sometime. Okay? Right now I'm going down to see Mr. Prado. Where you come in—I'm gonna knock on his door, he don't open it then I might have to kick it in. I mean the business I got with him is that pressing. So you can give me a key and maybe save yourself a door. What do you think?"

Moran said, "You can knock on the door. But if he doesn't open it you don't go in. You can talk to the cops and we'll see how good you are."

"Oh, man," Jiggs Scully said, sounding tired, leaning on the counter again. "I notice that thing on your arm. Once a Marine, always a Marine, uh? Gonna stand your ground. Okay, pal, he don't open the door I'll go home, watch Monday Night Football. How's that sound to you?"

*   *   *

Jerry stayed inside by the window, within reach of the phone. Moran would give him the high sign if he had to use it. Right now it was quiet out there. The two men had gone down to oceanfront Number One, knocked, waited, knocked again and the door opened. Now they were inside. Jerry looked at the clock. Twenty past ten. Now they'd been in there only a couple of minutes. Jerry opened the office door now. He called out in a low voice, "George?"

The figure near the shallow end of the pool didn't move; he was watching the end apartment. Beyond it was darkness and the ocean. Jerry stepped outside. He closed the door behind him quietly and crept up to Moran.

"You able to hear what they said?"

Moran shook his head.

"That wind out there, you can't hear yourself think," Jerry said. "The piano player opened the door, then seemed to step back, didn't he? Like he was inviting them in?"

Moran didn't say anything. He wished Jerry would go back inside.

"Maybe they're from the finance company, gonna repossess his car. I didn't like 'em at all. That type," Jerry said, "they come in a place, you know they're gonna take whatever they want. First I thought it was a stickup."

"You better stay by the phone," Moran said. "You look up the number?"

"Seven eight five . . . seven eight five two nine . . . Or is it nine two one one?"

"I don't know what it is," Moran said, "but you better be sure." He saw the door open. "Jerry, they're coming out."

Jerry hurried off.

Moran watched the younger guy, the Latino named Corky, appear, then the piano player and the woman. The Irish-looking guy, Jiggs Scully, closed the door and turned the knob to make sure it was locked. They came in single file now along the front of the apartment wing, heading for the alcove next to the office where the Coke machine and ice maker were located. They could go through the alcove to the street. They were about twenty feet away, passing him now.

Moran said, "Mrs. . . . ." He didn't know what to call her. He said, "Is everything all right?"

Jiggs Scully, a barrel shuffling along, bringing up the rear, looked over. "Everything's lovely, George. Go on back the ball game."

Moran said, "Mr. Prado?"

The Latino guy, Corky, said something in Spanish and laughed. Jiggs Scully said, "George, you're paid up, you got nothing to worry about there. We're gonna go out have a few pops. We'll see you later. Have a nice evening."

Moran followed them as far as the alcove. He watched them walk past the line of angle-parked cars, past the woman's gray Mercedes, Nolen's rusting-out blue Porsche. He didn't see the piano player's car. All four of them got into a two-tone red and white Cadillac and drove away.

Moran had to go to the office to get the key to Number Five. Jerry said, "Nolen's in there. He's been in there all evening."

"I guess he's asleep," Moran said.

"But why would he know anything about them?" Jerry said.

Moran didn't answer, already going out the door. He stepped over to Number Five, listened—there were faint sounds coming from inside. He knocked hard, three times. When nothing happened he used the key to open the door. The place smelled like a bar.

The TV was tuned to the football game. Nolen sat in the room's one comfortable chair facing the set, eyes closed, head lying on his shoulder, snoring a little. Moran shook him, taking the empty glass he held in his lap.

"Hey, Nolen?"

He woke up right away. "What's the matter?" He rubbed his hand over his face and saw Moran placing the glass on the table, by the scotch and the box of crackers. Moran came back to the chair.

"Two guys came in. Looking for the piano player."

Nolen didn't say anything.

"You hear what I said?"

"What time is it?"

"About ten-thirty. They came out with Prado and Anita, said they're going to have a drink, but I don't think so. They put 'em in a car and drove off. A red and white Cadillac."

"There you are," Nolen said.

"What do you mean, there you are? They took 'em somewhere."

"Forget about it," Nolen said. He still hadn't moved, sitting low in the chair.

"One of them, his name's Jiggs Scully. The other guy was Cuban—I don't know, Latin."

"The guy told you his name?"

"He gave me his card. Jiggs Scully."

"You believe him?"

"He gave me his *card*."

"You're paid up," Nolen said. "Forget about it."

"You sound like the guy Jiggs," Moran said. He turned around and walked out.

When he got the key to Number One Jerry wanted to go with him, but Moran told him he'd better stay in the office in case there was a call. He didn't want Jerry along. He was afraid he'd see something in the apartment and Jerry would ask questions and he'd end up telling Jerry the woman was Andres de

Boya's sister and then Jerry would ask more questions and Moran would have to stand there saying, "I don't know," over and over, Jerry driving him nuts. It was true, he didn't know what was going on. They could be good friends and the guy was kidding about kicking the door in. The woman hadn't yelled. She could have run or at least yelled out when she saw him standing by the swimming pool.

He had a funny feeling going in the apartment, the wind blowing, then quiet as he closed the door—the place empty but all the lights on, every one of them.

It still surprised him the woman hadn't yelled something. A woman like that, she would have demanded help if she needed it, then complained if he didn't jump right away.

The apartment seemed in order, music playing softly on the radio. If they didn't turn the radio or the lights off, that could mean something. Forced to leave without any fooling around. Or it could mean they didn't worry too much about bills from Florida Power. People who owned places along the beach were always comparing their electric bills. An ashtray was full of long cigarette butts. A few Coconut Palms illustrated postcards lay on the desk. There was an empty champagne bottle in the trash can. He didn't see the brandy bottle, the one Lula said was down a couple inches every morning

when she cleaned. Lula said they tore the bed up;
but both double beds were still made. A pink negli-
gee hung in the bedroom closet. Moran wondered
if he should take it; he was pretty sure he would
never see them again. There didn't seem to be anything that belonged to the piano player. Moran
turned off the radio and the lights before he left.

They didn't come back during the night. When
Moran walked out to the street, early, before seven,
he saw the woman's gray Mercedes was gone. He
thought, Well, that doesn't mean anything. All of
them still could be friends. They got back late and
the woman decided to go home; the lovers never
spent the night anyway. Maybe they'd be back at it
this afternoon . . . Just about the time Moran
would be at Miami International boarding the
Eastern flight to Santo Domingo.

He waited until after nine before calling the
number on the business card that bore the name
Jiggs Scully and *Consultant* beneath it.

A woman's voice said, "Good morning, Dorado
Management."

Moran said, "Mr. Scully, please."

The woman's voice said, "Mr. Scully?" As
though she didn't recognize the name. "Just a
minute." There was a silence on the line for about
ten seconds. The woman's voice came back on and

said, "I'm sorry, sir, there's no Mr. Scully with the company."

Moran said, "I've got his card. Your phone number's on it."

The woman's voice said, "I'm sorry, sir, there's no one here by that name," and hung up.

Moran didn't see Nolen until ten-thirty. He came out to the cement wall with a beer in his hand, stringy hair blowing in the wind, and raised his face, eyes closed, to the overcast sky.

"Beautiful morning."

Moran said, "They didn't come back last night."

"They never do."

"I called the guy's number. Scully? There's no one there by that name."

"He lied to you," Nolen said, "didn't he? But, in any event, the lovers will come back sometime or they won't. What else can I tell you, buddy?"

Moran was ready to jump on him. "You can cut the buddy shit and tell me what's going on. Why'd Anita and the piano player pick this place? There a thousand motels they could've gone to, they pick this one. Why?"

Nolen took a drink of beer without opening his eyes. "It's halfway between them—I don't know."

"But you were told to come here, weren't you? You didn't follow them here."

"Marshall gave me a postcard picture of the place, when it had palm trees."

"De Boya gave it to him?"

"I guess so."

"He tell his sister to come here? Good place to shack up? Come on . . ."

"Maybe she saw the postcard at her brother's house," Nolen said, in pain, persecuted. "She tells the piano player to meet her here 'cause it's the only place she can think of. How's that?"

"Something's going on," Moran said, "and I'm standing in the middle. Does de Boya think I know his sister? I invited 'em here?"

"I don't know," Nolen said, "I really don't. I was hired to watch Anita." He sucked in fresh ocean air, still not looking at Moran. "And sort of keep my eyes open."

"For what?"

"See who comes to visit you." Nolen glanced at Moran and could not have liked the way Moran was staring at him. "Marshall said—you want his exact words?—he said keep your eyes open for a broad."

"Go on."

"With sort of blond streaked hair, good-looking."

"About thirty-two?"

"Yeah, he said around thirty."

Moran kept staring at him. "What else do you

do for money? Anything you're told, huh?" He walked off toward his bungalow.

Nolen said, "George?" and waited for him to look around. Nolen raised his beer can. "You got any cold ones?"

Moran looked tired. He said, "Come on," with a halfhearted wave of his hand.

Nolen followed him inside.

Jerry Shea watched the black Cadillac pull up in front. At first he thought Moran had called for an airport limo. But then realized this car wasn't any ride to the Miami airport. This was the real thing, a personal limousine with no-glare windows that were almost as black as the car and a driver who wore a buttoned-up dark suit that could pass for a uniform.

Jerry Shea said, "Oh, my God," out loud.

The driver was the Latino guy who was here last night, the one the other guy had called Corky. Now he was a chauffeur. He stood holding the handle of the rear door, ready to open it.

Now the other one, Jiggs Scully, who had given Moran his card, came out of the passenger side of the front seat. He wore a dark suit and stood pulling up his pants and sticking his shirt in, adjusting himself.

Jerry picked up the phone but didn't dial.

The driver, Corky, was opening the rear door.

A man about sixty got out. A man with a broad, tight expanse of double-breasted gray suit that he adjusted smartly, pulling the jacket down to appear even tighter. The man was Hispanic but very light and had a certain bearing, immovable, built like the stump of an oak tree cut off at about five nine. He reminded Jerry for some reason of a labor leader, a guy high up in the Teamsters, a Latin Jimmy Hoffa. Though this guy was more polished. That word was in Jerry's mind because the guy looked like he darkened his hair with black shoe-polish, the way it was shining in the sun, like patent leather.

The man was taking a pair of sunglasses from his inside pocket as he looked up at the Coconut Palms. He didn't seem too impressed.

Moran was half-dressed, packing his canvas carry-on bag. Two pair of pants, five shirts, a couple of light cotton sweaters . . . he wasn't sure how long he'd be down there. Four or five days maybe. When the phone rang Nolen looked up. He'd been sitting with his beer, grateful, not making a sound. He heard Moran say, "They're back?" Then heard him say, "Jesus Christ, yeah, that sounds like him . . . It's okay, Jerry, I'll see what he wants." Moran was looking toward the side window as he hung up.

Nolen said, "What's going on?" Watching

Moran pull on a dark blue sport shirt and move to-ward the door.

"Stay where you are," Moran told him. He swung the door open and stopped.

The Irish-ex-cop-looking guy, Jiggs Scully, was standing outside the door, pushing his glasses up on his nose. He said, "George, how we doing? Your team won last night, uh?"

Moran stepped out, pulling the door closed behind him. He started past Scully and stopped.

"Which one was my team?"

Scully gave him a wise grin. "The Lions. You're from the Motor City, aren't you?"

"What'd I do?" Moran said.

"I don't know, George, you tell me. Or tell Mr. de Boya there. He wants to ask you something."

Moran moved past Scully, buttoning his shirt, approaching Andres de Boya now who stood near the far end of the cement walk, looking out at the beach with his hands locked together behind his back. He turned to watch Moran coming, then squared around again to face the beach as Moran reached him.

"How much frontage you have?"

It stopped Moran for a moment. He opened his beltless khaki pants and tucked in his shirttails, zipped as he said, "The same I had the last time. Was it a hundred and twenty or a hundred and thirty feet? I forgot."

".You're talking about a difference of two hundred thousand dollars," de Boya said to the ocean. His voice was soft, but with a heavy accent.

"Numbers aren't my game anymore," Moran said. "How's your golf?"

De Boya didn't answer or move a muscle.

Moran wondered what would happen if he kicked the guy ass-over the cement wall into the sand, and walked away. He attempted again to nudge him with, "If you're looking for your sister, she isn't here . . . You already know that, huh?"

Hard-headed guy, he refused to come to life.

"Am I getting warm?" Moran said. "I'll tell you something. If you think I had anything to do with her coming here, you're wrong. I never met your sister before the piano player and I've only talked to her once, if you could call it that."

"How much you want?" de Boya said, out of nowhere.

"For what? My place?"

"I give you . . ." de Boya paused. "Million six hundred thousand."

"You serious?"

"How much you want?"

"The real-estate guys that call about every week now are up over two million."

"I give you two million and two hundred thousand."

De Boya's gaze came past him and Moran smiled. Was he serious? The man's gaze continued on, sunglasses like a hooded beacon sweeping the beach; black hair parted in a hard line, showing his scalp.

Moran said, "You want me to go away, Andres? Come on, what's your game?" He wanted to keep it light and not let the guy get to him. "Whatever it is, the Coconuts isn't for sale." And looked out at his beach, at the surf pounding in. "I like it."

"Why?"

Moran waited; he wanted to be sure.

"I ask you why."

The man had turned and was almost facing him now. He had asked a question that had nothing to do with real-estate value or numbers and seemed interested in getting an answer.

"I live here," Moran said. "It's my home."

De Boya looked past him, toward the stucco bungalow. "You live in that?"

"I live in that," Moran said.

"How much you make here?"

"A lot," Moran said.

"How much? A few thousand?"

Moran said, "I don't know your sister and I haven't seen your wife in over a year. I want you to understand that. I never made any moves on your wife. Never."

De Boya seemed to be staring at him, though might have been sightless behind the sunglasses, the wax figure of a former general.

He said, "Get three offers on real-estate letter paper. I give you a hundred thousand more than the best one."

Moran looked at him closely. Maybe you had to hit him on the head with a hammer to get a reaction. Moran imagined taking a ball peen and the man's plastic hair that covered his one-track mind flying in pieces.

He said, "You serious, Andres? You want to build?"

"Of course, build," de Boya said, more animated than before. "What else do you think?"

And maybe that's all there was to it, though Moran still had his doubts.

He said, "Well, we could sure use another condominium," turning to look at his property. "There's room for forty units you go up ten floors. Sell them for around three and gross twelve million. Cost you about eight and a half to build it, say two for the property, add on this and that, cost of tearing down the Coconuts, you net maybe a million, million and a half. I could do the same thing. But it seems like a lot of trouble to go to. I mean what do I get out of it? Pay half to the government. I'm the owner so I live up in the penthouse with a great view of the Atlantic Ocean but have to take an elevator anytime I want to go outside." Moran nodded toward his bungalow. "I already have a view of the ocean. I got a living room, a bedroom. I got a color TV . . ."

The Dominican former general, cane grower, head of the secret police or whatever role it was that made him rich, stared at Moran. Maybe he understood; maybe he didn't.

But either way, Moran thought—packed, ready to take off on his adventure—what difference does it make?

He said, "Andres, all I'm trying to say to you is, there's no place like home and no friend like Jesus."

Moving away Moran's gaze came to the two figures standing at the opposite end of the walk, in front of the bungalow, Nolen and the Irish-looking guy, Scully. As Moran got closer he saw they were each holding a can of beer, *his* beer; Nolen acting, telling a story, Scully grinning, getting a kick out of it.

There you are, Moran thought. You gonna worry about these people?

4

ALL OVER THE WORLD, Moran decided, the past was being wiped out by condominiums.

There were condos now on the polo grounds west of the hotel, where Amphibious Task Force helicopters had dropped off Marines from the U.S.S. *Boxer*, the grounds becoming a staging area for Marine patrols into the city. There were condos and office buildings rising in downtown Santo Domingo with the initials of political parties spray-painted on fresh cement, PRD and PQD; but only a few YANQUIS GO HOME now, on peeling walls out in the country, old graffiti Moran had noticed coming in from the airport.

There were young wives of ballplayers sunning themselves at the hotel pool—where the Marines had set up their water purification tanks—the young wives talking about housing and travel while their husbands, down here to play winter ball, took batting practice and went off for a round of golf.

There were no open fields near the hotel now.

The gardens were gone, where the first group of Marines had dug in. The Kentucky Fried Chicken place on the corner of Avenida Washington and Socorro Sanchez was gone. The mahogany trees on the street south of the U.S. embassy were still there; the trees looked the same.

They had gone up this street beneath the arch of trees, wide-eyed in the dark, all the way to Nicolas Penson in a war where the street signs were intact and they found their way with a Texaco road map. In the morning they saw people in the streets, crowds of people lining Washington along the oceanfront, like they were watching a parade. They were—waving at the tanks and amtracs. Even with the FUERA YANQUIS signs painted on houses most of the people seemed glad to see them.

The next day, filing back to the embassy, a Marine walking point was shot dead by a sniper; Item Company, at Checkpoint Charlie north of the embassy, drew heavy fire and soon there were snipers working the whole neighborhood, what was supposed to be the International Safety Zone, using bazookas as well as small arms, even old water-cooled 30s that pounded out a heavy sound and at first were thought to be .50-caliber. The Marines moved crosstown, east, establishing a Line of Communication with the Eighty-second Airborne troopers coming into the city across the Duarte Bridge. The LOC held the rebels cornered in the old section of the city and kept the loyalists from getting at them. But it didn't stop the snipers.

A battalion officer told them, "You got your Friendlies and you got your Unfriendlies." He told them most of the snipers were hoodlums, street gangs who'd armed themselves when the rebels passed out guns the first day. These people were called *tigres* but were not trained or organized, not your regular-army rebels. The *tigres* were out for thrills, playing guns with real ones. "So don't fire unless you're fired on." That was a standing order.

Wait a minute. You mean there're *rules*? Somebody said, "We're *here*, man." Two Marine battalions and four Airborne. "Why don't we go downtown and fucking get it done?"

The question was never answered. By the end of the first month of occupation nineteen U.S. military had been killed in action, one hundred eleven wounded.

Moran said to his driver today, in the early evening sixteen years later, "I have a friend who was here with the Eighty-second, the paratroopers. He believes we could have gone into the rebel area, the old section, and ended the whole thing in about fifteen minutes."

"Yes, I believe it, too," the driver said.

"You were here?"

"Yes, I always be here."

"What side were you on?"

"This side." The driver, who was an old black man with Indian cheekbones that looked as though they had been polished, tapped his steering wheel. "Three taxicabs ago, the same Number Twenty-four. Chevrolet, but not new like this one." They were in a '76 Chevrolet Impala, Moran in front with the driver, the windows open, Moran now and again smelling wood smoke and the smell would take him back to that time.

"You were glad to see the Marines?"

"Yes, of course. To have peace. I drove press-mens from the United States. Yes, we come to a corner, a street there, we have to go fast or those rebel fellas shoot at you. One time the bullets come in this side where you are, they hit here"—he slapped the dashboard—"and go out this way past me, out the window." The driver's name was Bienvenido. He was born in 1904 and used to Marines from the United States. He said to Moran, "You want to see where Trujillo was killed, yes?"

"Tomorrow," Moran said.

"And the old quarter, Independence Park."

"Tomorrow," Moran said. He was silent a moment and then said, "Do you know a woman by the name of Luci Palma?"

The driver thought about it and shook his head. "No, I don't think so. Luci Palma . . ."

They followed the drive into the grounds of the Hotel Embajador, past the front lawn where the

American civilians had waited with their luggage to be evacuated. Moran said, "Will you do something for me?"

"Yes, of course."

Moran took a piece of notepaper from his shirt pocket and unfolded it. "I want this message put in the newspaper. In *Listin Diario* or *El Caribe*, I don't care, whichever one you like better. All right? Tell them to put it in a box. You know what I mean? With lines around it. So it'll stand out. Okay?"

"Yes, okay."

"In English."

"Yes, in English."

"Just the way it's written here. Okay? See if you can read it." He handed Bienvenido the piece of notepaper with the hand-printed message on it that said:

CAT CHASER

> is looking for the girl who once
> ran over rooftops and tried to kill
> him. Call the Hotel Embajador.
> Room 537.

Moran waited for the driver to ask him a question. Bienvenido stared at the notepaper, nodding his lips moving.

"You understand it?"

"You want a girl to call you?"

"The girl I met when I was here, before."

"Yes."

"She'll recognize 'Cat Chaser.' If she sees it."

"Yes."

"That was the code name for my platoon. When I was here. I was Cat Chaser Four, but she'll know who it is. I mean if she's still here." It didn't seem enough of an explanation and he said, "This girl shot at me, she tried to kill me. I don't mean it was anything personal, it was during the war. Then, I was taken prisoner by the rebels and I got a chance to meet her . . . You understand what I'm saying?"

Bienvenido was nodding again. "Yes, I understand. You want this girl. But if you don't find this girl, you want another girl?"

Mary de Boya watched Moran enter the lobby. She watched him pick up his key at the desk and cross to the elevators. She was aware of an instant stir of excitement and in her mind, concentrating hard, she said, *Look this way.* She said, *Moran, come on. Quick. Look this way!*

The elevator door closed behind him; he was gone.

Maybe she was expecting too much. It was dark in the hotel cocktail lounge. Even if he'd looked over he might not have been able to see her. Or their telepathy was rusty.

A few years ago Mary de Boya could stare across the lounge at Leucadendra and make Moran feel her eyes and look at her. Moran could do the same. In the dining room or the club grill she would feel it. Raise her eyes to meet his and something would pass between them. Not a signal, an awareness. They could smile at each other without smiling. Raise eyebrows, almost imperceptibly, and make mutual judgments. Aloud they could make comments removed from reality that would whiz past her husband, his wife, and they would know things about each other that had nothing to do with their backgrounds, both from the same city. That was a coincidence, nothing more. Though it was handy if needed, when Andres drilled her with his secret-police look and wanted to know what they'd been talking about. "Detroit." When in fact they'd been talking about nothing in particular, nothing intimate, nothing sane, for that matter, "Detroit" was the safe answer. "We just found out both of our dads worked at Ford Rouge, but George lived on the northwest side and I lived downriver, in Southgate." The look between them had remained harmless. Still, each knew it was there if they wanted to make something of it.

Mary smiled thinking about it now, realizing she missed him.

It didn't seem possible to miss someone you saw only once or twice a week over a period of a few years; but she had continued to picture him and think about him and what she felt now was real. You know when you miss someone.

Before today she hadn't seen Moran since his divorce. Since his father-in-law drummed him out of the club, ripped the crest from his blazer. Mary saw it that way in fantasy, in flashes: Moran standing at attention in his beard and sneakers, expelled for refusing to wear white patent-leather loafers with tassels, and matching white belt. Out. Refusing to talk about real estate, grain futures, tax shelters, more real estate. Out.

She should have jumped up and yelled and run across the lobby. Nine hundred miles from home . . .

Call his room.

An outfielder with the Cincinnati Reds' Triple-A farm team came over to where Mary sat at the first table inside the lounge and asked if she'd have a drink with him. Good-looking, well built, at least ten years younger than she was. Mary smiled and said, "I'd love to. Sit down."

Giving her something to do, so she wouldn't have to make an instant decision. For all she knew Moran was meeting someone, a girl . . .

They talked about the World Series in New York

and Guerrero, the L.A. Dominican, hitting the home run Sunday, the outfielder telling how everybody in the lounge watching it on TV had practically freaked out, their boy coming through. She flirted with the outfielder a little, because she could see he was taken with her and it made her feel good. The mysterious American woman in expensive casual silk, alone in Santo Domingo. The muscular, curly-haired outfielder sat with his big shoulders hunched over the table eating peanuts one at a time, holding back.

Mary de Boya, at thirty-four, was quite likely the best-looking woman the outfielder had ever seen in real life. Her blond honey-streaked hair fell in soft waves to her shoulders framing delicate features, a fine mist of freckles, startling brown eyes.

She asked the outfielder what it was like to stand at the plate and see a hardball coming at you at ninety miles an hour. The outfielder said it didn't matter how fast it came, you had to stand in there, you couldn't give the pitcher nothing. He said it was the curveballs that were more apt to do you in. Curves low and away. The outfielder asked Mary if she had ever been down here before. She told him a few times, for polo matches at Casa de Campo. He said oh, was that what she was down for this time? Mary paused. She said no, she was meeting her lover. The outfielder said oh . . .

"Now I've got to run," Mary said, and left the outfielder half in, half out of his chair. At the front desk she asked for Mr. Moran's room number.

The clerk said, "Mr. Moran," and looked it up. "Five three seven."

"How long is he staying?"

The clerk had to look it up again. "The twenty-ninth. Four days."

Mary turned partway, paused and turned back to the desk again. "I think I'd like a room."

"Yes," the clerk said, "we have a very nice room. Or we have a suite if you like a sitting room, too."

"That's fine," Mary said, though she didn't seem quite sure about something. "I don't have my luggage with me." She looked at the clerk now for help. "It's at Casa de Campo. If I give them a call, can you send someone to pick it up?"

"Yes, but it's seventy miles there," the clerk said. "I don't know how rapidly they can do it."

"Do the best you can," Mary said. She filled out the registration card using her maiden name, Mary Delaney, and an address in Miami Beach off the top of her head, committing herself now, beginning to make her move, thinking: If you're meeting someone, Moran, I'll kill her.

The view from Moran's room was south, past the swimming pool area directly below and down an

abrupt grade to a postcard shot of white colonial
buildings and palm trees on the edge of the Caribbean. In this time when dusk was becoming night,
color gone from the sky, he could hear voices,
words in clear Spanish and bikes whining like
lawnmowers: the same distinct, faraway sounds
they listened to sixteen years ago in tents on the
polo fields. The sounds of people doing what they
did despite the other sounds that would come suddenly, the mortar and rocket explosions, five klicks
removed from the everyday sounds, off somewhere
in the city of Santo Domingo. He didn't like those
first days, not trusting the people, not having a feel
for the terrain. He studied his Texaco map by flash-
light and memorized names of the main streets,
drew red circles for checkpoints, Charlie and Delta,
the embassy, the Dominican Presidential Palace,
the National Police Barracks. Take Bolivar to Independence Park, where burned-out cars blocked in-
tersections, and duck. Beyond this point you could
get killed. He liked it once he had a perimeter and
was able to tell his fire team what they were doing.
None of them had been to war.

He would walk those streets tomorrow . . . and
hear the voices again on the field radio . . . "Cat
Chaser Four, you read? Where the fuck are
you?" . . . And the girl's voice coming in. "I know
where you are. I see you, Cat Chaser . . . Hey, Cat
Chaser, come find me . . . You no good with *tigres*.

All you know how to hunt, you Marines, is pussy. Come find me, Cat Chaser Four, whatever your name is . . . This is Luci signing off."

Luci Palma, the sixteen-year-old girl who gave them fits with an M-1 carbine from World War Two. The girl who ran over rooftops . . .

The room-service waiter came with a bucket of ice that held three bottles of El Presidente beer. Moran signed, gave the waiter a peso and said, "Were you here during the revolution?"

The waiter didn't seem to understand.

"Hace dieciséis años," Moran said.

"Oh, yes, I was here."

"What side were you on?"

Again the waiter hesitated.

"Que lado? Los generales o los rebeldes?"

"No, I don't fight," the waiter said. "I like peace."

"No one I've talked to was in the war, the *guerra*," Moran said. "I wonder who was doing all the shooting."

The phone rang.

"I was in Samaná," the waiter said.

"Everybody was in Samaná," Moran said. "Thanks." He walked behind the waiter going to the door and stopped by the nightstand next to the bed. As the phone rang for the fourth time he picked it up.

"Hello."

The voice instantly familiar said, "Moran? What're you doing in Santo Domingo?"

He said, "I don't believe it. Come on . . ." grinning, sitting down on the bed. "What're you doing here?"

"I asked you first."

"Where are you?"

"About twenty feet above you. Seven thirty-five."

"I don't believe it." He sat up straight and wanted to make his voice sound natural, casual, as he said, "Mary? . . . Is Andres with you?"

"He can't come back here, George. He's afraid somebody'll shoot him."

"Gee, that's too bad. I mean that you couldn't bring him." He heard her giggle. "Well, who're you with?"

"Nobody. I'm all alone."

"Come on . . . I don't believe it."

"Why're you so amazed?"

"You kidding? I don't believe *this*. I'm not sure I could even imagine something like this happening."

She said, "Are you alone?"

"Yeah, all by myself."

"I mean are you meeting anyone?"

"No, I'm alone. Jesus Christ, am I alone. I don't believe it," Moran said, getting up, having to move around now, excited. "You know I recognized your voice right away? What're you doing here?"

"I saw you in the lobby. A little while ago."

"Yeah? . . ."

"If you're not busy, you think we could have a drink?"

"If I'm not *busy?* Even if I was . . . Listen, I've got three cold bottles of El Presidente sitting right in front of me, unopened."

She said, "Why don't you come up and see me, George? Bring your beer with you."

"Right now?"

"I'll have the door open."

She did, too.

Waited just inside the sitting room for him so that when he appeared in the doorway and entered the short hallway past the bathroom and closet he would have to come to her and she would open her arms. . . . Except that he was carrying the ice bucket in front of him with both hands and when she raised her arms he didn't know what to do and they stood there staring at each other, anxious, aching, until she said, "Make up your mind, Moran. Are you going to hold the beer or me?"

He hurried past her into the sitting room, placed his bucket on the coffee table next to hers that held a bottle of champagne. Now they could do it. Now as he turned she came into his arms like it was the most natural thing in the world, wanting to hold and feel each other close after only looking at one another for all those years and keeping a distance between them, sometimes inches, but always a distance. There. It felt good, better than imagined, and from that moment something more than two old friends meeting. Their mouths came together, unplanned, but this too seemed natural, their mouths seeking, brushing, fitting softly as their bodies relaxed and began to blend. . . .

Abruptly, without a flicker, the lights in the room and in the hall went out.

They pulled slightly apart, still holding each other. Moran said very quietly, "We must've blown a fuse. Generated too much electricity."

"I'd believe it," Mary said, "if I hadn't been here before. They run low on power and have to black out parts of the city."

"For how long?"

"I think fifteen or twenty minutes. Didn't you notice a candle in your room?"

"No . . . Where you going?"

"To find the candle. I saw it somewhere . . ."

"I can't see you."

"I think it's in the bedroom."

He followed the sound of her voice, moving carefully now in total darkness, hands ready in front of him. His shin hit the coffee table and he heard the ice bucket rattle against glass.

"Where are you?"

"I'm in the bedroom," Mary said. "I think."

He moved in that direction, around the coffee table, and came to a doorway that seemed darker than the dark sitting room. Entering cautiously, a room he'd never seen, with nothing to picture from memory, Moran extended his arms like a man sleepwalking. He caught the scent of her perfume, moved a cautious step and felt her hair brush his face. She was between his arms and he closed them around her now, feeling her hands slide up over his ribs.

He said in almost a whisper, "You find the candle?"

"No. It must be in the bathroom."

He said, "Do we need it?"

He felt her hands, her breath—this slim girl, not as tall as he'd remembered her, the image of her across a room. He felt the silky material covering her bare skin, the skin smoothly taut, her body delicate but firm pressing into him, their mouths brushing, finding the right place again, and this time drifting into a dreamlike kind of consciousness, Moran aware but not seeing himself, Mary moving against him, moving him, guiding gently, and Moran knew where they were going, feeling the foot of the bed against his leg and it was all the bearings he needed. They bailed out in the dark and fell into the double bed in the excitement of each other. She said, "You don't know how long . . ."

He said, "I know." Barely moving their mouths apart to speak. She said, "God, I want you." He said, "How do you get this off?" He said, "Shit, I tore it." She said, "I don't care, tear it," pulling his belt apart. He said, "Can you wait, just a second?" She said, "No." He said, "I can't either. Jesus." She said, "Don't talk." He said, "One second . . ." and got on his knees and pulled off her sandals and slacks and somehow got out of his pants, pausing then, catching his breath to pull his shirt over his head and when he sank down again into the bed they were naked, with nothing to make them hold back all that longing they could now release. The lights came on as they were making love, a soft bed-room glow that was just enough and could have been cued as Moran said, "Oh, man," and had to smile as he saw Mary smiling. Now they could see each other and it wasn't simply an act of their bodies, they were identified to each other, finally where they wanted to be more than anywhere. Moran's urge raised him stiff-armed, raised his face to the headboard, to the wall above them and he groaned, letting go that was like, "Gaiii-yaaa!" and brought Mary's eyes open, but she closed them again, murmuring, moving, and remained in irides-cent sparkling dark as he came back to her again, winding down, settling.

She felt moisture on his back, his shoulders. She said, "Oh, God," as though it might be her last breath. Then opened her eyes to study his face in repose, his eyelashes, his eyelids lightly closed.

She said quietly, "Well . . . how have you been?"

"Not too bad."

"Do you always do that?" Her words a soft murmur.

"What?"

"I thought you were in pain."

"I was, sort of."

"You really throw yourself into it."

"That was the first time I ever heard myself do that. It just came, so to speak." He opened his eyes. "You do an analysis after?"

"No, but I've always wondered about you," Mary said. "Do you know how many words we've spoken to each other, counting today?"

"We didn't have to use words. That was the spooky part about it. I always had the feeling we knew each other when we were little. Little kids who played together, then didn't see each other for about thirty years."

"I'm not that old."

"You're old enough. You know what I mean," Moran said. "I don't have to explain anything to you."

"No."

"Boy, you are really something."

She said, "There's more to it than that, isn't there?"

"There's way more," Moran said. "I don't mean just in bed. Will you tell me what you're doing here?"

"I came down with some girls from the club. Polo buffs. Or that's their excuse to get away and party, maybe play a little tennis. Actually they came down yesterday, but I couldn't make it till today."

Moran said, "Yeah, I ran into them at the airport. They looked sort of familiar—one of 'em's name is Philly?"

"Right, Philly, Marilyn and Liz, my old tennis court buddies."

Moran said, "You're staying here, this place? I don't think it's very *in*."

"No, what happened," Mary said, "my friends drove in from Casa de Campo to meet me and go to a cocktail party at the Santo Domingo Country Club. Mostly embassy people."

"Yeah? . . ."

"Then I was supposed to drive back to Casa de Campo with them later. The polo matches start tomorrow." Mary paused. "But I left the party."

"Why'd you come here?"

"Well, you told Philly you were staying here . . ."

"Yeah? . . ."

"I thought I'd stop by and say hi."

Moran said, "Really?" And began to smile. "You came to the hotel just to see me?"

"You want the truth?" Mary said. "I came to Santo Domingo just to see you."

"But you said—"

"I lied," Mary said. "I didn't plan to make the trip. But then Philly called last night to coax me, tell me about the embassy party and happened to mention she saw you at the airport." She said, "There, I've bared my soul to you, Moran."

"It's a nice one," Moran said. "I'm getting excited all over again. But what about the polo matches?"

"I think polo's boring," Mary said. She smiled and he smiled. "I sent for my bags. For the time being I don't have any clothes."

Moran said, "You don't, huh?" Still smiling.

5

SHE SAID, "You're getting tired of me already."

"What, because I said we ought to go out? Room service is okay, but it's still room service."

"I have to admit, George, you're a lot more romantic than I thought you'd be."

"I hear myself sometimes," Moran said, "I sound like I'm about seventeen."

She said, "You don't look much older, except for the beard. I love your beard. I love your body."

Even after he had told her why he was here and she was fascinated and wanted to walk the streets of his war with him, they remained in the hotel for the next two days. They needed the intimacy of being alone together, to look at each other with no one watching now and realize, no question about it, they were right. Boy, were they right. Meant for each other. They could say it and it sounded fine. They could say, I love you, earnestly, though so far only in the midst of love, perspiration glistening on their bodies, and I love you sounded pretty good, too. They lay in the sun at the hotel pool, a breeze coming off the Caribbean. She touched him and told him he could be one of the winter ballplayers. He told her she was way better looking than any of the young baseball wives, looked around, realized it wasn't even a contest and widened the scope to include all the girl movie stars he could think of. He believed it. They talked, never having to think of things to say, and were at ease with each other in silence.

"I remember times at the club I'd see you staring off in space," Mary said, "like you were planning to go over the wall."

They lay side by side at the deep end of the pool, facing the afternoon sun, their lounge chairs touching.

"I got pardoned," Moran said. "If I hadn't, yeah, I would've done it. I could feel it coming."

She said, "Can we get a few things out in the open?"

"It's all right with me."

"Okay. Why'd you marry Noel?"

"I think it was her heinie," Moran said. "That high, insolent ass, like it's got a personality all its own."

"Are we going to only say nice things?"

"Well, you know her as well as I do. Sometimes

the things that attract us are the things that sooner or later turn us off. I should've looked at her stuck-up ass and known."

He turned his head to see Mary's slender body in the yellow bikini, the delicate line from armpit to breast, her belly a shallow basin between the small-bone mounds of her hips. He wanted to jump on her.

"You asked me because you knew I was gonna ask you. Where you stand."

"I suppose."

"Okay, where are you?"

"Well, not too long ago I almost asked Andres for a divorce. I had the words ready, exactly what I was going to say . . ."

He was aware of his instant reaction: *great*. He didn't tighten, begin to feel trapped. No, he liked what she was saying.

"But I chickened out."

"How come?"

"Well . . . I felt sorry for him."

Moran didn't say anything.

"Or I felt sorry for myself—I don't know. I thought, if I'm gonna leave, I should be going to something I want to do. But even if there *was* something, I don't want to just walk out. I want to talk to him, so he'll understand how I feel. But we don't talk. In the six years we've been together"—she turned her head to look at Moran—"if there's a gale blowing out of Biscayne Bay in the hurricane season we might get in a good exchange about the weather. We don't even see each other that much. We have dinner together about three times a week. Half the time he doesn't get home till late, or we meet at the club."

"What'd you marry him for, his money?"

"I might've."

"I was kidding."

"No, you weren't. But that may be the real reason, security," Mary said. "At first I was fascinated by him. General Andres de Boya. In a way I thought he was cute."

"Jesus Christ," Moran said.

"I did, at first." Mary pushed up on her elbow, getting into it. "Usually—well, you know—he's very formal, he's the boss, you have to do things his way. But then when you see a vulnerable side, just a glimpse, you realize he's a person like everyone else."

"Regular guy," Moran said.

"No, he's not a regular guy. That's what I mean. He was a soldier in the Dominican army, worked his way up to general, then lost everything. He came to Miami with practically nothing and did it all on his own."

"I heard he escaped with a fortune."

"You heard wrong. He put fifteen thousand

down on an apartment house in South Miami and that was everything he had."

"You stick up for him."

"George, what do you want to believe? That story—he came with millions on a private yacht, that's baloney. He escaped with his life, very little else. But I know one thing, if he ever has to make a quick exit again he's gonna be ready."

"He keep his money under the mattress now?"

Mary paused. "It sounds funny, but to Andres it's real life. He thinks there's always somebody out to get him, so we have full-time security guards, armed. They never smile."

"Well, I guess you were head of secret police for Trujillo," Moran said, "and now you're sitting on all that dough . . ."

"That was political," Mary said, "we're talking about the man now."

Moran could argue the distinction—the man was still responsible for a lot of people dying—but he let it go.

"All right, you're telling me why you married him."

"I'm trying to think of a good reason," Mary said. "I was twenty-eight and all the good guys were taken. And he talked me into it."

"I hope you can do better than that."

"I was ready to get married. I didn't like what I

was doing. My dream, always, was to get married some day." She paused, thinking. "He's not bad-looking really, and he's very romantic."

"Jesus Christ," Moran said.

"Well, he thinks he is, but most of it's in Spanish. He's very, you know, serious, a heavy breather."

"I'm not gonna say anything," Moran said.

"On the other hand he's extremely cold, aloof," Mary said. "Sometimes smirky. If I want to see him I practically have to get an appointment. But he's a rock, George."

"I won't argue with you there."

"He's absolutely reliable. If Andres says he's going to do something, believe it. Whatever it is."

"He wants to buy the Coconuts," Moran said. He had told Mary about Andres's sister and the piano player, without going into much detail. "He came—I was gonna say yesterday, but it was three days ago. Anyway he made an offer and I said, 'You trying to get rid of me, Andres? Come on, what's your game?'"

It brought her upright. "You didn't. What's your *game?*"

"Listen, the other day I beat a guy playing tennis, a young hotshot, I said to him, 'You're all right, kid.' I'm starting to say things I've always felt like saying. But try to get anything out of your husband—I think you could punch him, he wouldn't make a sound," Moran said. "Maybe when you married him you thought you could change him. Turn him into a teddy bear. He's not at all cute, I'll tell you, but you thought you could make him cute."

"No, you're wrong," Mary said. She eased back to lie flat on the lounge again. "I was working in that law office typing one profit-sharing plan after another, pages and pages of figures, pension plans, trust funds, all due at five o'clock, always, and I had to get out. Andres came along—it was his lawyer I worked for. He'd divorced his first two wives. He has four grown children, a girl who's married and lives in California, three sons in Madrid who're in business together—those are the legitimate ones. He let his mistress go . . . I think. And I decided he was fascinating. I thought the difference between us might make it all the more interesting, maybe even fun. I thought, well, assuming there's a person under that cold, formal exterior, why don't I try to bring him out?"

"How'd you do?"

"Well, the only thing I can figure out," Mary said, "he puts on the front so no one will know what a real asshole he is."

"So walk away," Moran said. "What's the problem?"

"I told you, I want him to understand why I'm leaving. I don't want him to think it's for any other reason than we shouldn't have got married in the first place. We made a mistake and I want him to realize it."

"What other reason is there? You don't like him, that's all."

"There's a good one," Mary said. "I signed a prenuptial agreement. I didn't want to but Andres insisted. In the agreement it says if the marriage ends in divorce, for any reason, I'm to be given a flat settlement of two million dollars."

Moran said, "You didn't want to sign it?"

"I felt like it was an inducement. I didn't want to make a *deal* with him. I wanted to marry him. I might've been dumb, but I was sincere."

"Well, it was his idea," Moran said. "But if you're worried about what he thinks—I mean you want to prove you're still sincere, then don't take the money."

"Yeah, except that I like being rich."

Moran studied her face, the fine bone structure, the delicate line of her nose, knowing the face would change and he would still want to look at it for a long time to come.

"You got a problem," he said.

They were silent now. His gaze moved past her to the shrubs that bordered the south end of the hotel grounds. After several moments he said, "My first night here, I slept in a hole. Right over where that hedge is . . ."

6

THE AFTERNOON OF the fourth day. The Chevrolet Impala moved in low gear through streets that were like alleys, past stone structures with wooden entranceways, tenements that dated only a hundred years—new housing in a town where the son of Christopher Columbus had lived in style. Mary stared at scarred walls. They could be in San Juan or Caracas. The heat pressed motionless in the narrow streets. She searched for something to hold her interest as Moran spoke to Bienvenido in English and pidgin present-tense Spanish. The oldest buildings of all, she realized, the ones that dated to the early sixteenth century, were the newest in appearance, clean, reconstructed among recent decay, with all the charm of Disney World.

When they left the car to walk, Moran would nod to people along the street and in doorways staring at them, staring longer at the blond-haired woman than at the bearded man.

Mary said, "You're sure we're all right."

Moran's gaze came down from the upper floors of a building to the narrow shops on the street level. "They look at you and it's instant love. Blondes have some kind of magic." His gaze lifted again. "Up by that corner window—those are bullet holes. My fire team came along this street . . . We shouldn't have been anywhere near this area."

"What's a fire team?" She pictured firemen.

"A third of a squad. Two riflemen, an automatic rifleman and the fire-team leader. Thirteen men in a squad, forty-eight in a platoon. The platoon was Cat Chaser. After we lost our sergeant I was Cat Chaser Four—if anybody wanted to call up and say hi."

"Mister!"

Moran turned to see the dark face close to him, teeth missing and brown-stained eyes smiling, the man holding up lottery tickets. Moran waved him away, moving past.

"You the Marine, uh?" the man said, stopping Moran again in his tracks. "I hear it on the radio, the marine looking for his girl. You the Marine, yes?"

"I was a Marine," Moran said.

They were standing now, people gathering around. Mary saw the eager expression on the man's face as he said, "This is the Marine!" Excited. "You looking for the girl Luci Palma. You find her?"

Mary watched Moran shake his head, with the same eager expression as the man's. "You know her?"

"No, I don't think so." The man turned to the other people and began speaking in Spanish.

Moran took Mary's arm. They continued up the old street past lingering people, piles of trash, children following them now, the children and the lottery-ticket man's voice raised, telling everyone something in Spanish, with feeling, like he was telling a story.

"What's he saying?"

"I ran an ad in the paper, looking for somebody," Moran said. "Evidently one of the radio stations got hold of it."

"Looking for somebody," Mary said.

"Someone I met after I was taken prisoner. One of the snipers."

"A girl?"

"She was about sixteen. Luci Palma."

"That's why you came here? To see her?"

"No, this is why I came. What we're doing now. But I was curious."

"I'll bet you are."

"She was a skinny little kid."

"She won't be now, though," Mary said, "will she?" Have you seen her since then?"

"This is the first time I've been back," Moran said. Coming to a corner he was looking at the upper stories again. Mary watched him turn to look off in the direction of the river. "There the grain elevators I told you about. See? Ten stories high. The Eighty-second sat up their with their cannons. Up on top."

Mary stared at the cement cylinders standing about a mile away, on the opposite bank of the Ozama River. She felt Moran's hand on her arm and they continued across the intersection. Behind them, Bienvenido's Impala came to a stop. Moran was pointing now. "That's the building. The one on the corner. Where I chased the sniper."

"The girl?"

"No, it was a guy in a green striped shirt. Green and white." Moran turned, looking at the side streets again, thoughtful. "They'd hide a gun in an upstairs room, take a shot at you, come out, walk up the street to an apartment where they had another gun stashed and let you have a few more rounds. You see how narrow the streets are, you have to look almost straight up. You feel exposed, looking up, trying to spot the window, the guy's already someplace else, drawing a bead on you . . ." He turned slowly back to the building on the corner and stared, squinting in the sunlight. "I stuck my head out of that third-floor window, right there. . . ."

* * *

It was the girl, Luci, who had brought him here, this far, and got him in a lot of trouble, though she was not the one he had chased. A sixteen-year-old girl playing with him, now and then taking shots at him. That was the trouble with the whole deal: After a while it was like a game and he would get excited and lose his concentration. He got chewed out for it more than once by the platoon sergeant who told him he was going to get fucking killed and go home in a bag.

A lot of it was boring and a lot of it was fun. More exciting than anything he had ever experienced before. Hugging a doorway under fire, then stepping out, seeing them running across the street down at an intersection and squeezing off rounds at them. Hearing the voices then laughing and calling you *hijo de puta*, son of a whore, that was the favorite; learning what it meant and yelling it back at them, though "motherfucker" remained the all-time any-situation favorite. (Ham and lima beans: ham and motherfuckers.) "Hey, motherfucker! Come on out of there! Where's your balls!" Kids playing. Working a street and finding a *cantina* open, Christ, and stopping for a beer in the middle of a firefight. Or stopping to let the trucks go through with sacks of rice and powdered milk, the U.S. military feeding the people they were fighting. Did that make sense? None of it did. That's why you might as well accept this deal as being pretty weird and have some fun. Though it wouldn't be fun now.

Mary walked back to the taxi. Bienvenido got out. He opened the door for her and she said, "I'll wait. Thanks." She watched Moran, on the other side of the intersection, then said to Bienvenido, "Do you remember General Andres de Boya?"

Bienvenido said, "Oh my. Oh my, yes. General de Boya, ouuuh, he was a devil, that man."

"Why do you say that?"

"Because he kill people with his *Cascos Blancos*. Everyone the enemies of them. They kill more people than the malaria fever."

Mary said, "Oh . . ."

"That fella was a devil. Yes, we very glad he's gone from here."

Mary got in the car. She sat in back, staring through the windshield at Moran across the street.

Once Luci picked up their radio frequency she kept cutting in on them. They didn't know what she was using and they didn't talk to her at first. They'd switch frequencies and there she'd be like Tokyo Rose, giving them the business. "What you doing here, Marines? You come to kill us? Why? We haven't done nothing to you. You afraid of Communists? We not Communists, but you turning us into Communists you stay here." Political at first, till she got to know the Cat Chasers that patrolled along Independencia as far as La Carreras in a jeep with a 50 mounted on it. He spoke to her a couple times, asking her name and if she'd have a beer with him. She said sure, come over to Conde Street, she'd meet him. Conde, where rebel headquarters was located.

They were almost ambushed and got in a fire-fight at the corner of Carreras and Padre Billini; the Cat Chasers gave chase, in and out of the buildings, and that was when he finally saw her the first time, running across a rooftop with her carbine.

He saw her from a window across the street, the window a story higher than the roof she was on. He put his M-14 on her and began to track and saw her look back, laughing, yelling at somebody, waving then, *Come on!* Then she was looking this way, surprised, and he saw her face clearly. There was a burst from a submachine gun. He saw a guy on the same roof now, a guy wearing a baseball cap, a pouch of magazines slung over his shoulder, the guy aiming at him. Moran hung in and squeezed off and the guy spun, grabbing at his side above the left hip, and went down behind the cornice of the building. The girl disappeared. They went up to the roof but all they found was some blood and a few 9-mm casings. The next day, over the radio, the girl's voice said, "You so slow, you Cat Chasers. You tired from chasing *putas*." She didn't mention the guy who got hit.

The second time was after the 106 fired from the silos across the river almost put him under, tore his leg up with shrapnel and he had an awful time getting down from the third floor with the stairway blown to hell. He should have stayed up there. He climbed through the rubble, slipped out the back thinking he was pretty cool and walked right into them. A gang of guys in sportshirts carrying old M-1s and Mausers. He'd always remember how they grinned at him. The fuckers, they weren't even soldiers.

They blindfolded and quick-marched him to a house he'd never have found again even if he could have seen where they were going; gave him a bucket of water and a dirty towel to do something about his bleeding and locked him in a room. Every once in a while the door would open and some more of them would look in to see the prize, laughing and making, no doubt, insulting remarks in Spanish. He told them to get fucked but they just laughed some more. When the girl came and stood in the doorway he knew who it was right away. Maybe it was the carbine she had slung over her shoulder, though he told himself later it was her eyes, the way she looked at him like they had met before.

She was skinny, without any breasts to speak of, but had beautiful eyes and chestnut brown hair.

He said, "Well, Luci, how you doing?" Taking a chance and hitting it on the head. She smiled. She looked like she'd be a lot of fun just to be with. She wore a T-shirt and jeans that were patched and faded. She left the carbine outside, came in and closed the door.

She said, "You're the Cat Chaser." Her whole face smiling.

"I'm one of 'em."

"You catching much lately?"

"Well, I didn't do too good today, I'll tell you."

She liked that; she smiled and went out and came back with a bottle of El Presidente and a dressing. She fooled around with his leg while he drank the beer, the leg not hurting yet, though it looked a mess. He asked about the guy he'd shot and she mentioned the guy's name, which he forgot, and said the guy was not hurt bad but had quit the war. She asked him where he lived; he said Detroit and she told him she had stayed in Miami, Florida for two months, visiting. She told him she loved Miami, Florida and wanted to go back there sometime. She asked him if he liked the Beatles or did he prefer the Rolling Stones? Everyone, she said, was in love with the Beatles. They discussed the Supremes, Freddie and the Dreamers, Sam the Sham & the Pharaohs, the Righteous Brothers,

Herman's Hermits . . . She did not care much for the Beach Boys or Roger Miller. He said he didn't either. Her favorite of all was Petula Clark. She sang a little of "Downtown" in English, snapping her fingers; she knew more of the words than he did.

When they took him out and put him in the panel truck she was there. He told her to take care of herself. She gave him a look that was sad and sort of longing and told him to take care of himself, too. She said, "I won't shoot at you no more." Some war.

They told him see, we're not bad guys; we're good to you. It's your government, your President Johnson we don't like. They handed him over to a Marine patrol on the west end of Independence Park. The Marines looked at him like he was some kind of weird freak and drove him to the field hospital at Haina.

It was the end of Moran's war.

Mary was patient because she enjoyed watching him and could feel the enthusiasm he tried to keep inside him. Like a young boy. Excited but self-conscious at the same time. It gave her a feeling about him that was tender and made her want to touch his face. But maybe she simply liked to touch him; she would watch him asleep, breathing softly, and the same feeling would come over her.

When he returned to the taxi and got in next to her, she said, "That's where you were wounded?"

He nodded slowly, several times, then cocked his head, looking out the windshield. "It seems bigger. You go back to a place where you lived or spent some time and it always seems smaller. But Santo Domingo seems bigger."

"It probably is," Mary said. "It's grown. A million people live here."

"I don't mean that way," Moran said. "I guess I mean it isn't as easy to understand as I thought it would be. Things aren't black or white, are they?" He shrugged and said, "Maybe it's me. I see it differently now."

With feeling, Mary thought. How many people did she know who spoke or looked at anything with genuine feeling? Without being cynical, on stage, trying to entertain. Without puffing up or putting down. She wanted to know what he felt and, if possible, share the feeling.

"What happened then?"

He hesitated for a long moment. "I was taken to a field hospital. Five days later I was evacuated. Home."

* * *

They returned to the hotel along the broad expanse of Avenida Washington with its tall palms, its view of the Caribbean on one side and the facade Santo Domingo presented to the world on the other: sun beating on walled colonial buildings and straw markets, the old giving way to solitary glass structures rising in the background. Mary said, "This is one section that's never blacked out." She told of a Dominican couple she'd met at the country club who paid twelve hundred dollars a month for electricity. Moran said it would be something to tell his neighbors in Pompano; they were into electric bills and loved to compare them.

He asked Bienvenido about the radio broadcast. Was it true, what the lottery-ticket man had said?

Bienvenido said, "Yes, all day it's on the radio about you. You don't hear it?" He began switching dials on the car radio, getting static and rock music until he found a voice speaking dramatically in Spanish. "There," Bienvenido said. "Listen."

"What's he saying?" Moran hunched over the front seat rest, laying his chin on his arm.

Bienvenido was leaning toward the car radio. "He say . . . the American Marine who fell in love with the girl name Luci has returned."

"What? Come on—"

"For many years since the way Captain Morón has been thinking of her, missing her . . ."

"*Cap*tain?"

". . . with his heart breaking, until now he has returned to find her."

"Jesus," Moran said. "They're making it up. I hardly even knew her." He turned to glance at Mary who sat composed. "They're making all that up."

"He say . . . if anyone knows where to find Luci Palma, tell her that the Marine, Captain Morón, is here who loves her very much and wants to take her to the United States to live. He is at the Hotel Embajador."

"I don't believe it," Moran said. "How do they know all that? I mean my name. I didn't give anybody my name."

"Captain Moron?" Mary said.

"Morón," Moran said. He poked Bienvenido's shoulder. "How do they know about me? What'd you tell the newspaper?"

"What you told me, only. I think the radio station call the newspaper and maybe the hotel," Bienvenido said, "talk to some people there. I don't know."

"But it isn't true. None of it." He turned to look at Mary again. "Do you believe it?"

Mary gave him a nice smile. She said, "I can't wait to meet Luci."

There were a dozen or more Luci Palmas scattered about the hotel lobby, some with relatives,

mothers and perhaps fathers; several more were in
the cocktail lounge talking to winter ballplayers,
doing all right, forgetting why they had come here.
There was no announcement. It was like a celebrity,
a movie star, arriving. A bellman nodded, holding
open the door, and all the Luci Palmas converged
on the bearded man with the stylish lady, who was
maybe his aide, his secretary. They called out to
him, "Captain! Here I am!" They said, "Oh, it is so
good to see you again!" They said, "My Marine,
you have return!"

Moran said, "Wait a minute! . . ."

The bellman said, "Can I assist you, Capitano?"

Mary slipped through the girls crowding in,
walked over to the front desk. She watched from
here, standing with a travel group of Chinese from
Taiwan who nudged each other, staring. Mary said,
"It's George Moran, the American film star," and
some of them raised their cameras and began taking pictures.

She watched Moran in a much different role
now, but the same Moran, surrounded by girls with
silky dark hair and woolly Afros, girls in dresses
and girls in tight jeans, girls with imploring eyes
trying to make themselves heard in both Spanish
and English—Moran in the middle, hands raised
close to his body, trying not to touch them. He was
working his way out of the pack now toward the

front desk, his eyes with a helpless look finding
Mary. She smiled at him.

Reaching her he said, "What do I do?" And
looked at the desk clerk who stood composed, almost indifferent.

"Will you tell them I'm not the one?"

The desk clerk raised his eyebrows. "You are
Captain Morón."

"I'm not a captain. I never was."

"I don't believe they care you aren't an officer.
You are Mr. Jorge Morón, are you not?"

"They're not old enough," Moran said.

The desk clerk seemed surprised. "You like them
to be older?"

"They're not old enough to be Luci Palma. It
was sixteen years ago. There isn't one of them over
thirty."

"Take a good look," Mary said. "There isn't one
of them over twenty-five."

Moran said to the girls, "Wait, stand still. Be
tranquilo, okay? I'll ask each of you one question,
una pregunta, all right?"

"I'll be in the bar," Mary said.

"Wait. Help me, will you?"

"You're doing fine, George. Ask your *pregunta*."

Walking away, working through the girls pressing in, Mary heard him say, "All right, I'm gonna
ask you how old you are. *Comprende? Quantos*

años tiene? . . . You first. Hi, how're you doing?"

She was aware of the tender feeling again: a comfortable feeling, even as she realized there was much more to Moran than a natural, easygoing manner. At times he seemed almost naive; yet he continued to surprise her.

She chose a table on the far side of the lounge, away from the entrance and the ballplayers at the bar, and ordered a scotch. The chair felt good; it was low, with soft cushions and casters; she crept it closer to another chair at the table and put her feet up, stretching her legs, brushing at the wrinkles in her beige slacks. When the waitress brought her drink she looked up to thank her. The waitress moved off and a man was standing at the table.

"If you'll permit me . . ."

"To do what?" Mary said.

"Speak with you, please." His manner was pleasant, unhurried. "You're the friend, I believe, of the Marine."

Mary nodded. "We're buddies."

The man's dark eyes relaxed in warm creases. He looked to be in his early thirties with a trimmed mustache and hair styled by a hotel barber, swept straight back from a high forehead: the look of light-skinned Dominican aristocracy, Mary judged. He wore a tailored white cotton shirt that hung free of his trousers like a light jacket, open enough to show some of his chest hair.

He said, "I like to have a woman who is a buddy. I didn't know it was possible."

"Why?"

"I don't know, I suppose the way we are, men and women, uh? The difference between us."

"How do you know the Marine and I aren't married?"

"I find out those things." He smiled.

More than pleasant, his manner was instantly familiar, confident, the Latin lover come-on. Mary sipped her drink; she'd been there several times.

"Excuse me. My name is Rafael Amado." He paused, giving Mary a chance to introduce herself, but she passed. "I think your friend should know that none of those girls could be Luci Palma."

"He knows," Mary said. "He's just having a little fun."

"Yes, that's good . . . My name is Rafael, but by most people I'm known as Rafi."

"That's cute," Mary said.

The Dominican smiled. "You like it? Good. I wonder if I may join you." He brought over a chair without waiting for permission and eased into it, careful of the press in his black trousers. "Thank you. May I buy you a drink?"

Mary raised her glass. "I'm fine."

He looked up, snapped his fingers and said

something in Spanish that was abrupt, without the pleasant manner, though it returned instantly as he said to Mary, "If I may have one with you."

She wished Moran would hurry up. She wanted to see the look on his face, coming in and finding her taken care of. It might tell her something. Then immediately doubted it. Moran wouldn't make assumptions, waste time being jealous. If he were to hesitate, appear to be just a little awkward, that would be good enough.

Rafi said, "When I heard on the radio about the return of the Marine I thought, Could it be? Then in *Listin Diario* I see the message, Cat Chaser is looking for the girl . . . and I thought, It is, it's the same one."

"The message," Mary said, "I haven't seen it yet."

"In the newspaper personal column," Rafi told her. "Cat Chaser is looking for the girl who ran over the roofs of buildings and tried to kill him. Call this hotel. It's very clever the way it's said."

"The girl named Luci tried to kill him?" Mary straightened in her chair, bringing her legs down.

"Well, she try different tricks, you know, to lure him."

Mary wanted to be sure. She said, "To *lure* him?"

"To bring the Marines where they shouldn't be.

Trick them. But that was a long time ago. It was the war."

"You said you were sure then he was the one. What one?"

The waitress appeared with Rafi's drink. He took it from her without a word, then leaned toward Mary, his expression grave.

"I was with Luci Palma. In the group of partisans with her. I was on the roof with her." He continued to stare at Mary before easing back in the chair. "He didn't tell you? The Marine?"

"What? I'm not sure."

Rafi placed his hands on his chest, fingers spread, an amber stone with a dull gleam on his little finger.

"On the roof," Rafi said, his expression still grave, "I'm the one he shot and almost killed."

7

ALL THOSE WHITE TEETH flashing at him, different scents of perfume, a couple of the Luci Palmas taking his arm and rubbing against him. At some other time in his life, not too long ago, Moran would have asked them more than how old they were, might have staged a mini-Miss D.R. pageant and chosen a winner.

Going into the lounge he was thinking of something to tell Mary—that he was getting out of the motel business to become a movie producer; at least a casting director. He saw Mary's hair and a guy in a white Dominican dress-up shirt and took it a little easier going over to the table. The Dominican guy saw him now and was getting up.

Mary said, pleasantly enough, "How did it go?"

"Well, it was different."

"If you're through casting . . ."

It amazed him, how well she knew him already.

". . . this is Rafi. I'm sorry I didn't hear your last name."

"Rafi Amado. I'm very pleased to meet you." Extending his hand across the table. "I'm honored."

Mary was looking up at him. "Really? . . . And this is Jorge Morón, Rafi. The infamous Marine."

Moran glanced at her, taking the Dominican's slender hand, the grip not too firm.

"What did I do?"

"On your last trip it seems you shot somebody on the roof of a building," Mary said. "Well, Rafi's the one you shot."

Moran stared at him now, not sure what to say, the Dominican giving him sort of a guarded look, like he wasn't sure what to expect.

Moran said, "You're the one?" He seemed awed now.

"I believe so," Rafi said. "A house on Padre Billini near Carreras? Up on the roof? I was with Luci Palma."

Moran said, "Boy . . ." He moved his hand over his beard, still not sure what to do in this situation. He said, quickly then, "Sit down, please. What're you drinking?"

"I have one. Thank you."

They sat down and Moran ordered a beer. It gave him something to do, time to settle, get used to the idea that he was looking at a man he had once tried to kill.

"You had an automatic weapon. Like a grease gun."

Rafi was nodding. "Yes, I forgot what kind. They gave out all types of guns the first day of the revolution, in the park. I had different weapons."

"You tried for me first," Moran said. He held up his hand. "I don't mean that the way it sounds. But I remember you fired a burst. I was in a window across the street."

"I believe so," Rafi said, "but I don't shoot too straight. Which is good for you."

"Listen, I'm really sorry," Moran said. "Were you hurt bad?"

"No, not seriously. You like to see it?" Rafi leaned forward unbuttoning his shirt, pulling it open now and thrusting out his chest, giving Mary a sly glance. He brushed at the hair covering his left breast to reveal several inches of white scar tissue. "The bullet went this way, across me, instead of *in*to me, which was good, uh? It took off the nipple," Rafi said, "but I wasn't using it, so it doesn't matter."

He chuckled and Mary smiled, seeing him glance over again. Mary said, "You're a good sport, Rafi."

Moran said, "I thought I hit you lower and more in the side. Down around the belt."

Rafi pressed his chin to his chest looking down, feeling his mid section as though to make sure.

"No, I don't think so. It seems all right."

"We went up on that roof," Moran said. "You were gone."

"Yes, I hope so. Luci help me to get down. Maybe without her, I don't know, I may not be here. She was the one take me to the hospital."

The waitress brought Moran's beer, half the bottle poured in a glass with a foamy head. He said, "Thanks," still looking at Rafi and let the glass stand on the table.

"You know where she is?"

Mary's eyes, mildly curious, moved to Moran and waited for his reaction as she heard Rafi say, "Luci? I didn't see her after that war. But, I didn't hear anything happen to her either."

Moran seemed to accept this calmly enough. Mary had thought he'd be sitting on the edge of his chair. He said, "You knew I was taken prisoner."

Rafi hesitated, somewhat surprised. "Is that so? No, I didn't know that. And they release you?"

"The same day," Moran said. "I found out later a guy from the Peace Corps worked it out."

"Ah, that was good."

"But I got a chance to talk to her. It's funny, I remember I asked about you."

"Me?"

"She said you were alive and would be okay. She told me your name . . ."

"Yes?"

"But I forgot it. She brought me a beer . . ."

Rafi seemed to relax. "Yes, she was very thoughtful of people. And very brave." He sipped his drink, placed it on the table again as though in slow motion, a thoughtful expression on his face. "You come all the way here to find Luci Palma?"

"No, not really," Moran said. "I wanted to see Santo Domingo again. As a tourist this time."

"It's much bigger now," Rafi said. "You live where, in what state?"

"Florida. Pompano Beach. It's about fifty miles north of Miami."

"Pompano," Rafi said. "Is a nice place?"

"George owns the Coconut Palms," Mary said, "a very exclusive resort."

"Yes?" Rafi appeared thoughtful again, nodding. "I think I heard of it. Like the Fontainebleu in Miami? Very big place, uh?"

"Not as big," Mary said, ignoring the look Moran was giving her, "but much classier, if you know what I mean."

Rafi brightened. "A swanky place, uh?"

"That's it," Mary said. "It's got a lot of swank." She gave Moran, shaking his head slowly, a look of wide-eyed innocence.

Rafi was saying, "Perhaps I can be of help." It brought them back. "Find out for you where Luci Palma is."

"Well, I doubt if she's still here," Moran said.

"Yes, if she's still here in Santo Domingo she must know about you. Everyone seems to," Rafi said. "So I think she live someplace else. La Romana, Puerto Plata . . . There isn't much mobility among the Dominican people. I can find out for you."

"I don't want you to go to a lot of trouble though," Moran said. "I'm curious about her, that's all. She seemed like a nice girl. Very eager, you know, full of life. I hope nothing happened to her."

Rafi looked at his watch. "Let me make phone calls, see what I can do."

As he finished his drink and got up Moran said, "Really, it's not that important to me."

Rafi said, "Put it in my hands," gesturing, glancing at his watch again. "Now I have business to do. I'll call you later." He gave Mary the hint of a bow. "And I hope to see the buddy of the Marine again. It was a pleasure."

He was walking off. Moran rose. He said on impulse, "How about dinner later? If you're free . . ."

Rafi made a circle with his thumb and index finger. He waved and was gone.

Moran sat down.

Mary said, "I'm surprised he didn't click his heels."

"Your Dominicans are very polite people," Moran said.

Mary gave him a look. "Tell me about it."

"That's right, you have one at home, don't you? You see his Rolex?"

"He'd like you to think it's a Rolex, but it's not."

"How do you know?"

"I know gold, George. I have some of that at home too."

He sipped at his beer in silence.

"If she's in Santo Domingo, fine. But I don't want to go chasing all over the country."

"Then don't."

"Yeah but, what if he busts his ass, goes to a lot of trouble, finds out she's in Puerto Plata . . . I don't want to go to Puerto Plata. I'm really not that hot about taking him to dinner."

"But you don't want to seem ungrateful."

"You shoot a guy's left nipple off," Moran said, "I think you ought to buy him dinner, at least. Especially if you're the owner of a swank resort."

"I couldn't help it," Mary said. "Are you mad at me?"

"The Fontainebleu. Jesus, can you see me running a place like the Fontainebleu?"

"You can't say he wasn't impressed."

"That's what I'm afraid of. I'm his new buddy."

Mary waited a moment.

"You don't seem to be as anxious about finding Luci. What happened?"

"Nothing. It was an idea, that's all," Moran said. "Something that happened a long time ago. Sixteen years." He looked at Mary. "What were you doing sixteen years ago? . . . What were you doing last week? The week before? . . . What're we doing sitting here?"

Rafi said to the desk clerk in English, "Let me see it again. The woman's."

The clerk looked past him at the lobby before taking out the registration card and laying it on the counter.

Rafi studied the card without picking it up. "I don't know if that's a one or a seven, in the address."

"*Siete,*" the clerk said.

"All right, take it. I'll fix it up when you want to score, man. Let me know the room and what time."

"Speak so I can understand," the clerk said.

"I'm practicing my American," Rafi said.

He walked past the uniformed guard into the hotel casino where there were players at the first roulette table and at several of the blackjack tables, though not much of a crowd this early in the evening. Rafi nodded to the young American in the three-piece gray suit, pointed to the telephone on the stand by the entrance and the young American, the casino assistant manager, gave him the sign, okay, though he seemed to hesitate and have doubts. Rafi picked up the phone and told the hotel operator the number he wanted, then turned his back to the room, hunching over the stand that was like a podium.

"It's Rafi again." He spoke in Spanish now. "Mary Delaney. Seven hundred Collins Avenue, Miami Beach."

The woman's voice on the phone said, "Wait."

Rafi turned to look over the room, though with little interest; he drum-rolled his fingernails on the polished wood of the stand. The woman's voice came on. "Rafi?"

"Yes." He turned his back to the room again.

"It's a jewelry store, that address, and there is no Mary Delaney in Miami Beach."

"Hiding something," Rafi said, pleased. "Can you look her up some other way?"

The woman's voice said, "I have directories—what do you think I am, the FBI?"

He could see the woman, imagine her sitting in her room that was like a gallery of photographs of important people: some of the pictures framed and enscribed, "To La Perla, with love," or "fondest regards," though most of the pictures, the ones in color, had been cut from magazines twenty or thirty years ago. La Perla had written about parties and scandals and was said to have been an intimate of Porfirio Rubirosa, the world's greatest lover. Now she sold pieces of her past and somehow remained alive.

"You have to see this one," Rafi said. "Anyone who looks like she does has to be somebody. I think I've seen her picture, but I'm not sure. I don't have your memory, like a recording machine."

"What does she look like?"

"An ice cream. I had a spoon I would have eaten her," Rafi said. "Listen. Be at Mesón de la Cava, nine o'clock, you'll see her."

"You're taking me to dinner?"

"Sit at the bar. Look at her and tell me who she is."

"I have to take a taxi there, five pesos," the woman said, "for you to buy me a drink?"

"I'll pay for the taxi," Rafi said. "You can have two drinks."

"I hope I don't become drunk," the woman said.

"Tell me what would make you happy," Rafi said.

"I want three daiquiris, at least," the woman said, "and I want the large shrimp cocktail."

"If she's somebody, you can have a flan, too. Nine o'clock," Rafi said, looking at his watch. He hung up and walked over to a blackjack table where the dealer, a light-skinned Dominican who wore the casino's gold jacket and vacant expression, stood alone waiting for players. Rafi hooked his leg over a stool and gave the dealer a ten-peso note for ten pink chips. As they began to play Rafi touched his chin and worked his jaw from side to side.

"My face hurts from smiling."

"All the sweetness gone out of it," the dealer said. "You want a hit?"

"Hit me . . . That's good." He watched the dealer turn over his cards, totaling fifteen. "Take one yourself."

"I know how to play," the dealer said, putting a card down. He went over twenty-one and paid Rafi his chips.

"I'm letting it ride," Rafi said. "Deal." They continued to play, Rafi winning again. "You think of her husband's name?"

"Who?"

"Who have we been talking about? Luci Palma."

"I still don't remember it," the dealer said. "They live in Sosua. That's all I know."

"I don't like her having a husband," Rafi said. "She have a good-looking sister?"

"Some brothers."

"Pay me again. I'm letting it ride," Rafi said. "I know she has brothers. Hit me. It was a brother I talked to. He knew the one who was with her that the Marine shot. I think I need a younger sister if I don't find a good Luci Palma."

"You're crazy," the dealer said, paying him for the third straight time.

"How do you know? Have I told you anything?"

"I don't want to know," the dealer said.

"Hit me," Rafi said. "Does the Marine come in here?"

"I haven't seen him."

"Again . . . What about the woman that's with him?"

"I don't know his woman."

"You haven't seen her? Once more. You're missing it. She's an ice cream. Butter almond. I look at her . . ."

"You wish you had a spoon," the dealer said.

"I think I need a girl about twenty. Very beautiful, very innocent. I mean with the appearance of innocence. I don't have that in my stable right now."

"Your girls look like the hotel maids," the dealer said, paying Rafi for the fourth straight time.

"I'm riding one hundred and . . . seventy pesos," Rafi said, holding out his original ten. "If I win this one then I'm going to win something else very big, maybe the jackpot of my life . . . Come on, give it to me."

The dealer gave him an ace and a queen. Blackjack.

"There," Rafi said, like there was nothing to it.

He watched the dealer turn up his own cards. Another ace, another queen. The dealer raised his eyes.

"The thing about it is," Rafi said, "you have to

know what is a sign and what isn't. You can be wrong about signs, sometimes interpret them the opposite of what they mean."

"You're still crazy," the dealer said.

Rafi used restraint. He said, "Am I?" and left the dealer with that, a secret smile that told nothing because it had nothing to tell. At least for the time being.

He would have to be more attentive in reading signs.

The Cat Chaser's notice in the paper and the business about it on the radio had alerted Rafi, immediately captured his interest. He talked to people who referred him to others who had taken an active part in the rebellion and there it was, once he put the pieces of the story together: an approach, a way to play a feature role in this, using an old knife scar to represent a bullet wound. He saw in his mind a crude scenario that went:

RAFI: I'm the one you shot sixteen years ago.

MARINE: Oh, I'm so sorry. What can I do to make amends?

RAFI: Please, nothing.

MARINE: I insist.

RAFI: Well, as one businessman to another (assuming the marine was now a businessman), I could tell you about a most unusual investment opportunity. . . .

Something, in essence, like that. Make it up, get his check; gone. But now the mystery woman had entered the picture and the scenario was changing before Rafi's eyes, the woman the Marine called Mary emerging to become, possibly, the key figure. So far it was only a feeling Rafi had. But to a man who lived by signs and instinct, what else was there?

8

THEY DESCENDED a spiral iron stairway fifty feet into the ground to dine in a cave, a network of rooms and niches like catacombs where tables were set with candles and white linen and Dominican couples danced to the percussion sounds of *merengues*. The old city and this place, no Coca-Cola or Texaco signs, Rafi said. This is Santo Domingo.

He told them he had begun to make inquiries about Luci Palma, but so far had learned nothing. It might take a little more time.

Moran tried to convince him it wasn't important, but Rafi insisted; he was curious about Luci now himself. What could have happened to her? He ventured the possibility she had become a full-time revolutionary and fled the country. Like Caamaño, who had led the revolt in '65; he left the country, returned and was shot. It happened.

They talked about that time sixteen years ago, the situation. Moran said it had been impossible to understand, being here in the middle of it. The rebels kept saying to them, "Can't you tell your government we aren't Communists?" It didn't begin to make sense. Almost all the people were friendly; still, guys he knew were getting killed. He read about the situation later and decided they had helped the wrong side—just as they'd been helping the wrong side in Latin America for eighty years. Like Nicaragua, helping that asshole Somoza against the Sandinistas, the good guys. Except look at the good guys now. They just shut down a newspaper for criticizing them; they were doing the same thing Somoza did. What happens to good guys once they get control?

Mary said they have the right to make mistakes like anyone else. Don't assume anything; don't label people. She said, What if a skid-row bum asks you for a handout? Are you going to qualify him, give him the money only if he promises not to spend it on booze? No. Once you give him the money—and it's your choice whether you do or not—then it's his, with no strings. He can spend it on anything he wants. He can screw up or not screw up, that's *his* choice. Unless you're buying him. That's something else.

Wine with dinner conversation: a bottle of red with the *sopa Dominicana* that was like beef stew with noodles; white wine with the sea bass simmered in a peppery tomato sauce . . . Rafi hanging on every word: Moran's basic sympathy with the underdog, the revolutionary, maybe with a few minor doubts; while the woman's analogy said don't expect too much, don't be surprised. Interesting; what Rafi considered the usual man-woman positions reversed. The woman using reason—at least, he assumed, until one got inside her pants. The man asking questions of what he's learned—but essentially, typically, an American bleeding heart.

Yes, it looked good.

Rafi excused himself. He visited the men's room, came out and entered the bar area that was set apart, like a passageway in the cave, only a few couples here having drinks. At the far end of the bar was La Perla with her daiquiri, holding the big snifter glass in both hands beneath a pink glow, staring into the glass, an old woman in theatrical makeup, amber costume jewelry; a gypsy fortune-teller, a magic act waiting to go on.

"Tell me," Rafi said, tense now, expectant.

"Yes, I have her picture."

"I knew it! Who is she?"

"You don't know anything," the woman, La Perla, said. "We have to negotiate this some more. The shrimp cocktail isn't going to do it."

Now Rafi had to decide whether to give in to his impatience or play with the old woman, croon a few false notes to her, put his hand on the curve of her narrow back. But he was tired and he didn't care to feel old bones. He said, "Buy your own rum," and started away.

"She comes to Casa de Campo . . ."

He paused. "Yes?"

". . . for the polo. But without her husband."

"Ah, she's married; I knew it. And he's rich, uh?"

"I'm starving," La Perla said. "I want the entre-cote, asparagus with hollandaise . . ."

Rafi raised a hip to the empty stool next to her, her perfume overpowering him as he leaned close.

"Why don't you order whatever you like."

"I still want the large shrimp cocktail."

"You should have it," Rafi said. "Who's her husband?"

"You won't believe it when I tell you."

"I promise I will," Rafi said.

"He's Dominican."

There was a pause between them; silence.

"But he can't come here with her," La Perla said.

"Why is that, if he's Dominican?"

"Somebody would shoot him. *Many* people would shoot him if they could."

It was a game. Rafi tried to think of names—expatriates, political villains—anxious now, trying too hard, as though a buzzer were about to go off and he'd lose.

"He's rich, isn't he? He has to be, with an American wife who likes the polo."

"You won't believe it when I tell you," the

woman said again. "I think I want a bottle of wine also. A full bottle of Margaux."

"When you tell me who it is," Rafi said, "have whatever you like. With my love."

The woman tapped the bar, rings rapping on the varnished wood. "Put the money here for my taxi and my dinner," she said. "But keep your love. I don't want to destroy my appetite."

There was not a noticeable change in Rafi when he returned to the table; they talked about Reaganomics and taxes and the price of automobiles. In Rafi's own mind, though, he was at once more cautious, even more observant. If the woman had turned out to be a film star or an international jet-setter he would be coming on to her now with subtle masculine moves, signs that he was available, a man who viewed pleasure as a way of life; far more sensitive than this former Marine who wiped his salad plate with his bread. Take him on *mano a mano* and go for the woman with nothing to lose.

But this woman was a celebrity in a much different light. Married to a man who was at the same time rich and a son of a bitch, accredited in both areas; a man responsible for the deaths of hundreds of people, perhaps thousands. (How many were thrown from the cliffs during Trujillo's time? The sharks still came to Boca Chica.) Married to the butcher and having a love affair with the bleeding heart.

Rafi was quiet now, cautious, because he saw himself in the presence of his future, the opportunity of a lifetime. Here you are. What can you do with this situation? The obvious, of course. But wait and see.

Though not for long. The conversation wound down and the woman covered yawns, smiling at the Marine with sleepy bedroom eyes, the idiot Marine sitting there fooling with his coffee spoon. In these moments, in the Mesón de la Cava, Rafi began to feel contempt for the Marine; he should take the woman away from him. A lovely woman wasted on a man like this was a mortal sin. Move in . . . She'll buy you gifts.

But on the other hand . . .

It was an either-or dilemma. Go for the woman, get her to turn those eyes on him and have her. Or, use the affair with the Marine to score far more in the long run.

Or do both. Was that possible? Bleed the bleeding heart. Yes? And *then* take the woman? It was a shame she wasn't married to the Marine and having the affair with de Boya. As it was there were interesting possibilities to think about.

Rafi cautioned himself again to go slowly and said, "I think I should see you two back to your hotel." There was no argument. "I'll call you tomorrow if I learn anything, all right?"

What else? It seemed enough for now. Don't be eager. At least don't appear eager.

They got into bed in Mary's suite and held each other in silence, tired and wanting nothing more than this closeness, until Mary said, "It's coming to an end. I can feel it."

He said, "Are you a worrier?"

She said, "No, not usually."

He said, in a soothing way, "You know what's coming to an end and what isn't. I don't think we have a choice, we're stuck with each other. But it's gonna be a lot harder for you than it is for me. I mean if we plan to see each other."

"We have to," Mary said.

"Good."

She said, "I've never done anything like this before. Have you?"

"When I was married? No."

"Did you ever have an affair with a married woman?"

"No."

"Then you've never done it either. We're amateurs. I've never even thought about it." She paused. "No, that's a lie. I used to look at you and think about it a lot."

"I did too."

"I used to stare at you and when you'd look over I'd say let's get out of here and go somewhere, be together."

"I would have gone."

"Would you?"

"I wanted to."

"Boy, we've come a long way." She said then, "Where will we meet?"

"You can always come to the Coconuts. Andres's sister and her boyfriend love it."

"We're not like that, are we?"

"I was kidding."

"We're not shacking up . . . Are we?"

"No, there's a big difference."

"God, Moran, I'm gonna have trouble handling this Sneaking around, not telling anybody. I've got to get it settled with Andres, but I don't want to involve you."

"He was suspicious before he even had a reason."

"He's not dumb. But I've got to make him understand why I'm leaving and that it's got nothing to do with you."

He said, "What about your friends at Casa de Campo?"

She said, "Oh, my God."

"You forgot to call them."

"I haven't even thought about them. When I left the embassy party I said I might change my plans

and Marilyn, one of the girls, gave me a look—ah-
ha, have fun. I'm pretty sure they have an idea
what's going on, but you're right, I ought to call,
get our stories straight."

"Are they close friends?"

"Not really, but we get along, play tennis a few
times a week."

"They wouldn't call your home—I mean to see if
you're there."

"No, but I'd better let them know where I am."
Mary said then, "Shit. They went home today."

"Is that a problem?"

"I don't know. I hope not."

"Call one of them tomorrow, at home."

"I'd better. How long are we staying?"

"You mean it's up to me? You don't sound too
worried."

"I am though. I'm starting to get nervous. And
this is just the beginning, isn't it?"

Moran went to sleep; maybe for only a few minutes, he wasn't sure. Lying on his side he held
Mary's back curled into him, his knees fitting into
the bend of hers. He said, "Mary?"

"What?" She was close to sleep.

"Rafi's left-handed. You said tonight you were
sitting with two southpaws and he didn't know
what a southpaw was.

"Remember?"

She didn't answer.

*   *   *

Moran opened his eyes to see the balcony in sunlight, the sheer draperies stirring, puffing in the breeze. Facing away from Mary he felt her move and get out of bed saying, "Yuuuk, I drank too much wine." Moving toward the bathroom her voice said, "What time is he going to call?"

"I don't know, maybe he won't . . . Mary?"

"What?"

"The guy I shot was right-handed."

She said, "You can remember that?"

He heard the bathroom door close. He lay staring at the clear sky framed within the balcony, hearing the water running in the bathroom, thinking of the swimming pool then and winter ballplayers. The bathroom door opened again and Mary's voice said, "I forgot. I brushed my teeth and drank the water." She came into his view, her slim body in the nightgown clearly defined against the sunlight. "If I'm gonna die I don't want it to be from drinking water."

Moran said, I can see him holding his weapon and he was right-handed. Somebody shoots at you you can close your eyes and see it anytime you want. He wasn't that far away."

She turned from the sunlight, eyebrows raised in question, her face clean and alive.

"He was wearing a Cincinnati Reds baseball cap," Moran said, "an old one. I can still see him."

In Boca Chica, twenty miles from Santo Domingo and twenty years ago, the home of a wealthy family close to Trujillo was confiscated soon after his death, turned into a clubhouse by the sea and passed along to a succession of young men who drank rum and looked for girls and sold goods on the black market. The house now stood in an old section of the resort community that was decaying, losing itself to debris and tropical vegetation. Nearby was a beachfront café that had once been a gas station but now seemed dirtier with its litter of paper cups and ice-cream wrappers that were never picked up. There was blue Spanish tile in the men's room where, to Rafi's recollection, the toilet had never flushed. Late in the morning he would walk from the house to the café for his coffee or sometimes a Coca-Cola and sit outside beneath the portico at a metal table. He made phone calls from the café and brought girls here that he picked up on the beach, to buy them treats and eventually talk business. In an informal way the café was his office.

This morning he was interviewing a girl by the name of Loret. She was seventeen and had some good points, some not so good. She was attractive, she seemed intelligent enough—at least not out of the cane—but she was sullen; her normal expression was a frown, almost a scowl.

"Smile," Rafi said.

Sitting with her can of Seven-Up, Loret bared small teeth. Her smile seemed defensive.

"Relax and do it again . . . That's better. Now relax your smile very slowly . . . There. That's the expression you want on your face. Very nice. And sit up straight; don't slouch like that."

For a girl so small her breasts seemed to fill her T-shirt and pull her shoulders forward with their weight.

"What do you use on your hair?"

"A rinse, I make it lighter." It was a shade of henna, too bright for her tawny skin.

"Maybe we'll put it back the way it was."

"I like this," Loret said, touching her wiry hair. "I don't want to look Negro."

This increased her sullen expression and Rafi told her, again, to smile. "You want to be rich, you have to learn how to smile."

"What do I get?" the girl asked him.

"The world," Rafi said.

She could have it. He'd settle for a home in the embassy section of town, a few servants, an armed guard at the gate he'd present with a cigar each evening as he drove out in his Mercedes.

Rafi had been hustling since he was seventeen

years old, since working the *aduana* trade during the revolution of '65 when they looted the custom-house and the docks along the Ozama and sold everything on the black. TV sets, transistor radios, tires, Japanese bikes. It had been a training ground: learning how to get ahead when you begin with nothing. But he was up and down, spending half what he earned on his appearance, to look good in the hotel lobbies, and he had nothing of substance to rely on for a steady income. The few girls he managed worked when they felt like it and cheated him when they did. He'd threaten to cut them with a knife and they'd give him big innocent eyes. Loret's look was more sulk than innocence.

"Push your lower lip out a little more."

"What do I get for this?"

He loved her more each time she said it. It was a sign she was moved by greed.

"Push the lip out . . . Yes, a nice pout, I like that. Aw, you look so sad. Let me see a little more— you're filled with a great sorrow . . . Yes, that's good. Begin to believe you're very depressed. You feel lost."

She said, "You better tell me what I get."

"Tell me what you want," Rafi said. "But not yet. You're too depressed. Something terrible happened to your sister that you loved very much . . ."

He cocked his head at different angles to study the sad little girl. Not bad. The breasts were a bonus. She would have to be rehearsed, of course; still, he knew he was very close to what he needed. Work with Loret the rest of the day. Present her sometime tomorrow.

In the meantime he should pay his respects. Call the Marine and tell him you're onto something but don't tell him what. You'll get back to him later this evening. Yes, you want to look industrious. You don't want to seem to be just hanging around.

He called the hotel and asked for 537.

When there was no answer he got the operator again and asked if Mr. Moran had left word where he would be.

The operator said, "Mr. Moran has checked out."

"What do you mean he's checked out? Give me the desk." He was sure there was a mistake. But when he spoke to the clerk he was told, "Yes, Mr. Moran has checked out." What about Mrs. Delaney? "Yes, she also."

Rafi said, "Did Moran leave a message—I'm sure he did—for Rafi Amado?"

The desk clerk said, "Just a moment." He came back to the phone and said, "No, there's nothing for you here."

9

HE TALKED TO JERRY for a few minutes, left him whistling "Zing Went the Strings of My Heart" and as soon as he was in the bungalow Nolen's smiling face appeared at the door.

"You're home. When'd you get in?"

Moran said, "When did I get *in?*" He dropped his bag on the kitchen counter. "You're watching me get in." He had left Mary exactly fifty minutes ago at the Miami airport where they stood holding, kissing in a crowd of people, as though one was seeing the other off. She got in a taxi and Moran wandered through the parking lot looking for his car, the white Mercedes coupe he'd owned for seven years.

Nolen said, "You wouldn't have a cold one in that fridge there, would you?"

"If you left any," Moran said. "Take a look." He wanted him to leave so he could call Mary. It could be the wrong time to call but he missed her and he couldn't imagine de Boya answering the phone himself; a servant would answer. And pretty soon his voice would become familiar to the help. Here he is again for missus. He'd have to make something up, give himself, his voice, an identity.

Nolen uncapped a couple Buds, placed one on the counter for Moran and slipped up onto a stool.

"I skimmed the swimming pool."

"Good."

"Didn't find any used condoms or anything. No alligators. The two broads from Fort Wayne left and the old couple with the Buick. In fact everybody's gone. We had a couple broads from Findlay, Ohio, work for Dow Chemical, they were here for three days. I asked 'em if they heard the one, the salesman from New York who's in Findlay, Ohio, on business and runs into a foxy broad at the Holiday Inn? One drink they're in the sack, it's beautiful. But this guy's a good Catholic so he looks up a church right away, goes to confession and the priest gives him five Our Fathers and five Hail Marys for his penance. He leaves for New York, meets another good-looking broad at La Guardia. They drive into town together, go to her apartment and jump in bed, it's beautiful. But now he's got to go to confession again before he gets home. He goes to St. Pat's, tells the priest what he did and the priest gives him a rosary. The guy says, 'Father, I don't mean to question you giving me a rosary, but I went to confession in Findlay, Ohio, for the same thing and I only got five Our Fathers and five Hail Marys.' The priest looks at him and screams, 'Findlay, *Ohio!*' Like he can't believe it. 'Findlay, *Ohio*—what do they know about fucking in Findlay, Ohio!' . . . Otherwise," Nolen said, "there's nothing new."

"How about old business?" Moran said, taking clothes out of the bag. "I'm a little more interested in what was going on when I left."

"The lovers?" Nolen said. "They broke up."

"And when we last saw the guy who broke them up," Moran said, "you were treating him to one of my beers."

"Jiggs," Nolen said. "He's all right, a nice guy."

"Yeah, good old Jiggs Scully," Moran said, "hands out phony business cards for laughs, but as it turns out works for de Boya."

"I'm gonna have to explain a few things to you," Nolen said.

Moran picked up his clothes and dropped them in a wicker basket. "Will it take long?"

"George, that's not nice . . . See, you'll be interested to know that Jiggs doesn't exactly work for de Boya. De Boya borrows him from time to time, for heavy work."

"The piano player, Mario, that's heavy?"

Nolen shook his head. "De Boya didn't hire Jiggs for that one. The sister did, Anita."

"I see," Moran said, telling Nolen he didn't see at all.

"You know the song 'Breaking Up Is Hard to Do'? It's like that," Nolen said. "Anita doesn't want to go through a lot of shit with Mario, she just wants to cut it off clean. So she hires Jiggs. The piano player thinks her brother sent him and he's not gonna have a tantrum or argue with the brother and get his legs broken, he wasn't that deeply in love. I said to Jiggs, 'You ever hear the guy play? You gonna break anything break his fingers.' But evidently the brother *did* find out about it and he sent Corky along. You got it now?"

"Have I got what?"

"Corky is Corky Corcovado. He's Dominican, he works for de Boya. But Jiggs, Jiggs you call when you need him."

"Not the number on the card he gave me," Moran said.

"As a matter of fact," Nolen said, "that *is* his number. But the girl on the switchboard won't admit it if she doesn't know who you are. You call him, you have to be a regular."

Moran thought a moment. "She said Dorado Management."

"Yeah, it's sort of a euphemism. She said Ballbusters Incorporated it would've been closer, but that doesn't sound right on the phone, it's too graphic."

Moran waited, letting Nolen talk. The guy was onstage.

"Dorado either manages or controls all the businesses—the restaurants, the furniture stores, dry cleaners—that were into them for shylock money and couldn't make the payments. We're talking about the wise guys. You understand?"

Moran nodded. "Yeah, go on."

"So Dorado, the wise guys, foreclose and take over the business. All I'm saying is things like that go on, you know that, Miami's very heavy into all kinds of shit. It doesn't have anything to do with what we're talking about, nothing. Except I want you to appreciate where Jiggs Scully's coming from, his background. He's like a bill collector. He's on call. Dorado has an outstanding debt or, say, they believe one of their drug dealers is skimming they call Jiggs and he straightens it out. De Boya is something else entirely. I assume he's been into deals with Dorado Management and that's how he got to know Jiggs. But I don't know anything about the deals and I don't want to know. Forget I even mentioned it."

Moran said, "What're you getting into?"

"I'm not getting into anything."

"You gonna start wearing a black overcoat. Pack a gun?"

"They don't wear overcoats down here, George. I'm telling you who's who, that's all. You want to know who Scully is, I'm telling you."

"You think he's a nice guy."

"I think he's funny," Nolen said. "He says funny

things." Nolen grinned. "He says, 'Something's wrong, what they teach you in school. How come, I'm an altar boy, I go to mass and communion every morning of my young life, I end up working for the fucking guineas, the fucking spics, carrying their bags?' "

"That's pretty funny," Moran said.

"You have to hear him, the way he says it."

"Well, it wouldn't bother me too much I never saw the guy again," Moran said. "And if you'll excuse me—I want to rest and get cleaned up."

"Hey, that's right—how was the trip?"

"I'll tell you about it later." Moving Nolen to the door.

"Yeah, good. You gonna be around?"

"I don't know yet. I might go out." Practically pushing him through the door.

"I want to hear all about it, George. What was your platoon down there? Ass Chaser? You get much this time?"

"Get out of here," Moran said and closed the door on him.

She had told him her phone number and he'd memorized it on the spot. He dialed and waited, standing at the counter, anxious, without a story for the maid or whoever answered. A woman's voice with an accent said, "Yes, may I help you?"

"Mrs. de Boya, please."

"May I say who is calling?"

Shit . . . "Tell her Mr. Delaney." When she came on he said, "Mary?"

She said, "Who're you supposed to be, a relative?"

"Do you have any?"

"Not around here. They're all up in Michigan."

"Then I'm visiting . . . I miss you already."

"I do too. I ache."

"Can you talk?"

"Not comfortably. He's home."

"Where are you?"

"I'm outside on the deck, having a glass of sherry. I'm nervous."

"I can hear a boat," Moran said. "Have you talked to him yet?"

"I just walked in the door."

"I mean have you seen him."

"Yeah . . . we said hello. That was about it."

"Did you kiss him?"

"On the cheek."

"I'm not good on the phone. I miss you."

"I miss you more. God, I miss you. Let's go back."

"Tomorrow?"

"Let's meet somewhere."

"I'll pick you up."

"No, let me think . . . Do you know where Matheson Hammock is, the park?"

"Yeah, just south of you, on the bay."

"Drive out to the point. To the left of where you go into the beach."

"I know where it is."

"I'll meet you there tomorrow at . . . what time?"

"Six A.M."

"How about noon?"

"I'll be there."

"I love you, George." She hung up.

He had to pace the room a few times before settling down, getting organized. Through the window he could see Nolen sitting by the pool, alone with his beer. The bit actor, part-time private eye who thought Jiggs Scully was funny. Turned on by the guy's deadpan involvement with businessmen who hired him to break legs and collect the vig on money owed. Moran moved from the window.

He had all he could handle for the time being. Nolen Tyner would have to look out for himself.

From the sun deck she could see the park and tropical gardens, a peninsula of jungle extending out of the coral shoreline a half mile to the south, where she would meet him tomorrow. The sky, streaked red above the jungle and fading, darkened as her gaze moved east into the ocean, to the faraway Cape Florida light at the tip of Key Biscayne. Looking at the ocean made her feel safer, above suspicion to anyone in the house watching her. Resting after a two-hour flight and the usual airport hassle. Innocent. Though not eager to talk to a husband she hadn't seen in five days. If not innocent at least honest. What was there to talk about? Andres made statements, issued commands, grunted . . . breathed through his nose when he made love, finished and left her bedroom. He might come to her tonight.

On the lawn that extended to the seawall a figure moved out of shadows, a stand of young acacia, crossed open ground to the dock where the de Boya cruiser was moored, then continued on in the direction of the swimming pool, secluded among tropical palms. Day and night armed guards moved about the property: either Corky or one of several serious young Dominicans Andres employed. More security guards than household help: millionaire self-sufficiency and thoroughly modern, from the weapons the Dominicans carried to the video scanner mounted above the front door.

Altagracia, their maid, served dinner: chicken breasts glazed with fruit flamed in brandy by candlelight, the shadow of Altagracia moving across polished wood, soundless. Mary said to her, "The next time I go down give me your mother's number and I'll call her. If you'd like me to."

Altagracia said, "Yes, señora. But she don't have a phone."

Mary said, "Oh." Altagracia finished serving them and left. "We haven't made plans to go back, but I thought if we ever did . . ." Mary let her voice trail. She raised her eyes to the candlelight, watched for a moment as Andres ate with his shoulders hunched over the table, lowering his head to the fork barely lifted from the plate—the can cutter who had become a general. "We had a wonderful time."

She could hear his lips smack. When they were first married she had enjoyed watching him eat, even to the way he sipped his wine with a mouthful of food, sipped and chewed; there was something romantically hardy and robust about it, for a time.

"The weather was perfect. A few afternoon showers, but they didn't last." Mary tried hard to remember more about the Dominican weather.

Andres said, "That friend of yours, the fat one with hair like a man. I saw her."

It was coming now. Mary sat very still, then made herself reach for the salt. He was watching her now.

"You mean Marilyn? She was with us." Bold now, getting it out in the open. "When did you see her?"

"Yesterday. I was going in the club."

"Then she told you I was staying an extra day."

"She told me nothing about that."

Mary could see his eyes in the candle-glow, age

lines making him appear tired, less rigid, the look of vulnerability she had mentioned to Moran. But it was the lighting, she realized now, that softened him, not something from within.

"She told me about polo. But she doesn't sound like she ever saw it. She doesn't know who was in the tournament."

"Well, I guess what we like," Mary said, "is the atmosphere more than anything else. Watching the people. Everybody all slicked up in their polo out-fits."

"You see anybody you know?"

It startled her. He had never asked a question like that before; he had never seemed interested enough.

"Philly got us invited to a party at the Santo Domingo Country Club. Mostly embassy people. A few I'd met before."

"Did you see anybody from here?"

"Outside of our group? No. I told you, didn't I, I was going with Marilyn, Philly, Liz? . . ."

"You didn't see—what is his name, he used to belong to the club. The one from your city." He seemed to stare now, as though daring her to say the name.

"Who, George Moran?" Once she said it she had to keep going. "What would he be doing in Santo Domingo?"

"You said you were at Casa de Campo."

"I thought you meant at the embassy party."

Then, trying to sound only mildly interested: "How do you know he was there?"

Andres said, "How do I know things. People tell me. Or I want to know something I find it out. He was there the same time you were, but you say you didn't see him."

Mary took a breath, let it out slowly as she picked up her wine. She wanted to begin now, say something that would lead to a confrontation, without involving Moran. She said, "Andres . . ." but felt Moran's presence already here and lost her nerve.

He said, "Yes?"

She hesitated. "Do you know why I stayed an extra day?"

"Tell me."

"I toured Santo Domingo. Saw all the old places."

"Yes, did you like it?"

"My driver told me about the war . . ."

"Oh? What war is that?"

"A few years after you left, the revolution."

He seemed in no hurry now as he ate, his eyes heavy lidded in the candle-glow, watching her.

She said, "I remember vaguely reading about it, seeing pictures in *Life* magazine. You were here then, but you must have followed it closely."

"I know all those people."

"So you must've leaned toward one side or the other."

"Did I lean?" Andres said. He held his fork upright, his arms on the table. "Do you know the difference between a loyalist and a radical insurrectionist?"

"Well, the driver explained some of that, but his English wasn't too good."

"Or your Spanish wasn't good enough."

"You're right. I shouldn't blame the driver."

"You want to know about it, ask your friend George Moran," Andres said, watching her in the candle-glow. "He was there with the United States Marines. Didn't he tell you that?"

She managed to say, "I can't recall he ever mentioned it. Are you sure?"

Andres seemed to smile. "Why would I say it if I'm not sure? The first time I met him, we were playing golf, he told me that. Very proud of himself. I bought a drink for him, because at that time he was on the side of the loyalists. Maybe he didn't know it, but he was. Now I think loyalty doesn't suit him. He believes only in himself."

Mary waited, not moving. She watched Andres raise his glass, a gesture, a mock salute.

"Good luck to him. May he become loyal again."

* * *

In darkness she pictured the drive from Cutler Road into Matheson Hammock Park, through the dim tunnel of mangrove to the booth where you paid the attendant a dollar and went on, suddenly entering the cleared expanse of crushed coral that reached to the ocean. She saw their cars standing alone at the edge of that open space, as far as they could go, cut off; one way in, one way out.

It was close to two in the morning when she called Moran, heard him answer sleepily and said to him, "He knows."

There was a silence and when he spoke again he was fully awake though his tone was subdued. "What did he say?"

"He knows you were down there."

There was another silence before he said, "The day Andres was here, I was packing to leave."

She said, "We can't meet at the park. It's too out in the open."

He said, "But I can't wait to see you. I can't sleep."

She smiled at that. "Yeah, I could tell." She was within the sound of his voice and for the moment felt secure, as though they could go on talking and say whatever came to mind. "I'll think of a good place and call you tomorrow, before noon."

"Why don't you come here?"

"I'm afraid to. Not yet." She lowered her voice

to almost a whisper. "I've never done this before, George. I don't know the ropes."

"How's it going otherwise?"

"I'll tell you tomorrow. Go back to sleep."

She hung up and lay back on her pillow in the dark, beginning finally to relax as she listened and heard only silence. She needed to see Moran, his face with the soft beard, and feel his arms around her. Just being held made everything else go away.

She called at eleven-thirty and said, "The Holiday Inn on Le Jeune Road. Do you know where it is? This side of Flagler."

He said, amazed, "The Holiday Inn?"

She said, "I've already made a reservation under Delaney. Okay? I'll see you about one."

It made him think of Nolen's salesman, scoring at the Holiday Inn in Findlay, Ohio.

But he told himself it wasn't like that and when he got there and he was holding her, moving his hands over the familiar feel of her and saying how much he missed her, barely bringing their mouths apart, he was sure it wasn't anything like Findlay, Ohio. They made love and drank iced wine in bed, in the stillness of the room. Touching each other. Looking at each other. Gradually getting to things they needed to talk about.

He said, "Come live with me. It doesn't matter what he thinks."

She said, "Why didn't I tell him before this? If I bring it up now he's gonna blame you, because you're on his mind. He *knows* we were together."

"All right. What do you want to do?"

"Wait a while."

"How long?"

"I don't *know* how long."

He eased off. "I'm sorry. You have to do it your way. I understand that. I'm anxious, that's all . . ."

She said, "God, I don't want to lose you . . . But I have to wait for the right time. A month ago I felt sorry for him. Now I'm afraid of him—I don't know how he'll react. But I know if he wants to make it difficult . . . well, we have to be very careful." Her tone was thoughtful as her mind sorted through images of her husband. "The right time will come. I don't know when but I'll feel it and I'll ask him for a divorce. I'll *tell* him I'm gonna get a divorce . . . or if he wants to file, that's fine, if it's a pride thing with him. He'll understand if I do it right, if I can keep you out of it." She gave him a weak smile. "I don't want to beat this to death, but more than anything I want you to understand."

He held her in silence.

"What're you afraid of?"

"*Him.* I don't know what he'll do."

"Do you sleep with him?"

"I don't know how to handle that either. Not since we got back," Mary said. "But do I lock my door? We've never even had an argument; but how can we if we don't talk? Do you see what I mean? I want to be fair."

"Don't be too fair."

She pressed against him, trying to get closer. "I don't know what's gonna happen."

He said, "Well, you walk out with a two-million-dollar settlement, you'll still be one of the richest ladies in Coral Gables—including wives and girl-friends of dope dealers. You're not gonna have to get a job as a waitress."

"That's been on my mind too," Mary said. "I don't think I should take the money. Assuming he'll still offer it."

"You've got a signed agreement, haven't you?"

"I don't think that would bother Andres too much."

Moran raised her face to see her eyes, dark, questioning. "I was rich once. I thought it was more of a pain in the ass than anything else. As a matter of fact the beer at the club never tasted right."

Mary said, "George, ten years ago I was making a hundred dollars an hour modeling." She gave him a quick couple of fashion-model expressions, mouth and eye movements from smile to pout.

"All that high-fashion New York-beautiful-people bullshit. I did lipstick, perfume, eye-makeup; I was gone before designer jeans. I quit and didn't look at myself for two years. I thought about going to law school until I worked for a lawyer and got pension plans up to here. I don't know what I want as far as a career goes; but the best thing is to just be rich and not worry about it."

He said, "Are we gonna get married?"

She raised her face, her turn to search his eyes.

"I don't know. Are we?"

"It's okay with me."

She pulled away from him. "What do you mean, it's okay? You just go along? You're not obligated, Moran. You can do whatever you want."

He brought her back to him gently, moving his hand over her, down her arm to the curve of her breast, soothing.

"Don't think so much. Let it happen. We'll know what to do when the time comes."

They met at the Holiday Inn each afternoon for the next several days, tried the Castaways on the Beach and went back to the Holiday Inn because it was familiar and they felt at home. Mary came in her tennis warmups. (Nolen Tyner asked Moran where he went every afternoon. Moran told him visiting.

Then Nolen got a surveillance assignment and Moran wondered if he was the subject; but it had to do with a child-custody case in West Palm.) They booked the Holiday Inn room for another week and brought wine and fruit. They talked about playing tennis sometime. They didn't talk about Andres or when or what if. They were together and it was enough. Mary said maybe being rich wasn't that important. Moran said not as long as you can afford motel rooms. But it was a shame to pay when he had an entire motel going to waste, the place empty except for one guy and he wasn't there during the day. Mary finally said all right, she'd come to the Coconuts. Tomorrow.

She came at one o'clock in her warmups carrying her yellow bathing suit. Moran introduced her to Jerry and showed her around; it took about five minutes. Mary said she loved it. They went into Moran's bungalow and he told her not to pay any attention to the tropical floral-print upholstery and the curved bamboo arms on the furniture, he was going to redecorate one of these days. Mary told him to forget it, his decor was back in. He showed her the bedroom next, where she could change, put on her bathing suit.

They were still in there a little after two when Jerry called. Jerry said, "There's a gentleman and a young lady here to see you."

Moran stood holding a towel around him.

"Who are they?"

Jerry said, "His name's Rafi Amado. He says he's from Santo Domingo."

10

MARY WATCHED THEM from a side window: Moran standing with his thumbs hooked in the low waist of his cutoffs, the bearded innkeeper, gesturing then, yeah, this is it. How do you like it? She could almost read his lips.

The red-haired girl seemed, if not impressed, at least satisfied by what she saw. A strange-looking little thing, attractive, but all her colors wrong.

Rafi, in a shiny black business suit, was squinting, cocking his head as he inspected the Coconut Palms' center court—doors to a dozen rooms in a plain white facade with aqua trim facing the small swimming pool—as though if he caught the right perspective the Coconuts would become the Fontainebleu, a place with real swank.

It's your fault, Mary thought, but had to smile. Rafi was nodding, trying to look impressed. The red-haired girl would roll her lower lip, then lick it and roll it out again. Very strange. She wore a blue and yellow flowered-print dress—giant mutations that might be daisies—the dress tight in the bust but several inches too long, below her knees. Miss Sugarcane.

That's not nice, Mary thought.

But did she have to be nice? Moran seemed to be handling the amenities, making them feel at home, inviting them now to take a lounge chair. He came toward the house as they sat down, Rafi with a stern expression saying something to the girl.

Moran came in and closed the door.

"Not a soul here, the guy shows up all the way from the Dominican Republic."

Mary came away from the window. "Who's the girl with him?"

"Loret. That's all I know." Moran went to the refrigerator. "She wants a Seven-Up."

"Are they staying?"

"He says he's got something to tell me. Like bad news, the way he said it . . . I don't have any Seven-Up. I knew I didn't have any, I don't know why I'm looking."

Mary said, "Should I come out?"

Moran brought two Cokes and a bowl of ice from the refrigerator and closed the door. "Whatever you think."

"Aren't you a little surprised to see him?"

"I'm very surprised. He says, 'And how is your buddy, Mary?' and gives me a wink. I said you're fine."

"You didn't tell him I'm here?"

"No." Moran was at the counter now mixing a rum and Coke for Rafi. "I've still got a funny feeling about him. In fact I've got more of a funny feeling than ever."

"Do you think he knows who I am?"

"It wouldn't surprise me."

"Should I come out? I've got to go home pretty soon."

"Shit," Moran said. "The one time I don't have anybody here. Maybe I can get rid of them."

"No, you can't do that," Mary said. "Assume he's straight, but keep your eyes open. I think I'd better just slip out."

"You can go around the other side to the street."

"I'd better. Unless you want me to help you entertain." Mary smiled. She walked over to him, raising her arms. "Our time will come, George. Hang in."

Rafi said, very quietly, "I like Loret to tell you if she can. She has trouble not only with the words but"—he gestured, touching his chest—"because of the way it makes her feel."

She didn't seem too troubled to Moran: leaning over to slip her sandals off, the bodice of the dress opening to give Moran a peek at her full breasts. She sat back wiggling her toes. They looked dirty.

"But let's see," Rafi said, his sad eyes moving to the girl. "Loret? Tell him who you are."

The girl looked at Rafi and immediately her expression clouded, her lower lip came out and her chin seemed to tremble. Rafi gave a small nod toward Moran. The girl turned to him, raising her head proudly.

"I am the sister of Luci Palma."

Moran said, "Well, I'll be." The girl looked nothing like the Luci Palma he remembered. He said, "You're a lot younger."

"Yes, twelve years," the girl said.

"Well, how is Luci these days? Where does she live?"

"She's dead," the girl said. She seemed to glance at Rafi before placing her glass of Coca-Cola on the ground and covering her face with her hands.

Moran heard muffled sobs. He looked at Rafi.

"She's dead?"

Rafi nodded. "I found it out the day you left. I spoke to someone who told me of Loret and I went to see her."

"How did she die? Was she ill?"

Rafi looked at the girl. "Loret, tell him how she died."

Her hands came away from her face; her eyes seemed glazed now, red with sorrow.

"She was kill."

"She was killed," Rafi said. "Shot to death."

Moran said, "During the war?"

"Loret," Rafi said, "he asks when she was killed."

"Four years ago," the girl said, "but I think it was yesterday. She was so good to me. I live with her and she send me to school, but now I got nothing. I live in a terrible place by the Ozama River. It's very terrible."

"Loret," Rafi said. "Tell him how she was killed."

"Yes," the girl said, "they took her from the house at night, beating her and put her in an automobile and took her away."

"Tell him who did this," Rafi said.

"The men of the government. Like soldiers."

"Regular soldiers?"

"The bad ones, the det squad."

"The death squad," Rafi said. "Continue."

"They took her out in the country and shot her twenty times. She was like my mother . . ."

"Someone found her and told you?" Rafi said.

"Yes, and then I went out there and she was dead. They rape her too. It was like I loss my mother. Now I'm alone."

"Tell him why . . ." Rafi began.

"They kill her because she was, she belong to the New Revolutionary Party . . ."

"The NPR," Rafi said.

". . . which she join because she want to do

something for the poor people, but they kill her and do terrible things to her." Loret's chin trembled. "She was my sister. I love her and miss her so much I don't know what to do."

Moran watched her cover her face again and begin to sob. He reached over to touch her shoulder. He wanted to say something, but felt Rafi watching him and wondered what he would say if Rafi—frowning, shaking his head in sympathy—wasn't here.

"She misses Luci very much," Rafi said. "Their mother died and Luci became the mother for her. But Luci"—Rafi sighed—"you know how she was, the spirit she had as well as kindness. When the revolution failed she began again, working for the new party . . . She wanted to go to Nicaragua." Rafi shrugged, weary. "It's a shame, a fine girl with spirit."

"Was she married?" Moran asked.

"Loret," Rafi said.

"No, she never get married," the girl said.

"Do you know why?" Rafi asked.

Loret paused. Then looked at Moran. "She never marry because, well, I believe she was always in love with you."

Moran said, "What? Come on—I hardly knew her."

"She told me," Loret said to Rafi, who gestured toward Moran with a quick movement of his head.

"She told me," Loret said, now to Moran, "she had a feeling for you in her heart. She want to write to you but was afraid."

"Afraid of what?" Moran asked.

"I think she didn't want to bother you. You happy living in the United States with everything you want. You don't need a poor girl to be crying to you."

She began to sob and Rafi gave her the handkerchief from his breast pocket. He said to Moran, "She becomes very upset with the reminding of it."

Moran was silent. He wanted to put his arm around the girl, comfort her, wipe the eye makeup smudged on her cheeks. She reminded him of a little girl playing dress-up in her mother's clothes . . . Except for those breasts that seemed to have a life of their own. And except for Rafi sitting in his business suit prompting, making sure she told it all, holding his drink in his left hand, sipping, taking small hesitant sips in the presence of sorrow.

It gave Moran a strange feeling, to be moved by the girl's performance while knowing it was part of Rafi's scam. The two of them working so hard but so obvious about it; amateur night at the Coconut Palms.

He asked Rafi, "Where're you staying?"

"We have no place yet. We came from the airport."

"Well, you've got a place now."

"No, I have friends in Miami if I can find them," Rafi said. "I don't want to inconvenience you."

Moran said, "How can you inconvenience a motel? We're not the Fontaineblue, but . . . ."

"No, you're not," Rafi said.

Moran called Mary at 10:30. She answered and he said, "Can we talk?"

"The great stone face went out in his boat. He takes business people out, entertains them."

"Do you ever go?"

"No, I think he entertains with girls. I'm hoping he falls in love with one of them . . . How did it go?"

He told her Loret's story, the way Loret recited and Rafi prompted. "But I really felt sorry for her."

"Do you cry in movies, George?"

"I choke up now and then."

"Where are they now?"

"Well, I told them they might as well stay here. Rafi wants to look up some old friends in Miami. I still don't know what he does for a living."

"Are you charging them?"

"Well, the place's empty anyway."

"You already bought him dinner. But that was for shooting him, right?"

"*If* I shot him. I bought another dinner tonight and found out Loret doesn't like Italian."

"That's a shame," Mary said. "Has Rafi made a pitch yet?"

"He's working up to it. But you know what?"

"You feel sorry for him."

"In a way, yeah."

"He's gonna try to take you, George."

"I know . . . but the poor guy, he's working his ass off and you can see it coming a mile away."

"Well, have fun. Are you gonna show them the sights tomorrow . . . while cute little Loret shows you hers?"

"No, I was planning on being at the Holiday Inn in Coral Gables at one. I feel horny."

"God love you," Mary said. "Stay that way."

Moran was watching the late news when Nolen stumbled at the door and almost came through the screen. Moran said, "Wait and I'll open it, it's easier."

Nolen made himself comfortable and Moran handed him a beer. Nolen said, "Well, if you insist." He drank the can down about a third and said, "That broad in the pool ain't from Fort Wayne or Findlay, Ohio, I know that much. She's got a pair of lungs on her she could float across the ocean on 'em."

"That's Loret," Moran said. "I didn't know she was a swimmer."

"She isn't, she's a floater. Fernando Lamas was nervous, kept telling her to get out, but she wouldn't. I think she told him to get fucked in Spanish."

"That's Rafi Amado."

"Yeah, he says you shot him one time. He showed me."

"What'd it look like to you?"

"It looked like he had one tit."

"The scar."

"It looked like somebody cut him."

"Yeah, and I hit him lower. You hit somebody at about thirty meters you remember it. You can play it back and look at it."

"What's he want?"

"He comes all this way—I don't think just so I can meet cute little Loret. He tell you about her?"

"I wasn't paying much attention; I was watching her float. She's the sister of the girl you went down there looking for and life's been dumping on her and he thinks you're a swell guy. Something like that. What else?"

"I'm waiting for the rest of it."

"So you don't trust this boy."

"Not too far."

"There's somebody doesn't trust you either," Nolen said, giving Moran a sly look. "The old Cat Chaser."

"What're you talking about?"

"Gimme another beer I'll tell you."

"You got one."

"Time you pop another it'll be gone."

Moran walked around the counter into the kitchen and got the beer rather than take Nolen by the throat and choke him. It seemed easier; the man was half in the bag and had something he wanted to tell. Moran came over with the can of Bud to where Nolen was sprawled on the sofa, neck bent against the cushion, his legs sticking straight out. He was wearing a pair of old curl-toed cowboy boots. Nolen handed Moran his empty and took the full one.

"Who is it doesn't trust me?"

"Well, Jiggs Scully wants to know—as Jiggs says, 'Tell me. Your buddy Moran, he working over in Coral Gables at the Holiday Inn there?'" Nolen raised his eyes, holding the beer can at his chin. "Sound like him?"

"That's very good," Moran said. "What's he following me for?"

"He isn't following you, he's following de Boya's wife. He sees her go in the Holiday Inn, he sees you go in the Holiday Inn. She comes out, you come out. Scully wants to know if it's a coincidence or what. He doesn't know what to tell de Boya."

Moran stared at Nolen for a moment, Nolen waiting with the sly look, then went to the kitchen

and poured himself a scotch with one ice cube. He
stood at the counter now looking across the width
of the room at Nolen.

"Scully says he'd rather talk to you than de
Boya. He doesn't like de Boya."

"How much does he want?"

"He's not shaking you down, he wants to talk."

"About what?"

"He's an interesting guy. I think you ought to listen what he has to say."

"Yeah, about what?"

"I'm not at liberty. At this point it's strictly between you and him."

"How long's he been following Mrs. de Boya?"

Nolen grinned. "We're very formal, aren't we? I
knew something was going on. Back when the guy's
sister was shacking up with the piano player—the
way you mentioned de Boya's wife, like she was up
for canonization, and all the time the old Cat
Chaser's meeting her on the side. Jiggs says you
have to have very large balls fool around with the
wife of a guy like de Boya. He says you mention
Andres de Boya to people that know anything
about him it shrivels their balls right up."

Moran sipped his drink.

Nolen was comfortable, having a good time.

"You're not saying, uh? Well, I don't blame you.
Afraid you'll get your laundry scattered all over.

But I think you should talk to him, Jiggs. It might be, you find out it's in your best interest."

Nolen wouldn't say any more than that.

Pulling into the Holiday Inn the next day, driving around to the side, to 167 at the rear of the building, Moran didn't see Jiggs Scully's two-tone red and white Cadillac or anyone sitting alone in the few cars that were parked here. He pulled in next to Mary's Mercedes, both cars white, his old Mercedes next to hers giving a before-and-after impression. He hadn't decided how much to tell her.

And for a while it wouldn't have mattered if de Boya himself were parked outside; they were together and there wasn't anything else, only faint street sounds they might have heard but were removed and had nothing to do with them. They lingered, making it last, until the present began to seep back and sounds outside became images of two-tone Cadillacs and limousines; with awareness came apprehension, waiting for something to happen.

She said, "What's the matter?" When he didn't answer she said, "We don't have to do this."

"Yeah, we do," Moran said. "We're way past that. We could say we're not gonna see each other, but we would."

She said, "He hasn't mentioned you since the day we got back. I've been rehearsing my lines, I'm almost ready to corner him." Her tone softened. "I'm not dragging my feet, I'm just scared."

He said, "I know."

She said, "You're off somewhere."

"No, I'm here. I'm resting."

"Tell me what's going on."

She wanted to know about Loret. He told her the story again in detail and the parts that bothered him: the twelve years difference between Luci and Loret, no mention of brothers and sisters in between; that wasn't a Dominican family. The revolutionary party Luci joined; he didn't believe it existed; the political situation there had been quiet for years. And the way Rafi put words in her mouth, prompted so she wouldn't forget anything.

Mary said, "And are they having fun at the Coconuts?"

He had put them up in oceanfront Number One and Number Two. He told Mary that Jerry said he was crazy, giving them a free ride and now he'd have to get Lula in to clean. Jerry called them "boat people," like the Cubans from Mariel; pretty soon they'd be taking over.

Mary said, "Bighearted George. Well, as long as you know what you're doing."

"But I don't," Moran said. "I'm not sure what's

going on. But he makes a pitch I can always say no, right?"

"I don't know, George. Can you? You know they want something, but you're still moved."

The afternoon went too fast; it always did. Mary slipped into her warmups. They said goodbye, holding onto each other for several minutes and almost went back to bed. Moran waited then by the door as Mary got in her car and drove off. Still no sign of a two-tone Cadillac.

Moran got in his car and drove out toward the front of the Holiday Inn. He saw Mary's car turn south onto Le Jeune. Then saw a familiar car come out from the portico in front of the building, out of the shade, and turn onto the street after her. An older-model, faded blue Porsche. Nolen Tyner's car.

Moran followed, seeing faint bursts of colorless smoke coming out of the Porsche's tailpipe as it accelerated. There was no doubt in his mind it was Nolen. He hung back, keeping the oil burner in sight, then caught the light at Miracle Mile and had to sit there as both cars continued on, disappearing in the southbound traffic.

He took his time now, worked his way over to Granada and followed the road through Coral Gables to the country club to see if she might have turned in there; but there was no sign of either car. He passed the street where he had lived for seven

years, drove through caverns of tropical trees to
streets that branched off into fingers of coastal
land, the houses built on a network of free-form
canals and hidden by walls of stone and vegetation,
stands of sea grape, hibiscus, jungles of orchids and
acacia trees. He came to Arvida Parkway and
rolled slowly through the gloom of foliage, catching flashes of Biscayne Bay in the late afternoon
sunlight.

The de Boya home stood on a spur of land that
curved out a few hundred feet into the bay, the
peak of its roof ascending steeply against the sky
like a tor, a landmark from the bayside but from in-
land only glimpses of bleached wood and glass.
Moran had called it Polynesian contemporary, the
home of a South Seas potentate. Mary said, "If not
a very successful cocaine dealer." She called it bas-
tard modern, neo-nondescript. The entire house,
she said, could only be seen from the dock at the
edge of the front lawn. Otherwise, and especially
from the road, only an idea of its astonishing angles
could be seen beyond the iron pickets mounted to
the low cement wall and through the forest of poin-
ciana and acacia that sealed off the front of the
property.

Stone columns marked an entrance to number
700. The driveway circled into the trees and came
out again at another pair of columns up the road,

without revealing the front of the house or cars that might be parked there.

All he could do was assume Mary was home now and Nolen had passed this way a few minutes ago. What would happen if he pulled into the driveway? What was he doing there if de Boya came out?

Moran took the freeway north out of Miami thinking of the afternoon motel room and the warm awareness in Mary's eyes as she called him bighearted George, touching him, understanding him. Good, that part was good. But his own image of a bighearted George was not the bearded guy in the motel room. Or the cement-finisher working in the sun. Or the fire-team leader in the narrow streets of Santo Domingo. Not the fantasized seventeen-year-old lover either. The bighearted George he saw in his own mind was a dreamer, the ideal dumb-guy mark. He caught every light in Pompano Beach going toward the ocean and the bridge raised across the Intracoastal; it was all right, he was patient now as he realized he was out of patience, tired of waiting, accepting, listening to people like Rafi and Nolen, with their angles.

There was no faded blue Porsche parked in front of the Coconut Palms, no sign of Jerry anywhere, no one sitting by the pool. Lula came out of Number One carrying dirty towels and a plastic trash bag. Moran waited for her, looking out at the beach, empty with the sun gone for the day though it was still light.

"That girl in there," Lula said, "nobody musta taught her to pick up after herself. She got clothes, and they pretty things, all over the place."

"Leave 'em," Moran said, "you're not her maid."

"She messy. Dirty all the dishes—they been cooking in there. It don't smell bad but it makes a mess."

"They'll be gone soon."

Lula cocked her head, frowning. "I still got that, like a nightgown the woman left? You can see through it."

"You want it?"

"Honey, I can't even get one arm in it, or nobody can I know. It's hanging in the laundry room."

"I'll take care of it." Moran looked over at Number One. "They both in there?"

"She's in there eating potato chips," Lula said, "getting 'em all over everything. That's all I seen her do is eat. The man, I don't know where he is."

Moran got a beer and came back outside with a canvas deck chair he sat in to look at the ocean, his feet on the low cement wall. He'd get things settled with Rafi before the day was over, put him against a wall and pull his pockets out . . .

Nolen said, "You drinking without me?"

He came up next to Moran running a hand through his thinning hair as the wind whipped it across his forehead. He raised the can of beer in his other hand.

"I got my own. I bought four six-packs today; two for you, two for me."

"You doing a little surveillance this afternoon?"

"No, I was off today. Listen"—he sat down on the cement wall hunching in close to Moran, anxious to tell something—"that broad, your little pal from Santo Domingo, she comes up to me—no, first she has her swim, her float. She gets out of the pool, comes over and sits down next to me in this little string number, her lungs about to come tumbling out—you wonder if the straps can hold all the goodies in there. She's sitting there—Isn't it a nice day? Get all that over with. You like Florida? Yes. She's sitting there very quietly for a couple of minutes, she goes, 'You want to have a party?' I ask her what kind of party. She goes, 'You know'—and looks around to see if anybody's watching—'do it, man, have a good time. Me and you.' I go, '*Do* it?' Like I just got in from Monroe Station, some place out on the Tamiami. 'What do you mean, do it?' She gives this surprised look and says, 'What do you think? Half-and-half for fifty dollars. Okay?' . . . That's your little orphan."

Moran said, "You do it?"

"I told her it had to be for love. I'm gonna catch her later. Little broad—she isn't eighteen years old she's a pro."

"When'd all this happen?"

"Couple hours ago. Before I went to the store. I bought her some potato chips. She can't get enough of 'em."

"Where else did you go?"

"No place. What is this? I told you, it's my day off."

"I didn't see your car out front when I got home."

"No, I loaned it to your buddy Rafael Amado. The guy's a hustler, you know it? He comes on with the manners like he's the chief of protocol, but just the way he asks if he can use the car, buy the gas, all that, you know he's a hustler. So be careful. He wants to sell you something, tell him no, you got one."

"When'd you give him the car?"

"This morning, around noon. He left almost the same time you did," Nolen said. "He was right behind you."

11

THE SHOCK OF SEEING HIM was instant, even before
he called her name. She had just now arrived home.
Turned from the front door to see Corky hurrying
toward the blue car in the driveway, Rafi getting
out, smiling—*there*, at that moment—knowing
who it was before she saw his face clearly but recognizing something about him, Corky shoving him
then, keeping him against the car, and Rafi was calling, "Mary, help me!"

Beaming then, all a joke, with a few words in
Spanish for Corky and he was coming to her with
outstretched hands—to do what, put his arms
around her? She took his hands, managed to smile
and said pleasantly, with a note of surprise,
"Well . . ." It was the best she could do.

"Mary, Mary, it's so wonderful to see you
again!" His head darted and he kissed her, almost
on the mouth, before she could pull back.

Mary said, "Well . . ." She said something that
sounded like, "What a surprise."

Altagracia served them chilled white wine on the sundeck. Rafi made a show of raising his to the fading sun and came close to rejoicing over the red hues reflected in his glass. He wore his tailored white Dominican shirt, the squared-off tails hanging free of his trousers.

"It's lovely," Rafi said then, "everything, your home, your—how should I say?—your taste in decorating, it's as I imagine it would be."

Mary said, "I didn't think you knew my name."

His gaze came away from the view, the boat dock, the sweep of lawn, smiling with that air of familiarity, confidence, she remembered from the first time they met.

He said, "Mary, a woman of your beauty begs to be identified."

She said, "Rafi, knock it off. Get to the point."

"I'm sorry," he said. "What?"

"Who told you my name?"

"You're well known, Mary. The wife of a man who was once very important in our government. You come to Casa de Campo . . . You're the buddy of a man who was a celebrity in Santo Domingo for a day or two, looking for his lost love." He stopped. "I can't imagine that, why he would look for someone else if he has you."

"We're friends," Mary said.

"Yes, I notice. Very good friends."

"Have you called him since you got here?"

"Who, Moran?" This brought a new depth of enjoyment. As his smile began to fade a trace still lingered. "You just left him, Mary, at, I believe, the Holiday Inn? Didn't he tell you I'm staying with him?"

Mary had stopped smiling some time ago, seeing it coming. And now here we are, she thought. She was ready and said very quietly, "How much are you asking for?"

Rafi seemed hurt, furrowing his brow. He said, "*Como?* How much do I *ask* for?" Overdoing it. Then let his expression relax, though still with sensitivity, misunderstood. "You don't believe I intend to make something of this, do you? Your affair with Moran? I think it's beautiful. I admire both of you very much."

Past Rafi's shoulder, far out in the bay, a powerboat was trailing a curving wake, coming in toward shore. Mary saw it and recognized *El Jefe*, the de Boya sixty-foot yacht, vivid white against the darkening ocean.

She said, "why did you bring the girl?"

"Loret? He's looking for her sister." Innocence now in Rafi's tone. "But she's dead. Gave her life in a cause, and now poor Loret has no one to take care of her. I tell this to Moran because of his feeling, if he wants to give something to Loret for her future, her education, something to help the poor girl. It's up to him."

"And how," Mary said, "do you put the bite on me?"

"That sounds good," Rafi said, "whatever it means. I'd give you some nice bites, Mary, if we were more than friends. But"—he gestured, a sad smile now—"what can I do? I'm not your lover. I can only approach you as a friend. Ah, but there, perhaps I can suggest a very profitable business investment in Santo Domingo that might interest you. Something you can come down to see from time to time. I show you and we watch it grow. Maybe something like that?"

"How much?" Mary said.

"The investment? I don't know, I have to show you the papers."

"Would you like to show my husband?"

"He has his investment, uh?" Rafi said. "You have yours. What's the matter with that? I wouldn't wish to take his valuable time, a man like your husband . . ."

"He's coming," Mary said, nodding toward the bay. "Tell him about it."

Rafi turned to see the prow of the boat approaching the dock, a heavy rumbling sound reaching them.

"I think you misunderstand me."

They could hear the boat's exhaust clearly as the white hull crept toward its berth and a deckhand jumped to the dock with a line.

"Really," Mary said, "tell him about your profitable investments."

"Well, I'd be happy to meet your husband, of course . . ."

"You don't sound too sure."

"General de Boya. Every Dominican knows of him. It would be an honor."

"He's not a general anymore," Mary said. "He's . . . I'm not sure what he is. Ask him."

Rafi had lost some of his confidence. He seemed apprehensive, watching de Boya, in a business suit, coming across the lawn toward them, and looked at Mary quickly.

"I don't want to take his time."

"He won't let you take his time if he doesn't want you to," Mary said. "Tell him whatever you like."

She glanced at Rafi preparing himself, squaring his shoulders; then waited until her husband was mounting the steps to the sundeck. He was wearing sunglasses, his grim expression in place.

"Andres, I'd like you to meet a fellow Dominican, Rafael Amado." And told him they had met at the Santo Domingo Country Club on her last trip. "Rafi's in investments. You two should get along fine."

She watched Rafi step forward and bow, eyes lowered, as he took her husband's hand, a commoner in the presence of royalty. But it was her husband's reaction that surprised her more. His posture seemed to be not the stiff formality he reserved for strangers, meeting someone for the first time, but the more guarded sense of suspicion he usually reserved for her. She wondered if he knew who Rafi was. They spoke in Spanish for less than a minute while Andres eyed him and Rafi looked off nodding, trying to maintain a thoughtful, interested expression; until Andres gave him a stiff nod for a bow, looked at Mary briefly as he excused himself and walked into the house.

Rafi now seemed dazed. He said, "I've met General Andres de Boya."

"And he didn't take you out and shoot you," Mary said. "He must like you."

It was as though Rafi took her seriously, his expression numb, a glazed look in his eyes.

"When I was little," he said, then paused. "Perhaps I shouldn't tell you. It might seem offensive to you."

Mary shrugged. "No more than anything else you've said."

Now he seemed wounded. "Have I hurt you?"

"When you were a little boy," Mary began. "What?"

"My mother would threaten me," Rafi said, "as many of the mothers of small children did at that time. She would say to me, 'If you're not good, General de Boya will come and take you and we'll never see you again.'" Rafi gestured with a weak smile. "That's all. As you introduced me to him I thought of it again."

"Well, it sounds like something to keep in mind," Mary said, "no matter how old you are."

There had been a list of POOL RULES on a board nailed to a palm tree, put there by the previous owner. *No running . . . No splashing . . . No swimming without showering first . . . No glass objects allowed on the patio . . .* A list of negatives Moran never cared for. So when the palm tree died and was removed the POOL RULES went with it. He did set an example, though, and when he switched after two cans of beer to scotch he poured it into a plastic party glass with ice and took his drink outside to sit in his deck chair and wait for Rafi.

It was dark now though still early evening. He had not seen Rafi all day. When he saw him again it would be for the last time. He did not have to prepare a speech; what he had to say was simple enough. Get your ass out of here.

He told himself he shouldn't let things get out of hand like this. He should never wait for things to happen and then have to clean up after. Maybe he should have put the POOL RULES up somewhere. But then he thought, no. Even if you said *No glass objects* people could still bring a glass out and break it; they could still cut themselves and sue you. No, rules were cold, unrelenting. You had to handle people individually, take each situation as it came. Just don't let them talk you into something you don't want to do.

He wished Mary were here looking at the ocean with him. Looking at the ocean at night made him think of himself in a quieting way. He felt the breeze with a smell of salt in it and thought of turning on some music. Start with Placido Domingo doing love ballads. She said he was more romantic than she'd expected and he told her he felt like he was seventeen. He did. Thinking about her now mellowed him. Start with Placido and work up to J. Geils.

So that when Rafi showed up, coming across the patio from the office, Moran waved—"Hey, I want to talk to you"—and walked toward the swimming pool where Rafi stood in the green glow of underwater lights.

"What'd you lay on Mary?"

"I'm sorry . . ." Rafi began, not understanding.

"I am too," Moran said. "Never buy a guy dinner until he proves you shot him." Rafi still looked puzzled—real or acting, it didn't matter to Moran. "You weren't on that roof with Luci anymore'n that little broad's her sister. So let's cut the shit. I don't care if you own up or not, long as you're out of here tomorrow."

Rafi seemed hurt now. "George, what is it? Why you saying this?"

"You can try it out on me," Moran said, "it was kind of interesting, see how you handle it. But you go for my friend, the fun's over. Take your little hooker and get out of here."

Rafi said, "My hooker?"

"Your *puta*. She's over there waiting for you." Moran nodded toward Number One, at the figure of the girl in the doorway, and it took him by surprise; the classic pose, the girl's body outlined in a soft glow of lamplight, inviting without making a move.

Rafi said, "George, you heard her story . . . I swear to you on my mother's honor . . ."

"You better keep your mother out of it," Moran said, "unless you want to hear some street Spanish about where you came from. You *comprende, pendejo?* Let's keep it simple. You brought the girl along so I'll feel sorry for her and you can make a pitch. Something for poor little Loret, living down there in the slums. And if I get your meaning you don't have to hold anything over my head. Then what? You parade her in front of Mary? . . . You knew who she was when we were down there, didn't you? Must've lit your eyes up. What'd you say to her today?"

Rafi took his time. "George, part of what you say is true. Yes, I recognize Mary. But I don't say

anything because I don't want to . . . surprise you
and you think the wrong thing."

"Bullshit, you had to come up with a scheme.
You followed me today, you followed her . . . You
tell her how much you want or you haven't made
up your mind yet?"

"George, what do you think I want?"

"Not *what*, how much. I know what you want.
Christ, the way you do it, you might as well wear a
sign. You're a fucking lizard, Rafi, that's all I can
say."

Rafi gave himself a little time. He sighed. "You
make it sound ugly, George, I'm surprise. A man
like you, run this kind of place." Rafi looked about
critically in the glow of the swimming pool, unim-
pressed. "You want me to believe it's very swank.
But soon as I come here I realize something,
George. You see a good thing you go for it. You ac-
cuse me, but, George"—with a smile to show patience and understanding—"I'm not the one
fucking General de Boya's wife, you are."

Moran hammered him with a straight left, aiming for the grin that vanished behind his fist and
Rafi stumbled back, over the side of the pool. He
landed on his back, smacking the water hard, went
under and came up waving his arms, gasping.
Moran stood on the tile edge watching him. Rafi
was only a few feet away but struggling, fighting the
water, still gasping for breath. Shit, Moran thought.

He yelled at him, "Take it easy! Hey—put your head back, you won't sink."

Rafi was trying to scream something in Spanish, taking in water, gagging, going under again.

"Relax, will you. Take it easy."

Moran glanced around to see the girl, Loret, next to him now, calmly watching Rafi in the water.

"Can't he swim?"

"I don't know," the girl said. "It don't look like it."

"Shit," Moran said. He pulled his untied sneakers off, hesitated, took his wallet out of his pocket, dropped it behind him and jumped in the pool.

As soon as they got him in the living room of the apartment Rafi slumped into the sofa, his Dominican shirt sticking to him, transparent. Moran yelled at him, "Not on the couch!" and grabbed an arm to pull him up. Christ, the guy was making a survivor scene out of it, saved from a watery grave, the girl bringing a blanket she'd ripped from the bed. Moran held her off and pushed Rafi toward the bathroom. "Get in there. You ruin my furniture I'll throw you back."

Nolen was standing in the doorway holding the screen.

"What happened?"

"Asshole fell in the swimming pool."

"He all right?"

"Who gives a shit," Moran said. He started out, then looked around at Loret. "Give me my wallet."

She hesitated, then reached behind her and brought it out of the waist of her jeans. "I holding it for you."

"Thanks," Moran said. "Now pack. You're going home tomorrow." He took his wallet and left.

Nolen watched Moran cross to his bungalow and go inside. For several moments Nolen stood with his hands shoved into his back pockets, looking about idly.

"Moran hit him then save his life," Loret said.

"Funny guy," Nolen said. He came in now, moved through the living room to the kitchenette, snooping, looking around. "What do you and Rafael drink for fun, anything?"

"They some wine in the refrigerador."

"I'll be back," Nolen said.

Loret began in Spanish and Nolen had to tell her to talk English or shut up. He listened to see if she had anything of value for him, but all she was doing was bitching at Rafi.

"I don't know why I come here with you. I learn what you tell me, I say it perfect."

"You don't say it perfect," Rafi said.

"I say it so good I begin to cry myself and he touch me. You see that. He reach over and touch me. I did it perfect. But you—you say something he push you in the *piscina*." She looked at Nolen sitting forward on the sofa, pouring himself a drink from the bottle of Scotch he'd placed close by on the coffee table. "You know how much money I didn't make since I start being with him? I'll tell you—"

Rafi said something to her in Spanish that shut her up.

"It's okay," Nolen said. "How much?"

"Two hundred dollar a night—all those nights I have to spend listening to him, it come to *dos mil*, two thousand dollar I don't make," Loret said. "Maybe more than that."

Nolen was getting up, hands on his thighs like an old man. "You're a cute little girl," he said to Loret, taking her by the arm, leading her to the bedroom, "but you talk too much. Stay in there and be quiet." He pushed her into the room and closed the door. When she pounded on it and began yelling in Spanish Nolen opened the door a few inches and pointed a finger inside. "I said be quiet, you hear? Or I'll have to get rough with you and I don't want to do that." He closed the door again and went back to the sofa. Easing himself down he said to Rafi, "I recited that line every night for two and a

half months. 'Be quiet now, you hear? Or I'll have
to get rough with you . . . ' Oh my, where were we?
That's right, we haven't started yet, have we?"

Rafi sat quietly in a straight chair turned away
from the desk. He seemed drained of energy after
his ordeal, his hair still wet, flat to his skull, his
body wrapped in the comfort of a brown velour
robe.

"First, you didn't do it right," Nolen said. "You
come rolling in like a medicine show, got your little
helper with you. Fine, except every guy to her's a
trick. You see it in her eyes, she can't wait to get
your fly open. Second, you picked the wrong guy. I
don't mean because he doesn't have any money, I'm
not talking about money. And I don't mean he's the
wrong guy in that you ever leaned on him seriously,
spoke right out and tried to blackmail him, he'd
beat the shit out of you. That's nothing. You've
been cut, you know what I mean. You get over it.
No, I'm talking about you picked the wrong guy
from the standpoint you didn't pick the *right* one.
Are you following me?"

Rafi was moving his tongue over his teeth or
touching his mouth gently with the tips of his fingers.

"You paying attention?"

Rafi didn't say. He seemed to nod.

"I'm not telling you this," Nolen said, "because I
think you need counseling. You're no more fucked

up than the rest of the pimps trying to get by, but you're not a pimp."

"I was never a pimp," Rafi said, as indignant as he could sound with a sore mouth.

"I mean you don't have the right stuff to be a good pimp," Nolen said. "You're not only about thirty years behind in your style you're playing the wrong part. You come on like a young Fernando Lamas when another type entirely, today, is selling tickets."

Rafi said, "What tickets?"

"Just listen," Nolen said. "What's going down in the Caribbean, in Central America, El Salvador now, ever since Cuba? Revolutions, man. They've always been big down there, but now they're getting more notice because they seem closer to home. Only an hour, two hours across the friendly skies and it scares the shit out of people. It's going on right in Miami with the Cubans, the Haitians, Colombians that come to visit—you got dope and international politics all mixed up with terrorists that use pipe bombs and automatic weapons, man, it's real and it's right here. You understand what I'm saying to you? You want to score today you got to get into the action that's going down, you got to spread a little terror."

Rafi was listening. He said, "Yes? How do I do that?"

"I'm glad you asked," Nolen said. "You've got

the background, the hot blood, all that shit. I think with a little direction, a good slogan, you could make a pretty fair revolutionary. *Viva Libertad*—you know, get excited."

Rafi frowned. "You want to start a revolution?"

"No, you do," Nolen said. "You want to make it look like you're part of a wild-ass revolutionary movement. You're an ace terrorist come here to do a job. You're a fanatic, man, you can't wait to blow somebody away. But, you want him to know it first. You want to make him believe he's got this fucking movement coming down on him, not just some muggers—you know what I mean?—some real gung-hoers, man, fire-eaters."

Rafi said, "What guy?"

"I thought so," Nolen said. "Right there in front of you and you don't even see it. You go after Moran and his girlfriend . . . what about the girl-friend's husband? He's the guy with the prize, not Moran. Moran's one of the good guys."

"Wait," Rafi said. "You have to explain this to me."

"In time," Nolen said. "First we got to think of a good slogan, something to get the guy squirming—he doesn't know what's going on, where it's coming from, but it looks like some pretty heavy shit coming down."

"An *eslogan?* . . ."

"Not a slogan—how do you say it?—a *grito de combate*. A battle cry."

"Yes? To say what?"

"How about *Muerte a de Boya?*" Nolen said. "That's got a pretty nice ring."

Rafi had stopped touching his sore mouth. He stared at Nolen, interested but uncertain, trying to put it together in his mind.

"You asking me to kill?"

"Would you like to?"

Rafi didn't answer.

"I want you to think about it," Nolen said, "get a feel for the part. You're Rafi Amado, the man from Santo Domingo, a no-shit revolutionary full of zeal, revenge, whatever revolutionaries are full of. You understand what I mean? Get in the mood and we'll talk about it some more."

12

JERRY WAS READING the *Sun-Sentinel*. He held it up as Moran came in the office.

"You see this? Right up at Hillsboro. Guy walks out of his condo, he's taking his morning exercise, look what he finds right out in front of his place." The headline of the newspaper read:

33 HAITIANS DROWN IN HILLSBORO SURF; SURVIVOR'S STORY DOUBTED BY OFFICIALS

The photograph that ran the full width of the page and was about five inches deep showed four naked swollen bodies lying on the hard-pack sand at the edge of the surf in early morning light. A Coast Guard helicopter hovered about twenty yards offshore.

"I'm telling you," Jerry said, "it's getting out of hand. People up there, they invest a lot of money in their retirement homes—this's what they got to put up with."

"What's the story the officials don't believe?"

"That they came all the way from Haiti in this rickety boat, sixty-something people. If they're not coming from Cuba it's Haiti now, we don't have enough Latins here, we got all this extra welfare money laying around. Oh . . . there was a phone call for you. You know how many Cubans they got in Miami now?"

"Who was it called?"

"Two hundred thousand. Over half the population. Some woman . . . she didn't leave her name. Plus a hundred and twenty-five thousand boat people, for Christ sake, half of them out of the Havana jails and insane asylums. They send 'em here for us to take care of . . . Here's the number."

It was Mary's.

"When'd she call?"

"Few minutes ago. We're different, we got us a couple Dominican freeloaders. Where you going? You just got here."

"I'll be back."

Moran shoved the slip of notepaper into his jeans and walked out into the sunlight, back toward his house. He was anxious.

Nolen, coming out of Number Five, stopped him.

"George, can I talk to you?"

"I got to make a phone call."

"Just take a minute." Nolen, his shirt open and

hanging out of his pants, got to Moran at the shallow end of the pool. "I got a request. How about letting your buddy from the D.R. stay a couple more days? He's afraid to talk to you."

"I hope so," Moran said.

"He's sorry. He said he made a mistake."

"I made the mistake," Moran said, "ever talking to him." He started to move away.

"George, he can't hurt you. Let him stay a while."

Moran stopped. "Why?"

"Why not? He's all right, just a little fucked up. He's an interesting type, I can study him."

"I know what you want to study," Moran said.

Nolen shrugged. "I think I can get a freebee, a libretito." His hair hung oily looking, he needed a shave, he looked terrible, forlorn, standing barefoot with his hands in his pockets. "She wants me to show her Miami Beach, all the beeg 'otels."

"Good," Moran said. "You take her down there we'll probably never see her again. Look, I don't have time right now. Tell her to clean up the kitchen before you go and tell Rafi he'd better stay away from me, not that I'm pissed off or anything."

"I'll keep 'em in line," Nolen said, "no problem." He watched Moran hurrying away. "Hey, one other thing . . ."

"Later," Moran said. He ran inside his house and locked the door.

Moran waited. As soon as he heard her voice on the phone he said, "What happened?"

"He's still here but he's leaving. Going out on the boat."

"Should I call back?"

"No, it's okay, he's outside. I can see him."

"What's the matter?"

"He told me this morning he doesn't want me to drive anymore. I can't go anywhere alone in the car. If I go out, Corky's supposed to drive me."

"Why?"

"Because he knows. Or he thinks he does—it's the same thing."

"What'd he say?"

"He said he wants me to take the goddamn limousine, but if I insist on using my own car Corky's still going with me."

"I mean what reason did he give?"

"Crime in the streets, the high incidence of muggings and holdups. It's for my own safety. I told him there aren't any muggings at Leucadendra or the Dadeland shopping mall, but you don't argue with him. I told you, he's a rock."

"Can he order you like that?"

"If I get in the car, Corky gets in with me. That's

it, or stay home. What're we gonna do?"

"You got to get out of there, that's all."

There was a pause. "I had sort of a talk with him."

"Yeah? What happened?"

"Not much. I'll tell you about it some other time, not now," Mary said. "God, I'm dying to see you."

"I'll be over in a little while."

"You can't come *here*."

"I've got an excuse. I'm gonna return something."

"What is it?"

"I'll be there in about an hour. Why don't you invite me to lunch?"

"God, Moran—hurry."

Nolen caught him again, coming out of the laundry room holding a grocery sack, the top rolled tightly closed. Moran was wearing a sport coat and good pants. Nolen looked him up and down.

"The casual Holiday Inn attire?"

"There times you can say anything you want," Moran said. "This isn't one of 'em. I'm in a hurry."

"Jiggs wants to talk to you."

"You told me."

"Give him the courtesy—what've you got to lose?"

"My good name, being seen with a kneecapper. There isn't anything he can tell me I need to know."

"I'm not asking you to go out of your way."

"I hope not."

"I'm not suppose to say anything," Nolen said, "but I'll give you a hint. It's got to do with freedom of choice and self-respect. Like not having to sneak in the Holiday Inn anymore."

"What I have to say to that," Moran said, "has to do with self-control. How I'm learning to stay calm, not pop anybody in the mouth, dump 'em in the swimming pool every time I get a little irritated. But it's hard."

"I know, stay out of your personal affairs," Nolen said. "But I feel I owe you something. You've been a buddy to me, even after we tried to blow you away with a one-oh-six. I mean it might've been me, though I hate to say it."

"Let's let bygones be bygones," Moran said. "Long as you pay your rent on time. I'll see you."

Nolen said, "Hey, George?" And waited for him to stop a few feet away and look back. "You're a beautiful guy. I just don't want anything to happen to you."

"Jesus Christ," Moran said, "leave me alone."

"Only three nights I got to recite that line," Nolen said. "You can see why the fucker closed."

He liked the trees in this south end of Coral Gables, the quiet gloom of the streets; the trees belonged

and were more than ornamental. It was old
Florida, the way he felt Florida should still look.
No way for a one-time cement-finisher to think, or
a man partly responsible for a half-dozen king-size
condominiums with majestic names. Maybe it was
guilt. Or maybe he simply liked a tangle of ripe
tropical vegetation. What was wrong with that? He
told himself not to argue with himself; he was one
of the few friends he had. He didn't care for what
he was doing right now. It was like going to the
dentist when you were in love with his nurse, but it
was still going to the dentist. He turned off Arvida
Parkway into the drive marked 700 on a cement
column and this time followed its curve up to the
house.

Mary was waiting outside. She brought him past
the three members of the home guard who stood in
the driveway and seemed disappointed. Moran recognized the one with the mustache. Corky. The one
trying to look mean.

From the front steps Moran said, "Keep an eye
on my car, okay?"

Mary took him by the arm. "Get in here." And
closed the door. "What's in the bag?"

Moran opened it and brought out a pink negli-
gee. "You like it? Anita de Boya's playsuit. She left
it."

"He's not gonna believe that's why you came,"
Mary said. "Anita lives in Bal Harbor."

"Do you want me to care what he believes?"

"You're right, it doesn't matter," Mary said. Tense today, inside herself.

She led him from the hallway that was like an arboretum of exotic plants and trees, past an almost bare living room that resembled a modern-art gallery, through a more lived-in-looking room done in rattan and off-white fabrics and out to the sundeck with its several-million-dollar view of Biscayne Bay and the Atlantic Ocean, what Miami money was all about.

Moran was impressed; but he could be impressed by all kinds of things and not have a desire to own them; he considered himself lucky. He took in the sights, the empty boat dock, the stand of acacia trees, then back again, across the sweep of lawn to the swimming pool, designed to resemble a tropical lagoon set among palm trees and terraced flower gardens. Clean that setup every day, he thought. But said, "I like it."

"I don't," Mary said. "I've got to get out of here."

She stood at the rail with him, wearing sunglasses now, looking out at the water. When she turned away he followed her to a half-circle of chairs with bright yellow cushions. On the low table in the center was a white telephone and the morning paper headlining the dead Haitians.

"Why don't you leave now? With me," Moran

said. He sat down. Mary remained standing, tan in her white sundress, silent, her slim legs somewhat apart, folding her arms now; protective or defiant, Moran wasn't sure.

She said, finally, "Rafi was here yesterday."

"I know, I had a talk with him," Moran said. "If that's what's got you clutched up, don't worry about it. Rafi comes on strong, but he's a twink at heart, he caves in."

"What did he say?"

"He's not our problem. There's a guy that works for your husband on and off, Jiggs Scully. You know him?"

"I know who he is."

"He's been following you. He knows what we're doing and wants to talk to me."

"Oh, God—"

"Wait. Nolen Tyner—I told you about him. He says Jiggs doesn't have his hand out, he wants to discuss something else entirely, but I don't see any reason to talk to him. Do you?"

"I don't know." Mary was wide-eyed now, gathering it all in. "If he saw us together and he works for Andres . . ."

"Nolen says he hasn't told Andres. You know why?"

"No."

"He doesn't like him. I feel like we're back in the eighth grade. Here's a guy—" Moran stopped.

"Well, that's beside the point. What Jiggs and Nolen are up to's none of our business. I hope. But I don't want to see us get dragged into it. We got enough going as it is."

"Dragged into what?"

"I don't know, but it's got to have something to do with your husband and they either want to use me—I'm guessing now, you understand—or they want some information from me, or they want me to get it from you."

"Oh—"

The way she said it, like an intake of breath, surprised him. She was thoughtful now, staring. Then took several steps without purpose, moving idly, though he could see she was concentrating, looking down at the boards as she paced toward the railing, aimless, and came back. As she turned again he stopped her.

"You have an idea what it might be?"

Mary sat down now. She eased back into the chair next to him.

"Money. What else?"

"I had that in mind," Moran said. "But what kind of money? How do you rip off a guy like your husband? I mean it's not like going to the bank, make a withdrawal. How do you get it? Extortion? They have something on Andres? It's a feeling I've got more than anything else. I think Nolen and this guy Jiggs are putting something together. But it wouldn't be a holdup, anything as simple as that. Nolen's not, well, he's a little shifty, but he's not an armed robber. I don't think he'd have the nerve to walk in with a gun. So it would have to be something he thinks is clever or he wouldn't be doing it. *If* they've got some kind of scheme in mind."

"There's money in the house," Mary said.

Moran waited a moment. "Is that right?" He waited again and was aware of the silence. "You mean a lot of money, huh?"

"Quite a lot," Mary said.

Moran looked out at the bay, at the dark shape of Key Biscayne lying five miles off, on the horizon.

"Is it money he has to hide? I mean, did he get it illegally?"

"I assume it's from his business. Andres's investments net, before taxes, three to four million a year."

Moran waited. If she wanted to tell him more he'd let her, up to a point.

Mary said, "Remember in Santo Domingo we were talking about Andres? You'd heard he came here in Sixty-one with a fortune. Everyone thought so—he was a millionaire general with a sugar plantation and God knows what else. But he lost all that. He had to run for his life and he came here with practically nothing."

"I remember."

"And I think I said something about he's never

gonna let that happen again. Have to run and leave everything behind."

"You said he'd be ready next time," Moran said. "But I would imagine he has money in a Swiss bank or the Bahamas, one of those numbered accounts."

"I'm sure he does," Mary said, "but if for some reason he's not able to leave the country or he has to hide . . . All I know is he's got quite a chunk of quick-getaway money right here . . . in the house."

He could see the two of them at the deep end of the hotel pool . . . the wives of the winter ballplayers in a group . . . "I asked you, where's he keep it, under the mattress?"

Mary was looking at him. She didn't speak right away; she didn't have to. Finally, in the silence, she said, "You want to guess how much?"

"I've got a feeling I know too much already," Moran said. "We've got to get you out of here. Why don't you pack a bag and leave him a note."

"Not yet. I'm gonna talk to him, George, if I have to hit him over the head. Last night, I had all the words ready. 'Andres, listen to me, okay?' Like talking to a child. 'This isn't a marriage. I'm not happy and I know you're not.' And that was as far as I got. He gave me papers to sign. 'Here'—like he hadn't heard a word—'read these and sign them.'"

"What kind of papers?"

"Business. I'm part of his corporation, one of

them. He made a business transaction out of the marriage with that prenuptial agreement and that's all it is, a deal. I'm a member of the board."

"Resign," Moran said.

"Now he's trying to use the agreement to threaten me. He'll amend it so there won't be a settlement if I walk out. I told him fine, I don't care. I said, 'I just want to talk. I want you to understand how I feel.'"

"That didn't impress him?"

"I'll tell you, George, I'm scared to death. You know that," Mary said. She seemed to clench her teeth. "But I'm also getting mad, goddamn it."

"Good," Moran said.

"I'm gonna write it down, everything I want to say. Then I'm gonna try once more. If he still won't listen then I'll hand *him* the papers this time and that's it, I'm through."

"You promise?"

"You have my word," Mary said.

"Stay mad."

"I *am*. I don't owe him a thing."

"If anybody owes anybody," Moran said, and let it go at that. It would be nice to sit with tall drinks and talk about nothing and enjoy the million-dollar view. But his presence was making her nervous. He said, "Write your letter." He touched Mary's shoulder as he got up and left his hand there until she put her hand on his. She was looking up at him through her round sunglasses. More than anything he could think of he wanted to touch her face.

He walked away.

Jiggs Scully was in the road next to his two-tone red and white Cadillac, the car standing within a few yards of the driveway. So that when Moran swung out onto Arvida he had to brake to a stop or run into the Cadillac's rear end. Jiggs came over to him.

He said, "George, how we doing? If you don't have a pair of the biggest ones in town, come right to the man's house there, I don't know who does. You getting reckless or you just had enough of this sneaking around shit, going the Holiday Inn?"

Moran didn't say anything. He wondered if Jiggs had slept in his seersucker coat. He wondered where Jiggs lived and wondered what he thought about when he was alone.

"I'm gonna buy you a drink, George. How about the Mutiny up on Bayshore? You know where it is there? Cross from the yacht basin."

"Okay," Moran said.

The room was still nearly full in the early afternoon, the tables occupied by men in disco sport shirts with dark hair and mustaches, a few in business suits, some of them wearing their sunglasses, some talking on phones brought to the tables. The waitresses, moving among them in skintight leotards, were experienced and familiar with the patrons, calling them by first names or the names they were using.

"You think it looks like a jungle, all the plants and shit," Jiggs said, "it *is* a jungle. This's where all the monkeys hang out. Jack a phone in there and make a deal, talk about the product; it's always the product now, and how many coolers it'll cost you. Use clean new hunner-dollar bills, George, a hunner K's maybe twelve inches high, little less. Put a million bucks in a Igloo cooler you look like you're going the beach. These guys kill me, all the hot-shit dealers." He was looking over the room, pushing his glasses up on his nose. "About every fifth one you see is making believe he's in the business and about every tenth one's a narc. The mean-looking ones are the narcs, with the hair and the bell-bottoms. Fucking bell-bottoms're out of style, they don't know it. Little guy there looks like he repairs shoes, he's the biggest man in the room. Looks like the Pan-American games, doesn't it? Spic-and-span. They're the spics, George, and me and you, we're the span." Jiggs raised a stubby, freckled hand from the table, fingers spread, and looked at it. "Distance between the tip of your thumb to the tip of your little finger, that's your span." He looked at the back of his hand, then turned it over and looked at the palm. "But I don't see nothing in it, do you, George? No, it's empty. The spics, they got the product, they got all these coolers we hear about. But we're sitting here with our fucking mitts empty. Why is that? They don't work any harder'n we do. Is it we let 'em have it cause we're kindhearted or what?"

A waitress with a blond ponytail brought their beer and asked Moran what his sign was. He told her Libra and she said, "I was right," not telling him if she thought it was good or bad. She gave him a look though and he smiled.

"You got a nice way with the ladies," Jiggs said. "I admire that. You're quiet, you mind your own business, don't you? Till somebody pushes you. I notice that the night I came by your place, run the piano player off. You stood right in there."

"I'm going," Moran said, "soon as I finish this beer."

Jiggs grinned; his teeth were a mess. "I get talking to my own kind I run off. You talk to these monkeys they stare at you. Subtle—you try and say anything subtle to 'em you get a blank stare. You get what I'm saying but you don't make a big deal out of it. I don't think anything I might say to you would even shock you; I think you been around a couple times. Tell me what you think I got in mind. I'd like to know."

"If it's a payoff so you don't tell de Boya," Moran said, "you're out of luck."

"Come on, George, give me some credit. That's

pussy, that kind of deal; I never stooped to that in my life. Jesus, I'm surprised at you, George."

"Forgive me," Moran said.

"What I do when somebody's paying me, I don't even think about it," Jiggs said. "But when it's my deal I try to be a little selective, stay away from the shlock. You have to understand there's all kinds of opportunity out there, George."

"I'm not looking for work," Moran said. "I've got all I want."

"All right, let me tell you a quick story." Scully hunched in, planting his arms on the table. "Not too long ago I'm out at Calder with Mr. de Boya and a gentleman by the name of Jimmy Capotorto, you may've heard of. He runs Dorado, very influential guy, does a little business with de Boya. Jimmy Cap'll send some cash over there, get it cleaned and pressed in some condo deal, but nothing big. We're at Calder. We're watching the races up in the lounge. I'm placing bets for 'em, getting drinks when the waitress disappears. I'm the gofer, you might say, I'm not sitting there in the party too much. De Boya wins a couple grand, it's on the table there, and Jimmy Cap asks him what he does with his winnings, his loose cash. They start talking about the trouble with money like a couple of broads discussing unruly hair'r split ends, Jimmy Cap saying in Buffalo he used to have a vault in the floor of his basement, but there aren't any basements here. De Boya says you don't need a vault, there a lot of places to hide money it'll be safe. Oh, Jimmy Cap says, like where? De Boya says oh, there lot of places. Jimmy Cap asks him what he needs to stash money for, he's a legitimate business-man, he doesn't deal in cash, what's he trying to do, fuck the IRS? De Boya says no, he always pays his taxes. Then he says, quote, 'But you don't know when you have to leave very quickly.' Jimmy Cap says use a credit card. I miss some of the next part, I'm shagging drinks. I come back, de Boya's saying, 'If I tell you, then you know.' Jimmy Cap says, 'You have my word.' The guinea giving the spic his word. But it's good. That's one thing I have to hand 'em, George. They give their word you don't need it written out and signed. De Boya says then, 'Put away what takes you a year to make and have it close by, so you can take it with you.' Jimmy Cap says, 'That the rule of thumb?' Like getting back to our span, George." Jiggs looked at his hand again. "How much does it hold? How much does a guy like de Boya put away in case he has to slip off in the night and show up in Mexico as Mr. Morales? You follow me?"

"I don't know," Moran said, "how much does he?"

"Later on I'm talking to Jimmy Cap," Jiggs said, "I ask him out of curiosity how much does he think de Boya makes a year—all the condos, all the land deals. Jimmy Cap says, 'Net? Couple mil, easy.' "

Jiggs waited.

"What do you want me to say?" Moran said.

"Tell me where he keeps it."

"How would I know?"

"You could find out. Ask his missus."

"Why would she tell me?"

" 'Cause she thinks you're cute, George. 'Cause she thinks her husband's a bag of shit. 'Cause she'd like to dump him and play house with you. 'Cause if I knew exactly where it was I could be in and out of there in two minutes and your troubles'd be over."

"Why would they?"

"Because Andres de Boya would be dead, George, and you and the missus could sail off in the sunset."

Moran actually saw a picture of a red sunset, sky-red night . . . but put it out of his mind as he said, "What about Nolen? Is he in it?"

"I tell you the deal, Nolen dresses it up, adds a little inspiration. He's like my p.r. man, George, get you interested. It's the only reason I talked to him."

Moran said, "You've been thinking about this for some time, uh?"

"Walking around it," Jiggs said, "scratching my head. Then you come along and I think, here's a chance to do something for the happy couple. If they'll do a little something for me."

"I think you're crazy."

"I know you do, George, at the moment. But what you got to do is examine your conscience. You Cath'lic?"

"Sort of."

"You remember when you go to confession you examine your conscience? Let's see, I had five hundred impure thoughts and I entertained the idea of killing Sister Mary Cunnagunda. Examine your conscience, George. Go ahead, and tell me if you're doing anything wrong. It's in the intention where the guilt is. Your intention is to give me information. What happens after that is out of your conscience and into mine and I think I can handle it."

"You might be from New York," Moran said, "but you didn't learn to think like that at Fordham."

"No, I never quite made it, George. But the inference there, what you're driving at—well, you want to get philosophical and discuss whether a blow job from a married woman is the same as committing adultery or you want to make your life easier? I can get the guys and go in with blazing six-guns and tear the place up, we'll find it. But that's the hard way and I can't be responsible if an innocent bystander, if you understand what I mean, gets in the way. Or we can make arrangements, do it quietly. It's up to you."

"Why're you telling me this?"

Jiggs was patient. He sat back, pushed his glasses up, then hunched over the edge of the table again. "George, correct me. Didn't I just tell you?"

"I mean how do you know I won't go to the cops?"

"With what, a story? Come on, George, whatever way this goes down, you think I'm gonna be a suspect? Guy like de Boya, you make it look political. Write on his wall 'Death to Assholes' and sign it the PLO or some spic revolutionary party, that's the easy part."

"He's got armed guards," Moran said.

"This town you better," Jiggs said. "No, that's something you take into consideration. But he's only got one guy dumb enough to stand in there with him, young Corky, and I'm taking that into account."

Moran sipped his beer, making it last. Maybe he had time for one more. Carefully then, thinking of what he was saying: "If this money de Boya's got, it's like an emergency fund?"

"Right, case he has to bail out in a hurry."

"Well, if he's ready to do it like at a moment's notice," Moran said, "why don't you spook him? Turn in some kind of false alarm."

"Yeah?" Jiggs said.

"He runs with it and you're waiting for him. Saves tearing his house apart."

Jiggs didn't say anything for a moment.

"That's not bad, George. That's not bad at all. Sounds to me like you're in the wrong business."

"Or maybe I could tell fortunes," Moran said. He picked up his beer glass and gazed at it. "I see a guy murdered in his house. I don't see anything about him being robbed, no money in the picture. But wait a minute. I see the police have been given information about a suspect. Ah-*ha*, guy runs a motel and is a good friend of the victim's wife." He looked at Jiggs. "That how it works?"

Jiggs said, "George, I offer you the stairway to happiness and all you gimme back're ideas. I'm telling you, you're in the wrong business."

13

SOMETIME BETWEEN 12:45 and 1:00 A.M. an explosion blew the boat dock at 700 Arvida Parkway into Biscayne Bay.

The charge took out the wooden surface of the dock, the heavy planks, the steel davits, ripped out a section of the cement retaining wall, sheared off the pilings to leave splintered stubs that barely cleared the surface of the water, and shattered a sliding glass door on the sundeck of the house. Fortunately Mr. de Boya's $350,000 yacht, *El Jefe*, was moored at Dinner Key where Mr. de Boya had picked up guests, business associates, earlier in the evening and had returned there to drop them off at the time of the explosion. It was heard in downtown Miami.

Coral Gables Police called Dade County Public Safety and a bomb squad was at the scene by 1:30. They picked up pieces of wood and metal strewn over the lawn and would find out through gas chromatograph tests of residue the explosive used

was C4 plastique. A Coral Gables detective said,
"The fuckers are at it again." He put 700 Arvida
on the computer to see if it was a hot address, if it
had ever been used as a "safe house" where marijuana and cocaine were off-loaded, and found no
reference. Andres de Boya's name went into the
computer and came out clean. They didn't notice
the graffiti, spray-painted in red on the cement pillars in front of the property, until daylight. They
thought about calling in the Bureau but decided to
wait. Dope or political, it was still within their ju-
risdiction and the graffiti could be either. Some
kind of Latin dramatic effect that said, on all four
of the cement pillars:

MUERTE A
DE BOYA

When Corky pulled up to the Jordan Marsh entrance to Dadeland the doorman was on the spot.
He offered Mary his hand and slammed the door as
Corky said, "Wait! . . . Mrs. de Boya?" She
stooped a little to look at him through the dark
glass, almost invisible behind the wheel of the
Cadillac. He was gesturing as he said, "I'm suppose
to go in with you. Wait, please. I have to park."

Mary said, "That's all right. I'll see you here in
about an hour."

She heard Corky say, "What? Wait, please!"

"Tell him, will you?" Mary said to the doorman. She tried not to run entering the store. But once inside restraint gave way to eager expectation; it hurried her through Jordan Marsh and down the length of the Dadeland Mall to an entrance near the east end. She sprinted now, out into sunlight, saw the old white Mercedes waiting and almost cheered.

"I'm late," Mary said, catching her breath now, inside the car, as Moran drove through the crowded parking area toward an exit.

"Five minutes. Boy, you look great."

"I'm perspiring."

"Good. We'll take a shower. You know we haven't taken a shower yet?"

She seemed surprised. "Where're we going?"

"A new place. Change our luck."

They drove up Dixie to the University Inn across from the U of M campus where Moran had already got a room and iced the wine, just right, waiting for them. He poured glasses as she slumped into a chair, legs apart, flattening her tan skirt between her thighs on the seat.

"Here."

She took the hotel-room glass of wine and drank half of it down before her shoulders sagged and she began to relax.

"You better love me, Moran."

"Look at me, I'm dying."

"I mean you better *be* in love with me."

"I *am*," Moran said. "Listen, if it was just getting laid there a lot easier ways." He'd better soften that and said, "You bet I love you. Boy, do I."

She said, "Do you, really?"

He wondered how a woman like Mary could have doubts about herself. He came over in the pale light and pulled her up gently, wrapped bare sun-brown arms around her and told her how good she made him feel and how he thought about her and couldn't be without her. She said again what she had told him before, "I don't want to lose you." He told her it wasn't possible. He told her they couldn't lose each other now. He paused. Was he holding back? No, he was running out of words. He told her they couldn't be pried apart with a crowbar or cut apart, they were sealed together for good. He believed it with the feeling she did too, now. Everything was all right; even with Corky waiting they could make slow love and lie in silence after, looking at each other. Save conversation. What more was there to say?

They talked while they were getting dressed.

She told him the police were in and out of the house all day yesterday investigating the explosion, questioning her, the help, Andres, mostly Andres. Their tone wasn't suspicious but their questions were, trying to find out what Andres was into, if Dominican revolutionary or anti-government factions had ever threatened him before. Moran let her tell what she knew, Mary standing at the mirror brushing her hair.

Then he told her about Jiggs Scully in the Mutiny Bar, and she put the brush down and stood very still. Moran ended with a flat statement.

"He knows Andres has at least a couple million hidden in the house. He wants us to tell him where it is. If we do he'll go in, take the money and he'll kill Andres, as a favor."

She said, "A *favor*," wide-eyed.

"We sail off into the sunset and live happily ever after."

The room was as silent as he could remember a room being silent, going back to when he was a little boy lying in bed during his afternoon nap, wide awake. Mary walked to a chair but didn't sit down; she turned to Moran again. He was sitting on the side of the bed with a tennis shoe in his hand.

"I have to tell him," Mary said.

He gave her time.

"You understand that, don't you? I have to."

"The only thing I'm sure of," Moran said, "somebody's trying to use us. A guy talks to me out of the side of his mouth like I'm one of the boys. Why? As far as he knows I'm a decent, law-abiding citizen. It's true you and I happen to have something going—"

"That's quaint, George. Something going."

"Something special, soon to be—you know—out in the open, aboveboard. Let me just tell you the rest, okay? The question is, first, why would he think we'd go along?"

"That's right, he'd be taking a chance," Mary said.

"A big one. But let's say we do. We tell Jiggs where the money's hidden and close our eyes. What happens then?"

"You just said—he'll kill Andres."

"Are we positive?"

Mary frowned, shaking her head. "I don't understand."

"What if the whole thing's your husband's idea?"

She hesitated now. "You think Andres is using Scully?"

"You go to your husband and tell him his life's in danger. What's the first thing he asks you?"

"God, you're right."

"You didn't hear it at the Dadeland shopping mall. But say you tell him," Moran said, "and now it's confirmed, Andres knows we've been seeing each other. What does he do then?" He saw a different look come into Mary's eyes. "You know him better than I do, but he doesn't seem the type that loses gracefully. What does he do to you when you tell him?"

Mary's reaction surprised him: the look of calm that came into her eyes as she listened.

"You're right, it sounds like him. It's the roundabout way he thinks . . . the son of a bitch." She sat down in the chair, thoughtful.

"But we aren't sure," Moran said. "There's the matter of your dock blowing up. Would Andres go that far?"

Mary shook her head. "No, he's not gonna do something that makes him look vulnerable. Unless— why would it have to be part of Andres's scheme?"

"All I know is," Moran told her, "Jiggs said he'd make the hit look political. Like some revolutionary group out to get your husband . . . But why does he tell me all this if there's a good chance I'm gonna tell you and you're gonna tell Andres?"

She said, "He must be awfully sure we'd go along. Or it's worth the chance. He can always deny it. Which brings us back to the only question that means anything. Do I tell Andres or not?"

Mary looked like a young girl sitting in the chair, biting her lower lip now, though more preoccupied than frightened: an imaginative girl wondering how to tell her parents she was pregnant.

She said, "If something did happen to Andres . . ."

He said, "Mary, we don't need help. We don't have to hope he gets a heart attack or falls off his boat. All we have to do is walk away."

She said, "I know. I'm not hoping for anything like that," and looked at him with clear eyes. "But it would be nice, wouldn't it?"

14

NOLEN AND RAFI HAD BEEN DRINKING the better part of two days and were both drunk when Moran found them in the early evening. Nolen was keeping it going. Moran saw it right away: Nolen had to stay up there because if he came down now he'd crash and burn.

They were having a private party in oceanfront Number One with scotch and rum, Coke cans, a bowl of watery ice and potato chips on the coffee table and the smell of marijuana in the room. There was no sign of Loret. They were wound-up drunk: Nolen bare to the waist, stoop-shouldered skin and bones, his slack cheeks sucked in on a joint; Rafi wearing a scarf rolled and tied as a headband, the ends hanging to his chest, his sporty Dominican shirt open all the way. Nolen was calling him Ché.

"You meet Ché? George, shake hands with Ché Amado, one of your premier fanatics, brought here by special request to combat the toadies of oligarchic imperialism, but don't ask me what it means."

"You didn' know that," Rafi said to Moran. Rafi sat slumped in a plastic chair, feet extended in glistening, patent-leather zip-up boots. "You think I come here to bite you for money. It work pretty good, didn' it? I had you fool."

"You had me fool, all right," Moran said. "I thought you were just a pimp. Which one of you did the job on the boat dock?"

"That was him," Rafi said, "he's the powerman." He squinted up at Moran and said, "What did you say before it?"

"That's powderman," Nolen said, "in the trade," and gave Moran a sly look. "I hear we're in business. Is that right? I heard it from a certain party, but I'd rather hear it from you . . . Where you going?"

Moran got a glass from the kitchen and came back to sit at the opposite end of the sofa from Nolen. He poured himself a scotch; he would probably need it.

"You're over your head," Moran said. He drank the scotch and poured another one.

Nolen was grinning. "So what else is new?"

"Stick to acting."

"It's what I'm doing, man. What's the difference?"

Aw shit, Moran thought.

He wondered why he'd ever had a good feeling about Nolen, why he'd been comfortable with him and went for that grunts together, old war buddies grinning their way through life bullshit; he wasn't anything like Nolen. Nolen was pathetic trying hard to be tragic and any more of him, Moran knew, would be a bigger pain in the ass than he could bear. He wanted to hear about it though, what they were into. He would hardly have to encourage them and it would come sliding out of their mouths with alcohol fumes.

"What'd you use," Moran said to Nolen, "on the boat dock?"

Nolen said, "On the dock?" focusing his eyes. "I was gonna go with ammonium nitrate and fuel oil, little dynamite, and light up the sky. But if these people're suppose to be pros, I thought no, you gotta go with a nonhydroscopic plastique, you dig? Slip in there in a Donzi, half-speed all the way. Me and my shipmate, this spic that steered—excuse me, Ché—guy was wearing sunglasses at night. You head due south from near Dinner Key where we launched till you get the Cape Florida light off your port bow, then hang a right and there you are. Drift in . . . I've already run the det-cord through the blocks, they got adhesive backing on 'em now, stick 'em flat under the boards but use a linear-shape charge on the pilings so it'll cut 'em off clean. Twelve pounds of plastique, could've done the

house. I'm scared of timers, so we drifted down by
Matheson Hammock and I blew it remote control." Nolen made an elaborate exploding sound
on the roof of his mouth with his jaw clenched.
"The dock's gone."

Moran said, impressed, "You remember all that
from your paratrooper days?"

"No, I did a bit in *A Bridge Too Far* and hung
around with the special effects guys. It's all make-
believe, George."

"What'd you blow it for?"

"Show him somebody means business."

"Who did the lettering?"

"Ché. Right, Ché?"

"*De nada,*" Rafi said.

"Don't put yourself down," Nolen said. "You
did it, man. Our silent partner goes, 'What's he
gonna write?' I told him don't worry about a thing,
this man's been writing on walls all his life, *fuera* or
muerte to whoever happens to be around that
pisses him off. The man's ace of the spray paint.
You see his work?"

"Your silent partner," Moran said. "Who you
talking about, Scully?"

Moran saw Nolen's fuzzed gaze shift to Rafi and
return to stare at him. Nolen shook his head from
side to side. The drunk being secretive. But Rafi
was even drunker and didn't notice; he was eating

his ice. Nolen pulled himself out of the sofa, took
Rafi's glass from him—Rafi still holding his hand
up, cupped—fixed another rum and Coke and put
the glass back in Rafi's hand. Nolen stumbled sitting down. They were both in bad shape.

Moran could not see Jiggs Scully bringing these
two into the game. Unless he had a special use for
them.

"We're gonna publicize Mr. de Boya's past sins,"
Nolen said and gave Moran a stage wink, obvious
enough to be seen in the back row, "unless he
comes across with a generous piece of change . . .
Isn't that right, Ché?"

" 'Less he pays," Rafi said.

"Tell George what the man did," Nolen said,
"when he was in charge down there."

"What he did?" Rafi said. "He was the head of
the Cascos Blancos, he sent out the death squads to
get people he don't like or people who talk against
Trujillo. He take them to La Cuarenta in Santo
Domingo for the torture. Sometime he take them to
Kilometer Nueve, the army torture place at San
Isidro."

"Tell him what de Boya did to people," Nolen
said.

"Well," Rafi said, "he like to sew the eyelids to
the eyebrows and put them in a light. He like to
beat them with Louisville Sluggers. He like to put

acid on them sometimes. He like to castrate people. He like to take the nipples and pull them out and cut them off with scissors."

Moran said, "Is that what happened to you?"

"No, no, he do that to girls. Cut the nipples off. Men he cut everything off with—how do you say it, these big *tijeras?*"

"Shears," Nolen said.

"Yeah, chears. Cut off your business with them. I had a uncle that happen to. Then when General de Boya finish with them he have them killed and thrown from the cliff into the sea to be eaten by the sharks. You want to find out what happen to somebody, you ask, nobody knows. They say he's gone to Boca Chica to visit the *tiburones*, the sharks. Or sometime to Monte Cristi. That was twenty years ago—the sharks still come looking for General de Boya to feed them. He like to put ants on people, too."

Rafi rolled his eyes back.

"I don't like to think about it."

"Have a drink," Nolen said. The answer to most things.

Rafi took a drink. "I don't feel so good. Maybe I go lie down; I'm feeling tired." He stood up unsteadily, spilling some of his drink.

Moran watched him. He wanted to get up but didn't have the energy; the scene was depressing. He watched Rafi shuffle into the bedroom, Nolen calling after him, "Don't throw up on the floor, Ché. You hear? Go in the *baño*."

He said to Moran, "I don't know what it is about them, partner, those people just don't hold the juice."

Moran watched Nolen pour himself another scotch.

"What're you gonna use him for?"

"He's our spray painter, man. You see his work?"

"But he doesn't know Scully."

"Jiggs wants to see how he works out first. So I told Rafi we got a guy on the inside, but he doesn't want his identity known just yet."

"I don't imagine he would," Moran said. "All right, what's the deal? What're you going after?"

"Jiggs says he told you."

"Come on, this isn't your kind of a thing."

"Is that right? Tell me what I'm saving myself for. It's the best part I've read for in ten years. Shit, I don't even have to act tough."

"He's using you," Moran said.

"Jesus, I hope so. I need to be used, man."

"You know what he asked me to do?"

"I sent you to him, didn't I, for the interview?"

"Come on—you know what he wants?"

"Yeah, he wants you to ask your lady where her husband hides his cash. What's hard about that? Shit, call her up right now."

"Jesus Christ," Moran said. He drank down his

scotch and sat back. "How does he know . . . Hey, you listening?"

"Yeah, I'm listening. What?"

"How does Jiggs know she won't tell her husband what's going on? How does he know *I* won't tell him?"

"Well, shit," Nolen said, "because I told Jiggs you're my bud, we see eye to eye. I said sure, George's the old Cat Chaser, we served down in the D.R., man. I told him it was me almost put out your lights with the one-oh-six and Jiggs got a kick out of that. He sees the humor in life, everybody busting their ass trying to score off each other. I told you he's a funny guy and I was right, huh?"

"Yeah, he's funny," Moran said. "But I still don't understand. Why would he trust me? Tell me a story like that?"

"I just told you. And you want the husband out of the way, don't you? Jesus Christ, or else I came in late and missed something."

"Look," Moran said, trying to keep Nolen's attention. "You listening to me?"

"Yeah, I'm listening." Pinching the roach, sucking his cheeks in with a sound like the north wind.

"I'm not in it," Moran said.

"What happened?" Nolen grunting the words as he held his breath. "You change your mind? There's nothing to be scared of."

"I never *was* in."

Nolen expelled smoke in a long sigh. "Well, Jiggs says you gave him a hell of an idea. He told me. Make the man run and head him off at the pass. I said to Jiggs, I told you he's good, he's a fighting leatherneck. Jiggs says he didn't think much of the idea at first, frankly, 'cause what if the man took off in his boat? Jiggs doesn't like to have anything to do with boats. He goes, 'I don't want no parts of them fuckers.' He gets seasick he goes out. But then, hey, with the dock gone the man can't bring his boat in, can he? He runs, he's got to go by car. And when he does, Jiggs says he'll be way ahead of him . . . He likes you," Nolen said.

Aw shit. Moran felt heavy, out of shape, and the scotch wasn't helping at all. He said, "Nolen?"

"What?"

"I'm not in. I didn't give Jiggs anything. You understand? What he's doing, he's using you. I don't know for what, but when he's through he'll dump you. He can't afford not to."

"We made a pact," Nolen said. "Us against them."

Moran tried again. He said, "You told me who he works for, what he does for a living, right? He leans on people. He breaks their bones. Isn't that right? That's what you told me."

"He used to."

"Okay. But does he sound like the kind of guy you can trust? You can put your life in his hands?"

"Jiggs says we're his kind," Nolen said. "He's sick and tired of the guineas and the spics raking it in, taking everything, guys like de Boya sitting on top. Look at the guy. He's a fucking death squad all by himself. And he's married to your lady. What more like incentive you want, for Christ sake?"

"Don't call her my lady, all right?"

"What should I call her?"

It annoyed him, "my lady." He never liked the expression; but that was something else. "Think a minute," Moran said. "What if somebody else put Jiggs up to this and he's playing a game with you?"

"That's it, man, a game." Nolen was half-listening. "It's us against them. Shirts against the skins, man. They're swarthy fuckers, but they got white legs . . . if you know what that means on the basketball court can figure it out." He gave Moran a feeble grin. Then came alive again. "We'll get little Loret some pom-poms, she'll be the cheerleader. *Muerte a de Boya*, Fight! The old locomotive. M-U, M-U, M-U-E-R; T-E, T-E . . . What do you think? Get her a short little red and white pleated skirt . . ."

"Where's Loret?"

"Jesus, that's right. She hooked up with some guy at the Fontainebleu, guy in the lounge smoking a cigar. She gives him the eye, says excuse me, going to take a leak and I haven't seen her since. I know, you told me. But don't say it, all right? I hate guys like that. Have to rub it in."

Moran said, "What am I gonna have to do to get you to understand something? You dumb shit."

Nolen grinned, eyes out of focus. He held up the dirty stub pinched between his fingers. "How 'bout a smoke? Good stuff."

"It makes me hear tires squeal when I'm barely moving," Moran said. "No, this'll do me." He raised his glass. "Like it's doing you in. I don't want to sound preachy—"

"Then don't."

"But I got to tell you. You're in a no-win situation. The best you can get out of this if you're lucky, I mean if you come out alive, would be something like fifteen to twenty-five at Raiford. Hard time."

"Don't sweat it," Nolen said. "I'm having fun."

Moran stared at him before easing back in the sofa. All right then. Okay. . . .

He was tired.

He saw Mary in his mind, in the room in the University Inn, her hands between her legs on the chair cushion and could see the line of her thighs beneath the tan skirt. He saw her looking at him with her look of quiet awareness, waiting. What did he need to talk to this shithead for?

* * *

Corky came out to the red and white Cadillac in the drive. He asked Jiggs, getting out of the car, then reaching in to punch the headlights off, what he wanted. Jiggs said, "If I thought I had to tell you, Corko, I'd be in pretty bad shape. Tell Mr. de Boya I'll be around back where you used to have a boat dock somebody took out while you're keeping an eye on it." And walked away.

He was inspecting the splintered stubs of the pilings, barely visible in the dark water, when de Boya came out to him. Jiggs turned very carefully on the crumbled edge of the retaining wall and stood with his back to the tide breaking in below him, giving de Boya a casual, death-defying pose.

He said, "Seems you got a problem here," with a grin of sympathy. "Jimmy Cap says take a look. He don't care to see any his friends get fucked over by parties unknown. Jimmy says it's like they're doing it to him."

De Boya was looking down at the water now, at the stump remnants of his dock.

"How do you think of it?"

Jiggs took cautious half-steps from the cement edge until he felt the safety of grass underfoot. "Well, my first thought when I read about it in the *Herald*, I think to myself, some dopers're having a disagreement and one of 'em sends his guy to the wrong address. '*Seven* hundred Arvida. Oh, I thought you said six hundred. Oh well.'"

De Boya's reaction: nothing. Like a statue with clothes on.

"But then I started asking around."

"Yes? What did you learn?"

"You understand we got contacts in Little Havana," Jiggs said. "I first come here they're referring to it in the company as Sowah Seda. This girl Vivian Arzola used to work there says, 'Go on over to Sowah Seda,' I'm supposed to see somebody over there. I ask her where Sowah Seda is. She says, 'Sowah Seda, Sowah Seda.' Finally it dawns on me. Oh, Southwest Eighth Street. She says, 'Yeah, Sowah Seda.' Well, I talked to a guy down there this time name of Benigno, runs a tavern, if he's heard anything. What's this shit, a man's dock getting blown up? He looks around see if anybody's listening. They got the salsa on so loud I can't even hear Benigno. He says it's the work of the FDR. I said FDR? Franklin D. Roosevelt? You said that name to my mother she'd genuflect. Christ, she'd have left home, all the kids, for FDR, he ever wanted to get it on. But, it turns out, Benigno says it stands for Democratic Revolutionary Front."

"It's Salvadoran," de Boya said. "It has nothing to do with me."

"That's what Benigno says, they're from El Salvador. But evidently these people, your different revolutionary groups, are getting together, helping each other out. They don't give a shit you're Dominican, you're Nicaraguan, you come from the ruling class you're one of the bad guys. What do they call it? The oligarchs. You're one of them and they're all working for Castro anyway, they don't give a shit. See, he's sending 'em here to spread a little terror."

"For what purpose would that be?"

"I check around, hear it from some other sources there," Jiggs said. "These people with little bugs up their ass, they come here to cause trouble, score a few big names."

"What do they destroy the dock for?"

"Get your attention," Jiggs said. "So you know it's coming. Like toying with you. Little terrorist foreplay. You go to the cops for protection you're all right for a while. Then when you aren't looking— whammo. They hit you a good one, for real this time and get their initials in the paper."

Jiggs felt de Boya studying his face in the dark, probably trying to look in his eyes, the truth test. De Boya said, "Yes, and what do you do for me?"

"Well, are the cops helping any?"

"They say they keep an eye on my house. They drive by."

"You hire any more people?"

"Not yet." De Boya turned abruptly. "We go inside."

"I know you like Corky, but get rid of the rest of

'em," Jiggs said, following de Boya, "and I'll send you over a couple guys, couple heavy-duty Cubans worked for the CIA when the CIA had a hard-on for Castro. Now these guys're freelance. Jimmy Cap says take care of you, that's what I'm doing."

"It's kind of him," de Boya said.

They went up on the deck, through the two-story hallway filled with plants and young trees like a path through the jungle, and into de Boya's study. Jiggs liked it, the oak paneling, the gun cabinet, the framed photographs of people in military uniforms all over the walls. There was a big one of Trujillo himself in a white uniform full of medals, shots of de Boya with different people, another one of de Boya in what looked like a German SS uniform, de Boya nonchalantly holding an old-model Thompson submachine gun. Jiggs paid his respects to the photographs, nodding solemnly, while de Boya went around behind a giant oak desk and sat down. There was a tape recorder on the desk, a tray that held a brandy decanter and glasses.

Jiggs finally took a chair. He said, "I wanted to ask you. I locate any of the party responsible, General, you're gonna want to prosecute, I take it."

"In my own way," de Boya said.

Jiggs said, "That's how I'd feel about it myself. You have 'em arrested they're back on the street in twenty-four hours." He said then, "I understand, what I've heard, you were the expert at getting people to tell you things they didn't want to. Back in the old days."

"Really? I'm surprised you hear anything about that," de Boya said.

"You kidding?" Jiggs said. "General, there certain areas you're a living legend among people that know anything about or appreciate the fine art of interrogation. It used to be, when I was a youngster on the Force in New York, we could use our own resources, so to speak, in extracting information. Now, the guy doesn't even have to tell you his name his lawyer isn't present. Fucking Miranda changed everything." Jiggs shook his head, began to grin a little. "Wasn't like that where you come from, I don't imagine."

"You say to get information?"

"Yeah, interrogate a suspect."

"The trick," de Boya said, "when you question someone is not to ask a question."

Jiggs maintained a pleasant expression. "You don't ask 'em anything?"

"No, never. You take the person's clothes off. Always you do this, strip the person naked, and sometimes it's enough. Or you subject the person to an unpleasant experience, increasing this gradually," de Boya said, giving his recipe. "The person wants to tell you something, but you still don't ask him. He pleads with you, he begins to say things, to ask the questions himself, yes, and then answer them, he's so anxious to please you if you'll stop the unpleasantness."

"The unpleasantness," Jiggs said, his face creased in appreciation. "That's not bad, general."

"But the information," de Boya said, "that isn't the important reason for interrogation."

"It isn't?"

"What do you wish to know?" de Boya said. "Where someone lives? Where they hide arms? Something they're saying about you, the government? No, the purpose of interrogation is preventive. What you do in the secrecy of the act always becomes known to others, to the ones against you."

"And it scares the shit out of 'em," Jiggs said, nodding. "I getcha."

"I like to think it gives brave men pause," de Boya said. "Remember, fear is of more substance than information."

"Yes sir, that's a good point."

"Information, it has degrees of importance at different times," de Boya said. "But fear, you can use fear always."

"Keeps your people under control," Jiggs said.

"Yes, they don't know what to do, so they do nothing." De Boya began to nod, a pleasant expression masking his thoughts, his pictures from another time. "I always do a good job at that." He gestured with his hands. "Well, it was my especiality, of course."

A few minutes past midnight Moran's phone rang. He turned off Johnny Carson and got to the counter, knowing it was Mary, feeling wide awake now.

She said, "Jiggs Scully was here, earlier this evening. They were in Andres's study with the door closed for almost a half hour."

Moran said, after a moment, "I know what you're thinking . . . But I talked to Nolen and now I'm leaning the other way, back to Jiggs."

"You think the whole thing's his idea?"

"I'm pretty sure. If Andres wanted to get the goods on us there's got to be a simpler way than all this."

"Then why did Jiggs come here? He must be working for Andres."

"For him and against him. Listen, you got to get out of there."

"I will, soon."

"Have you written down what you want to say?"

"I'm working on it."

"Does Andres know I was there today?"

"He didn't mention it, but I'm sure he does. He

got home late." Mary paused. "Wait a second, okay?"

"What's the matter?"

"I heard something. Hold on."

Moran waited, standing straight up now. He heard it then, away from the other end of the phone connection, sounding like shots, glass breaking. He pressed the phone to his ear and heard a voice far away, someone shouting. He heard Mary's voice, closer, call out, "What is it?" Then nothing. He waited. He heard jarring sounds close, as though she might have dropped the phone picking it up. Now her voice in the phone was saying, "I'll call you back."

"Wait a minute. Are you all right?"

Her voice came as a whisper now. "I'm fine, but I can't talk now."

"What's going on?"

"Andres is upstairs."

"Just tell me what happened."

But she'd hung up.

15

MARY DIDN'T CALL BACK during the night.

Moran phoned her in the morning. The maid with the accent said Mrs. de Boya was not at home. It was only nine o'clock; Moran didn't know what to say next. He asked what time she was expected. The maid said she didn't know. He asked then, "Is Mrs. de Boya all right?"

The maid, Altagracia, said, "Yes? I think so."

He took a chance and said, "What was all that noise last night?"

The maid hesitated. She said, "I don't hear any noise."

He tried again a little after ten.

A recorded voice answered to say, "The number you are calling is temporarily out of service. Please try again later." He dialed again to be sure and heard the message repeated.

What in the hell was going on?

He got the number of the Coral Gables Police from Information, 442-2300, dialed and a male voice answered. Moran said, "Hey, what was all the noise over on Arvida last night? Up at the end of the street."

The male voice said, "Who is this speaking, please?" Moran said he lived in the neighborhood and was just wondering . . . The male voice said, "Could I have that address and your name, please?" Moran hung up.

He knocked on the door to oceanfront Number One, waited and banged on it. Then got the key from Jerry, Jerry in a lighthearted mood whistling "I'm Going to Live Till I Die," and went back to let himself in.

The apartment was empty, still a mess from the night before: the bottles standing on the coffeetable, the bowl of water, bits of potato chips all over. The bed Rafi had slept in was unmade, the light spread and sheet in a tangle on the floor.

Nolen, in Number Five, was popping open a can of beer. He said, "Stand back. Don't say anything yet."

Moran waited in the doorway to watch.

Nolen poured a good four or five ounces of Budweiser down his throat. When he lowered the can and looked at Moran with grateful wet eyes he said, "Oh Jesus. Oh my God Almighty." He raised the can again and finished it in two tries.

"I'm gonna live."

"Till you die," Moran said. "Jerry'll whistle it for you while you're going down the tube."

"Fuck you," Nolen said.

"If you know you're gonna be hung over—"

"And if *you* know I'm gonna be," Nolen said, going to the gas range where a saucepan of chili with beans was starting to bubble, "what're you asking me for? You want to be useful, open a couple of beers."

Moran sat with Nolen while he ate his breakfast, chili laced with catsup to sweeten it and drank several ice-cold beers, the sorrow in his watery eyes giving way to a bleary expression of contentment.

Moran commented. "You having fun? You dumb shit."

"Don't judge," Nolen said, "till you walked a mile in my moccasins."

"Few weeks you'll be down to Thunderbird."

"Or Chivas. I'm making my run."

"Bullshit, you'll be down making love to the toilet bowl."

"I never throw up, George. I value my nutrition."

"What time'd you go to bed?"

"I watched black and white TV, you cheap fuck, and hit the sack early."

"Where's your pal Ché?"

"Who?"

"Rafi, your spray painter."

"He borrowed my car to go look for Loret."

"He expect to find her, Miami Beach?"

"Rafi expects—Jesus, this hits the spot, you know it? I doubt Rafi's expectations have anything to do with the real world. He's a twinkie."

"You finally realize that?"

"I've always known it. But he's got to learn on his own, right? I'm not gonna lead him by the hand."

"You bring him into the deep end, now it's up to him to get out, huh?"

"It's hard out there," Nolen said. "You can strike it rich or break your pick. It's up to you."

"That from a play or a movie?"

"It's an outtake. I'm on cutting-room floors at all the major studios. So I'm going into a different field."

"You remember anything I said last night?"

"Every word. I never experience blackouts."

"But you don't want to talk about it."

"I don't care. Get me a beer, I'll listen."

"Jiggs was at de Boya's last night." Moran waited.

Nolen spooned in bright red chili, his face down close to the bowl. "Yeah?"

"Why do you think he went there?"

"I think to tell de Boya some dirty Comminists want to kill him. Also set the stage for what's coming up in the next couple of days. Time's getting short, George. Then you know what I think he did?"

Moran had to ask because he didn't expect all this.

"What?"

"Then I think he gave this crazy Cuban—the one drives his Donzi at night with sunglasses on? I think he gave the Cuban five bills and a twenty-two rifle and told him to take a run past de Boya's house and see if he can bust a few windows, then throw the twenty-two over the side, deep-six it, whether anybody comes after him or not. That's what I think, George. What do you think?"

He thought of Mary, little else. He went back to his house, called Leucadendra and had her paged in the grill and at the tennis courts, knowing she wouldn't be there. He thought about calling the Holiday Inn in Coral Gables; but would that make sense? He tried anyway. There was no Delaney or Moran registered. In the afternoon he tried her home again and listened to the recorded voice tell him the number he was calling was temporarily out of service. He thought about driving over there but knew he'd better wait. Mary would get in touch with him when she could.

It was a dismal, overcast day. The surf came roaring in making a spectacle of itself, but failed to interest him. Grocery-shopping at Oceanside didn't either. Until he was putting a six-pack of Bud in his cart and remembered something Nolen had said. Something about setting the stage for the next couple of days . . . time getting short. Christ, were they ready to move? He'd better put Nolen against the wall and get some facts.

But by the time Moran got home Rafi had returned and Nolen was gone.

Rafi said, "No, I didn't find her. But I went in the Fountainebleu and let my eyes see the most beautiful hotel in the world. I think I like to stay there before I go home."

Moran said, "There's a Miami to Santo Domingo at one tomorrow afternoon, they give you your lunch. Why don't you get on it?"

Rafi said, "Oh, am I being ask to leave? You have so many people staying you don't have room for me? Certainly, I'll be happy to leave a place where they don't want me."

Moran said, "Rafi, you're full of shit, you know it? . . . Where'd Nolen go?"

Rafi said he didn't ask him and if this was the way Moran felt he would leave as soon as he made arrangements to move to a resort that suited him. In the meantime, because Loret had taken his money, could he borrow a few dollars for something to eat? Moran gave him a ten and checked with Jerry, just before Jerry left for the day, to see if he'd had any calls.

None. He tried Mary and got the recorded message again. All right, he'd wait until later tonight—after the maid was in bed and hope de Boya didn't answer—and if the phone still wasn't working he'd drive over there, or drive past at least; he wasn't sure what he'd do. He fixed half of a yellowtail with tomatoes, onions and a touch of garlic for dinner, sautéed it, trying to keep busy, looking at the clock. He read. He watched a little TV. He read the latest on Stevie Nicks and an interview with Lee Marvin, former U.S. Marine, in *Rolling Stone*. Still looking at the clock. Anxious. Looking at it a few times each half-hour, waiting to call about eleven. It was the reason he would remember Jiggs Scully came at exactly 9:40.

Moran opened the door and Jiggs said, "You not doing anything I'd like you to come see somebody." Moran stood with his shirt hanging out, barefoot. When he didn't say anything Jiggs said, "Mr. de Boya wants to have a word with you."

Moran said, "You serious?"

"Put your shoes on. I'll take you, bring you back."

Moran said, "What about?"

Jiggs said, "George, come on. We get there you can play it any way you like. But don't try and shit a shitter, okay?"

Moran put on his sneakers and stuck his Hawaiian shirt into his jeans. He walked with Scully in silence across the patio and through the dark office to the street. Corky was waiting by Jiggs's two-tone Cadillac. Corky got in back as he saw them coming.

Walking around the front of the car, Jiggs said, "Sit in front."

Moran had the door open before he saw Rafi in the back seat with Corky, Rafi hunched forward. He said, "George? I don't want to go nowhere." Trying to sound calm but scared to death. "George? Tell them, please."

Jiggs said to Moran, "It's okay. Get in the car."

The servants would be speaking to each other in Spanish and stop when Mary entered the room. They always did this; but today, for some reason, it had an air of conspiracy. The phone would ring. Altagracia would tell Mary it was someone for Mr. de Boya. Only once did she call Mary to the phone. She spoke to a man from the company replacing the window panes, half-listened to an involved tale of glass availability, why they couldn't come out until later in the day. Twice she tried Moran's number and got no answer.

And after that, for no apparent reason, the phone went dead. She called the telephone company on Andres's private line, in his den, with Corky standing by. Several times she returned to the den to try Moran again and each time there would be Corky. Finally she said, "Excuse me, will you? I have to make a call." But he didn't move.

Corky said, "I have to stay here if Mr. de Boya wants me. He say not to leave for any reason."

She said, "It'll take me two minutes."

He said, "Yes, please," offering the phone. "But I have to stay here until the other phone is fixed."

She said drily, "Mr. Corcovado, if he can't reach you while the line's busy, why do you have to stay here?"

Corky said, "It's what he told me."

Is this your house? Mary thought. She said, "Well, in that case I'm going out. Do you stay by the phone or do you have to drive me?"

He said, "I'm sorry, Señora. Mr. de Boya say we not suppose to go out. Because what happen last night."

She said, "That's not the reason."

Mary went into the kitchen to speak to the cook about dinner, tell her not to bother, and came face to face with two men she had never seen before. They sat at the butcher-block table having coffee. Hispanic, confident, shirts open beneath summer jackets, both wearing strings of red and white beads. They looked her over but did not get up. Mary left the kitchen.

She felt she was in someone else's house. Corky, sitting behind Andres's desk now, told her the two were the Mendoza brothers, Chino and Nassin. They had been hired to replace the two Mr. de Boya fired after the boat dock was exploded. He told her the Mendoza brothers were Cuban and only one of them spoke English, but not very much.

Mary said, "Do they know who I am?"

Corky said, "Yes, of course."

"Who was it shot at the house last night?"

"We don't know that. It happens."

"And cut the telephone line?"

"The repairman tell the Mendozas he think it was a storm."

"There was no *storm*."

"Yes, then maybe it broke itself."

"Why can't I make a phone call in private?"

"I don't know." Corky shrugged; he seemed to be getting used to her. "Why don't you ask your husband?"

She mixed a vodka and tonic and took it out to the sundeck, in the early evening, the sky clearing now that the day was almost past, the wind down to a mild breeze stirring the acacia trees. The two new ones, the Mendozas, watched her from the seawall, where the dock had been. They moved off in opposite directions still looking toward the house. Mary felt a knot of anger. She wanted to scream something as she sat ladylike, yell at the Mendozas, "What're you looking at!"

And waste it, she thought, on bodyguards who wouldn't understand or care if they did. Save it for Andres. The hell with writing down what she wanted to say—writing neatly in her precise up-and-down script. Let him have it with simple truth, you're leaving and that's it. Tell him right out, face to face. If he asks if it's because of Moran say *yes*. Absolutely. She was in love with Moran. She was so in love with him it didn't matter what other reasons there might be. Right now Moran was the reason. And Andres would say . . . The hell with what he'd say! Tell him and get it over with. Andres would think what he wanted to think anyway.

Which was pretty much what she had done six years ago. Talked herself out of all her misgivings, talked fast with the lure of everlasting security in the back of her mind and rationalized up front, telling herself marriage to Andres would be—God help her—fun. If she had known Moran then—if they'd been simply good friends, which would have been impossible, but just say they were—and she had announced she was going to marry Andres, Moran would have said . . .

With a straight face he would have said, "You're gonna marry a general, uh?" That's all.

And that would have done it.

She wanted to keep her anger intact, ready to level it at Andres when he got home. But she couldn't think of Moran and stay mad. She smiled to herself for a time. She looked out at darkness smothering the sunset and felt the smile dry up within her.

Fear was something else.

She'd have to ask him: Can you be afraid of something you think is absurd? No, she wouldn't have to ask, she knew the answer. If the thing that's scaring you doesn't know it's absurd you can laugh all you want, that won't make it go away.

Mary was upstairs when she heard the double horn beeps: Andres's way of announcing, when he drove himself, he was home. She went into Andres's bedroom, the lights off, and looked out a front window to see his immaculate white Rolls in the drive below. Andres was already out of the car talking to the two Mendoza brothers. She didn't see Corky with them. After a few moments they walked off toward the side of the house. It surprised her at first; then decided Andres was showing them around the property. But where was Corky? She hadn't seen him in some time.

Sitting in darkness her gaze moved to the massive shape of Andres's king-size bed mounted on a marble pedestal and remembered her reaction, the first time, sitting on the edge—a *waterbed?*—trying not to smile. And Andres's serious expression, Andres saying to her, "It's more than a bed . . ."

The bed delighted him without altering his expression. He came to her sitting on the bed, raised a knee awkwardly and pushed her back. His face close to hers he murmured, "We make love on millions of dollars," and finally smiled. But it was morning before he explained what he meant. *Making love on millions* . . . talking to his new bride in a boastful way, playful for Andres, but not failing to impress it was their secret, uh? His lidded gaze staring into her eyes. "No one else must know." She wondered now if his words had implied a threat. Or if making love on millions was still possible to do.

She would make love to Moran on cement. On nails.

And began to think of another bed not so large . . . the lights going out in her hotel suite, Moran calling to her in the dark, finding her as she slipped into his outstretched arms. She thought of them falling into the bed together, Moran trying to get their clothes off as she held onto him . . .

She saw the beam of headlights in the trees and moments later Jiggs Scully's Cadillac rolled up the drive toward the house. It came to a stop behind Andres's car and the inside light went on as the doors opened.

Her breath caught as she saw Moran get out.

Now the others came out of the car. She recognized Rafi. The car doors slammed and they were in darkness. As Mary watched, the four figures moved off toward the north side of the house. But why? The gravel path on that side led through the garden to the swimming pool.

"He asks you," Moran said, close to Rafi, "you don't know anything, what he's talking about."

"All I did," Rafi said, his whisper hoarse, straining, "I write something, that's all."

"No, you didn't. You don't know *any*thing."

Corky was waiting for them at an opening in the hedge and Moran shut up. He could hear Jiggs Scully behind them on the gravel. He wasn't worried about Jiggs. It had been a quiet ride all the way and there was no reason to start talking now. Past the hedge they followed patio lights that were hooded and eerie in the close darkness, dull spots of yellow, misty in the tropical growth. The path brought them to the swimming pool, illuminated pale green among ledge rock and palm trees, the man-made filtered lagoon that looked to Moran like a movie set. Though the figure standing at the end of the pool were real enough, de Boya and two men Moran had never seen before. The two, the Mendoza brothers, came this way as Corky turned

and gestured to Rafi, saying something to him in
Spanish. Rafi didn't move.

Scully was next to Moran now. He said to Rafi,
"I think Mr. de Boya wants to ask you something;
that's all."

Rafi looked around, helpless, as though in pain.

One of the Mendoza brothers gestured now,
pointing, and Rafi moved away from Moran to the
edge of a curved section of the free-form pool, the
water clearly illuminated to its tiled depths. Rafi
looked down, then across the curved corner to de
Boya who stood with his hands in the deep side
pockets of a linen jacket.

His voice low Moran said, "Giving us the stare."

"That's what it is," Jiggs said, barely moving his
mouth, "the old Santo Domingo stare. Suppose to,
you look at it long enough, shrivel up your balls."

Twenty feet away de Boya stood without moving, the pale reflection of the pool lights shimmer-
ing on his white jacket, part of his face in shadow.

It began to look like the village players to
Moran. Were they serious? He said, "Hey, Andres,
what's going on?"

De Boya didn't answer.

If he gave a nod Moran didn't see it. He was
looking at de Boya in the same moment one of the
Mendozas stepped in behind Rafi, gave him a hip
and Rafi went into the pool screaming a sound or a
word in Spanish. He came up flailing the water,

gasping, trying to scream, his eyes stretched open. Moran was yelling now, "He can't *swim*," trying to get to the edge of the pool, but both the Mendozas turned to hold him off. He yelled again, "He can't *swim*, goddamn it!" and tried to get through the two Mendozas with shoulders and elbows, grabbing at a shirt and feeling a string of beads come apart in his hand. As he tried to lunge past the other one stuck a gun in Moran's stomach. He felt the barrel dig in as he saw Rafi struggling with his head thrown back, helpless, going under and coming up, going under again. Moran saw Andres watching, Corky watching, the two Mendozas turned from him watching. None of them moved. When Rafi's arms stopped flailing and he began to sink deeper they continued to watch in silence, without moving, staring at the string of bubbles coming out of Rafi's mouth, his body settling to the bottom now, rolling gently from side to side, eyes sparkling in the pool lights, eyes looking up at them sightless as the last air bubbles rose from his open mouth.

Moran listened to the sound of a single-engine plane in the night sky, the sound taking forever to fade. He didn't try to think of anything to say. He felt a hand touch his arm. He saw de Boya staring at him. He heard Scully's voice very quietly say, "Come on."

He saw de Boya staring at him.

He felt the hand grip his arm tighter. "George?

Let's go." Still looking at de Boya staring at him.
He was thinking now, Yes, he'd better go; turned
and walked off with Scully, Scully saying, still quietly, "Let's take it easy now, George, not do anything you be sorry for, okay? Let's just get out of
here before you say anything. Then you can say
anything you want, that'll be fine, George, but not
right at the moment . . ." Scully's voice soothing
him, talking him all the way out to the car.

They were on Interstate 95, heading north to Pompano before Scully spoke again. He said, "That little spic makes a point he makes it, don't he?"

Moran was thinking of things he might have
done or tried to have done. He was thinking of
Mary in that house. He was thinking of what he
would say when he called the police. He remembered the number, 442-2300. He wondered if the
same impersonal voice would answer and if the
voice would change, indicate a person inside, when
he said he wanted to report a murder.

Jiggs said, "George, don't do what you're thinking. They get those funny calls all the time. Sergeant
puts his hand over the phone. 'Who knows a guy
name Moran? Got a swimming pool murder.' No,
George, our friend Rafi Amado's on his way to the
Gulf Stream right now and I don't mean the race-
track. The cops go to Seven hunner Arvida Park-

way, nobody knows what you're talking about there. 'Somebody drown in the pool? Well, the pool's right outside here, officer, you want to take a look.' "

Moran said, "Tell me something."

"What's that, George?"

"How'd he know Rafi couldn't swim?"

Jiggs took a few moments. He said, "George, in the light of eternity, what difference's it make? The guy comes flying in from Santo Domingo with the hot setup, he's gonna try to make a score, right? It's called to my attention and I think to myself, What is this? This guy know what he's doing?"

"And you hired him," Moran said.

"Well, actually I never met the guy in my life till tonight. He was Nolen's boy."

"You're using Nolen," Moran said. "What's the difference?"

"George, you got a suspicious mind and now you're getting off on something else," Jiggs said. "What we're talking about here, all the guy does is spray-paint some bullshit on de Boya's gatepost. It doesn't matter the guy can swim or not, what I want you to look at here is the way de Boya handled it. He call the cops? It's an act of vandalism, you get a fine, maybe ninety days chopping weeds for the county—uh-unh, de Boya believes in capital punishment."

"You delivered him," Moran said.

"You want to look at it that way," Jiggs said, "I offered him up, like a sacrifice so you can see where we're at here."

Moran opened the car door.

"George, just a minute. Let's consider the documented fact you got something going with the guy's wife."

Moran slammed the door closed and Jiggs raised his hand, a peace sign.

"I'm not questioning your intentions, George. Where I live down on the South Beach—Hotel Lamont, sounds like class, uh? You should see it—down there you fall in love with some old Jewish broad on food stamps or you go uptown a mile and find a hooker. No, true love is beautiful, George; but in seeking it you got to be sure and keep your nuts outta the wringer." Jiggs paused and the inside of the car was quiet except for a faint ticking sound, the engine cooling down. "I'll bet you asked his wife—I'll bet it came up in conversation and you asked her where the general keeps his going-away money. Am I right?"

Moran opened the car door again.

"The only point I want to make about this evening, George—de Boya does that to a spray-painter, what's he gonna do to a guy he finds out's been jazzing his wife, room one sixty-seven the Holiday Inn? He's already pretty sure. The man'll believe anything I tell him."

Moran got out of the car this time. He said, looking in at Scully, "You want to tell him, Jiggs? Tell him." He swung the door closed and walked off toward the motel office.

Maybe it was the only way. Let it happen.

16

TRUJILLO HAD SAID he was riding a tiger and if he ever fell off the tiger would devour him.

"Please don't talk like that; put it out of your mind," Andres had told the old man, the Benefactor, who not only ruled his country for thirty years he owned it and was worth—with his sugar, his rice, his sisal, cattle, cement, his tobacco—some $800 million the day he fell off the tiger and was devoured.

Andres had tried for the next few days to transfer bank accounts and titles to property, searching for people he could trust to help him, and finally had to run for his life to Miami by way of San Juan with less than twenty thousand in cash and a cardboard box of photographs.

They hung in his study, all that was left of that time. Photos in black and white of Andres with Trujillo, with Peron, with Batista, with Anastasio Somoza, with Pérez Jimenez of Venezuela. A photo with U.S. Marine officers taken when U.S. Marines maintained tranquility and could be trusted. There

was the photo of Andres holding the submachine
gun that belonged to Trujillo's brother, Arismendi.
They would go out on Trujillo's yacht—Andres and
Arismendi, who was called Petán—and fire the submachine gun at the sharks off Monte Cristi, the
sharks gorging on the rotten meat the sailors threw
over the side, the two of them having a splendid
time blowing the man-eaters to pieces.

Here it was another kind of boat-ride with a different species of shark circling, waiting for the boat
to tip over. Riding this boat or riding a tiger it was
the same end if you weren't careful. Trujillo had got
old and failed to listen, failed to keep his enemies
frightened of him. Which was easy enough to do.

Choose one from a group of suspected enemies
and shoot him. Or drown him, it didn't matter. The
others would look at the ground or close their eyes,
not wanting to meet the eyes that would choose the
next one.

But he had stared at Moran and Moran had not
looked at the ground or at the man drowned in the
pool. Moran had stared back at him. Perhaps he
should have given Moran to the Mendoza brothers
to be taken to sea with Rafi. It was possible Moran
was not involved in the plot, but Jiggs Scully had
made a point saying, "Either way you got to do
Rafi. So let Moran watch and have second thoughts
in case he *is* involved. Give him pause, as you say."
Jiggs said he had questioned Rafi and there was

nothing to learn from him, he was a "third stringer." Whatever that meant.

Jiggs said he had discovered Rafi through informants and was closing in on the others. Jiggs saying so much, Jiggs finding out about this plot and the people taking part in it. Jiggs giving, he said, all his time to it. But not saying anything about being paid.

Andres, the day before, had called Jimmy Cap to discuss this with him, to say he appreciated Jimmy Cap's concern, sending Jiggs to help. See if he had actually sent him. But Jimmy Cap was in Buffalo for several days and could not be reached.

So now late at night Andres sat behind his seven-foot desk drinking Cognac, staring vacantly at his past life in photographs, wondering what was taking place in the present.

Trying to see it clearly without interruptions.

First Corky. Corky in the doorway, a manila envelope under his arm, saying the business with Rafi Amado was finished. Then, remembering the manila envelope, coming into the study only far enough to place the envelope on de Boya's desk next to the brandy decanter, Corky reaching out, not wanting to intrude himself. "It came today from Marshall Sisco." The door closed. Andres picked up the envelope marked PERSONAL & CONFIDENTIAL.

Almost immediately the door opened again and Andres put the envelope down.

Now Mary stood in a white dressing gown that

reached to the oriental carpet. She said, "Who was here?" She said, "Andres, what's going on?" Curious, perhaps alarmed.

But not without insolence. The way she always stood with her thin legs apart, one foot pointed out, shoulders slightly drooped. Demonstrating the bored insolence of American women as she asked her insolent questions. "Will you please tell me?"

He walked over to her.

"Andres—"

And closed the door in her face.

He returned to his desk trying to remember at what point he had left his mind, interrupted— ignoring for the moment the envelope Corky had brought—yes, he remembered now.

The cartridge was already in the tape machine on his desk, the recording of a phone conversation made earlier this evening at his office in the Biscayne Tower. A conversation with an old friend, Alfonso Silva, who was Cuban and zealously anti-Castro, a survivor of the Bay of Pigs, a former agent of the CIA and member of Leucadendra Country Club. Andres pushed the ON button, listened patiently to their voices, sipped cognac, then began to stroke, gently, his dark cap of lacquered hair as he heard:

ANDRES: You know the one named Scully who works for the ITALIANS. Tell me again what you think of him.

ALFONSO: He does what we have spoken of before. Anything you want. If you trust those people you trust him. It's a decision you have to make.

ANDRES: But his appearance . . . How is he able to get information on the street? He's not one of us.

ALFONSO: With money. How else? Miami is a city of informants. What do you want to know?

ANDRES: He sent me two brothers, Mendoza . . .

ALFONSO: Ave Maria.

ANDRES: You know them? He said they worked for the CIA.

ALFONSO: They went to Cuba to do some work and were arrested and put in prison. Now they come back on the boatlift from Mariel. They wear red and white beads?

ANDRES: Yes, I believe so.

ALFONSO: To protect them from police. They belong to Changó, a cult of bandits and convicts, very bad men. They believe they have a dispensation to kill, given them by African gods.

ANDRES: Can I trust them?

ALFONSO: They're not of the revolution; there's no money in it, thank God and His Mother. They work for the one who pays the most.

ANDRES: I want to know about someone else. George Moran. He was a member of the club at one time.

ALFONSO: Moran . . . let me think. Is he the one you believed wanted your wife?

ANDRES: I want to know if he's active in a cause.

ALFONSO: I hear nothing of him.

ANDRES: Rafael Amado, a Dominican.

ALFONSO: No, I don't know him. But the one named Moran . . . I hear something in your voice. What is it now, still the wife? You get something in your head, Andres. . . .

He turned off the recorder, poured himself another Cognac.

It was more than something in his head, his imagination. It was Moran coming here. It was Moran calling his wife on the phone. He had instructed Altagracia, finally, to tell him his wife wasn't home. Then, mysteriously, the telephone was dead, the outside wire damaged. Security men on watch and something had happened to the wire. He questioned the Mendoza brothers and one of them said it must have been caused by the shooting the night before, a bullet struck the line and weakened it. Or it was old. The Mendoza brothers said they had no knowledge of telephone wires. They said the man from the telephone company who came fixed it, but didn't seem to know much himself, how it could break.

He had not told Alfonso Silva any of that. He could phone him now, tell him Rafi Amado had

gone to sea and was no longer a problem. He could
tell Alfonso how Moran stared back at him, not
looking at the ground or closing his eyes. Ask Alfonso if that was something in his head.

He opened the manila envelope marked PER-
SONAL & CONFIDENTIAL, feeling the tape cartridge
inside, letting it slide out on the desk, but in his
mind still seeing Moran staring back at him. Andres
snapped the cartridge into the recording machine—
a conversation with Marshall Sisco the investigator, remembering some of it from two days ago—ran
the machine forward and stopped, listened; ran it
forward again until he found the part that began:

MARSHALL: . . . answer to your question, no.
The latest report, I don't see any radical affilia-
tions, any close friends of Hispanic origin. Guy
worked for a cement company before he went
with Sutton Developments. Now he runs his
motel and that seems to be all he does. His
credit's not bad and neither Broward or Dade
have ever issued a warrant on him, even a mis-
demeanor.
ANDRES: He has affairs with women . . . married
women, doesn't he?
MARSHALL: If he does he's superdiscreet about it.
ANDRES: When he was in Santo Domingo . . .
MARSHALL: Yes sir, I've got that right here.
Stayed at the Embajador. Got his name in the pa-

per as a war hero looking for a girl he fell in love
with sixteen years ago, the time Johnson sent in
the troops. They got very excited down there
about him looking for the girl, but evidently he
didn't locate her. Her name's Luci Palma. He was
seen in the company of an American woman
staying at the hotel and returned to Miami with
her on the same flight.

ANDRES: What's the woman's name?

MARSHALL: Guy I talked to wouldn't say. You
want it documented I'll have to send somebody
down, spend a few bucks.

ANDRES: Do it. I want to know exactly . . .

Andres turned off the recorder. He picked up the
manila envelope again and brought out a sheet of
Marshall Sisco Investigations, Inc. letterhead that
bore a handwritten note Andres didn't bother to
read. Folded inside the sheet was a photocopy of a
hotel registration card.

The name on the card in block letters read
MARY DELANEY. The signature, very clear, precise, familiar, also read *Mary Delaney*.

Andres poured another Cognac. From the middle drawer of his desk he brought out a typewritten
sheet that bore his attorney's letterhead, the sheet
stapled to several copies of a legal-size document.
With a paper clip he attached the photocopy of the
hotel registration card to the legal papers.

Before getting up from the desk Andres sipped his Cognac and sat for several moments looking at the photograph of himself with Petán's submachine gun, the old Thompson. He had loved that gun, the feel of it jumping in his hands, hearing Petán's hoarse laughter, the sharks thrashing in a frenzy as the water turned a rust shade of red . . .

Mary's eyes came open with the sound of the door banging against the wall. Andres was at the bed, a shape outlined in the light from the hall, ripping away the sheet before she had time to move. As she tried to roll away from him his hand caught the back of her nightgown, tore it from her body and pulled her by the hair from the bed to the floor.

Mary screamed his name, once. Then silence. She could hear his breathing, grunts of effort.

She came to her feet submissive, looked in his face and cracked him as hard as she could with an open hand, seeing only his face, a flush of color rising, the moment before he hit her with a fist, drove it hard into her mouth and she saw pinpoints of light explode, falling, and felt him pull her again from the bed, locking an arm around her neck as she tried to butt him and dragged her naked from the room, across the hall and into his bedroom. The door slammed. Lights came on. When he threw her at the bed her knee struck the marble pedestal and he had to lift her, breathing through his nose, getting a knee between her bare thighs and now threw himself with her onto the bed, pushing to his knees to open his clothing, Mary feeling the wavy movement of the water bed beneath her, still aware of it, sinking without sinking, his weight pressing down on her again. He smelled of brandy, breathing through his nose, getting all of him between her thighs and using his hand, his fingers to pry and push himself into her, her legs stretched aching with the grinding of his hips. Now face to face as Andres levered his body to look at her, Mary staring back, dull eyes locked like arm wrestlers, Andres breathing with the labor of his body; and when he pressed his mouth against hers, when he gasped, sucking his breath in, she smelled his brandy with the taste of her own blood, felt it slippery wet on her face against his until his face slipped from hers to the pillow. He lay on her without his arms beneath him now, dead weight. Mary didn't move. She waited and would wait as long as she needed to. It was over now, there was nothing more he could do. She turned her head and saw their reflection in the wall of mirrors that covered the doors to Andres's closet. Saw her face strangely painted, blood-smeared. Saw her thigh upright against the mass of his pale naked hips. Saw the hem of the bedspread hanging and the marble pedestal that had the appearance of a solid block beneath the water mattress. *Making love on millions* . . . now raped on millions to mark the end of a marriage, Andres having the last word. Let him.

When he pushed up, throwing her leg aside as he got off the bed to stand with his clothes open, wiping a hand over his face, he looked at her and said, "Whore. Does he do that to you?"

She got up and walked out of the room, aching, feeling her front teeth, testing them with her fingers. In her bathroom she turned the light on to stare at her reflection, slipped on a terry-cloth robe now as she studied a face she had never seen before. God, she was a mess, mouth swollen, teeth aching with a dull throb. She bathed her face with warm water. It surprised her to realize she was alert, more relieved than resentful, a feeling of confidence giving her new energy. Then jumped in spite of her calm as Andres's face appeared behind her in the mirror.

"I'm not finished with you."

He gestured to her to come with him. When Mary hesitated he took her by the arm through her room and across the hall into his bedroom again. "Goddamn whore," he said, "go over there," and pushed her toward a bank of low dressers. She saw the legal papers, a gold ballpoint pen. "Read them or don't read them, I don't care," Andres said, "as long as you sign."

She saw her name in block letters on the copy of

the hotel registration card, knowing at once what it was, feeling some of her confidence slip away. She picked up the photocopy and looked at it, remembering the moment—standing at the desk and writing in "700 Collins Avenue, Miami Beach," making up an address but using her actual maiden name—thinking of Moran in the same hotel five floors above her. Thinking of him now . . .

"Sign it."

Andres was coming out of his walk-in closet carrying luggage, a full-size Louis Vuitton fabric suitcase in each hand. He swung them in Mary's direction to drop in the middle of the floor.

"Sign each copy. Then pack your clothes, everything you own, and get out." He turned and went back into the closet.

Mary picked up the legal papers, saw the heading, *Amendment to PreNuptial Agreement*, and glanced through the typewritten page, familiar with the legal terms, the ponderous sentence structure. She looked up as Andres came out of the closet with a second pair of Vuitton suitcases.

"These I give to you," he said, dropping the luggage. "There are more in the closet, all you need. Take them and get out."

"Let me be sure I understand this," Mary said, with cold composure, nothing to hide now, nothing to lose. It had begun as a business deal and was ending as one. "The divorce settlement is now an option?"

Andres was moving toward her. "That's correct." He picked up the pen from the dresser.

"And it's up to you whether you want to honor it or not."

"Yes, I have the privilege of not paying a wife who whores with other men."

"Before, it didn't matter," Mary said, composed, but with an effort now. "You insisted on a two-million-dollar agreement, regardless of what might cause a divorce."

"Now I change my mind," Andres said. "You get nothing in settlement, you get nothing in my will, no matter when I die. So if you're plotting my death with your lover you been wasting your time."

The words stunned her, yet were believable coming from Andres. She could study him six more years and still not understand the twists and turns of his mind, the man refusing to accept reality, or still living in another time.

She said, "You've got a lot of class, Andres. You know how long I've been trying to talk to you?"

"I would believe," Andres said, "since you began fucking in hotel rooms."

God—she wanted to hit him and tried to, bringing up her hand, but he caught her wrist and

slapped her hard, slapped her again and forced her
over the dresser, face stinging, eyes blurred, and
worked the pen into her hand.

"Now sign it!" Holding her head bent with his
fist tangled in her hair.

She wrote her name and he turned to the first
copy.

"Sign it!"

She signed twice again, writing *Mary de Boya* in
a scrawl that seemed as unrelated to her as the
name itself, *Mary de Boya*, signing an identity that
was no longer hers.

Once she finished he was finished. Andres pulled
her upright, his hand still knotted in her hair, and
threw her to the floor, discarded. He walked over to
his closet, threw out another suitcase, then went
through his dressing room to his bath and slammed
the door closed. Within a few moments Mary heard
the shower running.

She lay on the floor among several thousand dollars worth of matched Louis Vuitton luggage, eyes
level with the pedestal supporting the king-size bed.
She moved, pushing up on her elbow, and saw her
shadow move on the dull sheen of Italian marble.
She was aware of a faint ringing sensation, a feeling
of pressure within her head.

But her mind was clear. A deal was a deal.

17

MORAN WALKED THE BEACH in a fine mist of rain, sky and ocean a blend of the same dismal gray, the day showing in faint streaks of light but not promising much. It was all right though. The solitude was like a vacuum, seamless; he could stand in the middle of gray nothingness with his mind at rest and soon a burst of revelation would come to him. Enlightenment. A cosmic reaction to his panting neurons. He waited, looking at nothing, trying hard to think of nothing. He waited and waited, calm. Still he waited. Then raised his face to the rain, to the murky wash of light, and yelled against the moan of the wind as loud as he could, "Fuck!"

After, he felt some relief but not much. It released maybe a few pounds of frustration and was better than slamming his fist into a wall, though the wall was still there and he'd be god*damned* if he could see a way to get through it. All he wanted to do at this moment was talk to her.

He'd phoned at eight and the maid, Altagracia,

had said, "I'm sorry, Mrs. de Boya is not here. She out for the day." Moran had said, "Please, okay? She wants to talk to me." And the maid had said again she was sorry. . . .

His sweater and jeans were soaked through, hair matted to his head. He had been wet before. He had come up against walls before. Had learned patience, he believed, in the Marines and could wait sitting on his seabag when there was purpose in waiting. He had learned about frustration in his war in the D.R. trying to tell Friendlies from Unfriendlies and it had been, up to now, the most gut-twisting time of his life—yes—frustrated on the one hand and set up and sucked in on the other, just like now, and he'd hacked and stalked his way through it—that's what you *do*. (Was it his revelation, the answer right there inside him all the time?) Yes—you don't think, you *do!*

Moran left the beach and went in his bungalow tracking sticky sand to the counter and dialed Mary's number. He felt pumped up. When the maid with the immutable tone said, "I'm sorry—"

Moran said, "Listen, you put her on the phone right now or I'm calling the police." Which made no sense to him but maybe it would to her.

Altagracia said, "A moment, please."

Moran said to himself, *Do,* don't think. But when de Boya's voice came on he was stopped. De Boya said, "Yes? Who is this?"

"Andres, it's George Moran. I'd like to speak to Mary."

"She's busy," Andres said.

"Would you ask her to call me?" Christ, saying it to her husband.

"You going to be busy too, very soon." Andres hung up.

For the second time since waiting for his revelation Moran felt a slight lessening of pressure. Mary was home. At least for the time being. All right. All he had to do was go get her. Then wondered what de Boya meant: he was going to be busy, soon.

Jerry, the morning paper under his arm, got his key out and unlocked the door to the office. He noticed the trunk of Nolen's car raised, then saw it go down and there was Nolen holding a grocery sack. Jerry watched in wonder because he had never seen Nolen up and about before 10:00 A.M. Jerry said, "I didn't know the liquor stores were open this early."

Nolen raised the sack. "Lemons."

Jerry said, "You gonna make lemonade?"

"I'm gonna squeeze all the vitamins out of 'em," Nolen said, "and make whiskey sours."

Jerry made a face as though he might be sick. At this point he saw the two Latins get out of a car across the street and start this way, one of them carrying garden shears.

Nolen had already seen them. He was moving Jerry into the office. "Call George. Hurry."

Jerry didn't understand the note of urgency. "I can tell 'em," he said, "we don't need any trimming done. The hell they want to work in the rain for?"

Nolen said, "Goddamn it, gimme the phone. He dialed the number looking out the window and said, "George, run. I mean *quick*."

Moran put the phone down. On an angle through a side window he saw the Mendoza brothers coming through the corner alcove past the icemaker and Coke machine, coming toward the bungalow. Both were wearing wool knit watch caps and leather jackets, one of them carrying a large pair of pruning shears with rubber grips. Moran got back to the phone. He said, "Call the cops."

Now Jerry was on. He said, "What do they want, George?"

"They want *me*. Call the cops—tell 'em it's an emergency." He hung up. Christ—he had to get something on; he'd showered and dried himself but wasn't dressed. Moran pulled on jeans, got a sweater out of the closet. He needed a weapon, a club. He didn't want a knife, he didn't know how to use a knife. Now they were banging on the door. He had to get out of here. They were banging on the door again. The side window was stuck, it was

always stuck. But he strained and raised it enough
to slip through the opening. He was walking away
from the side of the house when the two Mendozas
appeared, coming around from the front. They
waved.

The one with the shears said something in Spanish. The other one said, "Come here. We want to go
inside."

Moran's ears strained for the sound of a siren.
He picked up the ten-foot aluminum pole that was
used, with an attachment, for vacuuming the pool.

"Got to work, *trabajo*," Moran said.

The Mendoza brother who had spoken English
held his palms up to the rain. "You don't work today, man. We go inside, out of this, the *tiempo*."

"I work every day," Moran said. "I love to
work. Got to get it done."

He glanced around, saw Nolen coming up on the
other side of the pool. Nolen was looking at the
Mendozas, saying, "Hey, you got the wrong guy.
This is a friend of Jiggs Scully, his *amigo*."

Moran said across the pool, "These guys work
for *Jiggs*?"

Nolen gestured, minimizing. "I think so . . . Hey,
we're *amigos* of Jiggs. You *sabe* Jiggs? Go call him
on the *telefono*, he'll tell you. You got the wrong
guy."

The Mendozas didn't seem to understand or
didn't want to. The one who spoke English had the

end of Moran's aluminum pole now. He tried to pull it hand over hand toward him, but Moran tightened his grip and they tugged back and forth for a moment about eight feet apart. The other one stood with the shears in both hands now, the blades pointing up.

"We go in the house," the one holding the pole said. "You suppose to give us something for Señor de Boya." He repeated it, Moran believed, in Spanish and the one with the shears laughed and continued to grin.

"You think I'm going in the house with you," Moran said, "you're outta your mind." He raised one hand to indicate the motel units. "There people here, they're all watching. You *sabe* witness? Shit, what was the word? *Testigo. Muchos testigos* in all the *ventanas*."

"Come on, we go inside," the Mendoza holding the end of the pole said, and gave it a quick jerk, almost pulling it away from Moran. But he got both hands on it and jerked back, his hands slipping on the wet metal, pulling, having a tug-of-war in the rain. When finally he heard the first high-low wails of a siren coming very faintly from Atlantic Boulevard, hearing it because he was listening for it, he let the Mendoza holding the pole pull him closer hand over hand until Moran was in reach, the Mendoza still gripping the pole when Moran let go and slammed a hard left hand into the astonished

Mendoza's face; the man sat down, stunned. With five feet of aluminum pole in front of him now, the rest dragging, Moran drove at the Mendoza with the shears and caught him in the belly—the siren wail much louder now—and jabbed at him until the shears came clanging against the pole; but Moran was going to get in and not let this man alter his life and when he caught the Mendoza's throat with the pole it stopped him, brought him up, and Moran was able to step in and belt him with a left and another left that brought blood from his nose, the Mendoza wobbly but trying to stick him with the shears. Moran gave him a head fake and went in high, got inside those jabbing blades, grabbed hold and drove. They went over the cement wall to land in wet sand, Moran on top, getting a hand under the wool cap now to grab hair, twist the guy's head facedown. He heard words snapped in Spanish above him. The other Mendoza had a knee on the cement wall, pointing a blue-steel revolver . . . But now a voice called out in hard Anglo-Saxon English telling the Mendoza to freeze, called him an obscene name and that was it for the Mendozas. The two Pompano Beach officers came hatless looking like young pro athletes with nickel-plated Smith & Wessons gleaming wet and it was clear they would use them.

Moran said yes, he would sign charges, assault with deadly weapons or assault to do great bodily harm, whichever was worse, and if the officers could think of anything else put it down. This kind of thing, Moran told them, was not good for the tourist business. He didn't tell the police he knew the Mendozas or that he had seen them assist in murder last night; he'd save that and maybe tell them another time. One of the cops said, "Well, you sure handled these fellas."

Moran said, "I was protecting something more valuable to me than I can tell you."

From his bathroom—cleaning up, changing his clothes again—he heard a familiar voice in the front room and walked out through his bedroom to see Nolen talking on the phone. Nolen raised his hand. On the counter was a pitcher of what looked like French-vanilla ice cream, melted and watery.

"Jesus, make yourself at home," Moran said and went back into the bedroom. Putting on a clean pair of jeans and a dark blue pullover sweater, he heard Nolen say "Jiggs" a couple times. When he went out again Nolen was off the phone, pouring the mixture in the pitcher into two glasses. He offered one of them as Moran came over.

"Breakfast," Nolen said. "Fresh lemons, bourbon and four eggs. A little powdered sugar. You don't provide a blender, I had to beat hell out of it by hand."

Moran took the glass Nolen offered and drank it, not to be sociable but because he needed it. It wasn't bad.

"So, they work for Jiggs."

"Listen, he's very apologetic," Nolen said, seated at the counter now, cowboy boots hooked in the rungs of the stool, starched safari shirt hanging out. For a change Nolen didn't appear sick this morning. "Jiggs sent 'em over to de Boya, like to help out with that piss-poor security he's got, but actually to help Jiggs, get the master plan rolling."

"You mean those guys are your partners?"

"Naw, they don't know anything. You wind 'em up and pay 'em, they do whatever they're told. Like yank out de Boya's telephone line. Screw up his head, he thinks the terrorists are closing in."

"Well, you know who they're screwing up," Moran said, "while I'm trying to get his wife out of there."

Nolen poured a couple more sours. "You got time."

"Is that right? Tell me about it."

"That was Jiggs, I phoned him. He says de Boya sent the Mendozas over cause he found out about you and his wife and had a fit. *Not* from Scully, from somebody else."

Moran said, "Wait a minute—put the goddamn glass down." He gave himself a moment, Nolen telling him it was okay, take it easy, but he could feel his heart beating against his chest and he didn't know how to slow it down or if he wanted to.

"He's kicking her out of the house," Nolen said. "You got no problem."

"When?"

"Now, today. He told her to pack and get out."

"How does Scully know? De Boya tell him?"

"Scully gets pieces and puts 'em together. The Mendozas hear something from one of the maids— they're sitting around the kitchen—about the wife getting beat up and they call Scully—"

Moran stopped him. "Wait now. Andres beat her up?"

There was a look coming into his eyes Nolen had never seen before and hoped it wasn't for him.

"Take it easy, okay? She's fine."

"He hit her?"

"They had a heavy argument with some pushing and shoving, that's all. The Mendozas tell Scully and he goes over to check, feel his way around; he doesn't want any surprises when the time comes. He get there—no Mendozas. De Boya'd sent them here. They're suppose to bring your shlong back in a Baggie so he can give it to his wife. Weird, but it's like what Rafi was telling us, they do it with shears, man. Jesus, I get goose bumps thinking about it.

The Mendozas, they don't give a shit they're not actually working for de Boya, it sounds like fun.
Scully says it was a misunderstanding and he says
he hopes you're okay. I told him the two guys're in
the Pompano city jail and Scully says that's all
right, he was through with them anyway." Nolen
raised his glass. "So here we are." He drank down
his sour. "And I might add, today's the big day."

Moran walked away, Nolen's voice following
him now into the bedroom. "You gonna ask me
what's happening?" From the dresser Moran got
his wallet and car keys, returned to the front room
and kept walking toward the door.

"Where you going?"

Moran said, "Where do you think."

"Wait now, you don't want to go over there. Let
her come here. Call her up."

"I'm through calling."

"He sees you he'll get a gun. Honest to God, I
mean it. He'll kill you."

Moran was still doing rather than thinking,
more pumped up now than he was earlier; but
Nolen's words and grown-up wisdom stopped him
with his hand on the door. He looked back at
Nolen.

"What happens today?"

"We hit de Boya. That's what happens."

Moran came back to the counter. Nolen seemed
to straighten on the stool.

"Your idea—flush him, make him run."

"How're you gonna do that?"

"Bomb scare."

"A real one?"

Nolen shook his head. He had Moran's interest now and could take his time. "One was enough. He saw his dock blown to hell, the man's a believer. Jiggs'll ask him about the telephone line being cut and who came to fix it. Is he sure they were from Southern Bell? Give him doubts. So when he gets a call his house's been wired to go up he grabs his money and runs."

"How do you know he will?"

"Because he's been looking over his shoulder for twenty years half-expecting something like this. I mean what's getaway money for otherwise? The man doesn't have to get hit over the head. He's ready to jump."

"Maybe," Moran said, "but he could be way ahead of you, have an idea what you're doing."

Nolen was shaking his head.

"Why not?"

"What convinces him it's real is who the call comes from." Nolen winked, feeling frisky. "The Coral Gables Police." He grinned at Moran. "Like it? I'd think you'd wish us luck anyway, clobbering the son of a bitch."

"That a line from a movie?"

"This is real-life drama now, George."

"You missed the big scene last night."

"Well, that was unfortunate, but guys like Rafi, that can happen. He overreached and didn't look where he was going."

"You used him."

"I had nothing to do with that."

"Are you drunk?"

"This's what I've had, right here. One beer when I got up."

"You were drunk I could understand you," Moran said. "Rafi was used and you're next, you don't even know it."

"Unh-unh."

"What's your part in it?"

"I make the anonymous call to the cops. Ready to go off around seven this evening. We want to wait'll the rush hour's over on the freeway."

"Then what?"

"I wait for Jiggs to call me. Bar out by Ninety-five."

"Go on."

"I meet him, wherever he's got de Boya."

"You mean wherever he's killed de Boya. Nolen, you dumb shit, he's not gonna let him live. You either. He'll take the both of you, fifty miles over to the Everglades, you're never seen again. Just tell me, is that a possibility?"

Nolen pretended to think about it, nodded once and took a drink.

"Well?"

"There's a certain risk," Nolen said, "I know that. But there's no payoff in this kind of action without risk, is there? See, I'm aware of that. You think I'm dumb. Jiggs, he uses me, yeah, for what I can do. But you're forgetting one thing." Nolen reached around behind him, dug under his shirttail and from the waist of his trousers brought out a Colt .45 automatic, winked at Moran and laid it on the counter.

"I was Airborne."

Moran saw Nolen's gleam, wet and bloodshot but still a gleam. He said quietly, "Nolen, that was sixteen years ago."

Nolen said, "I've jumped out of airplanes, George, and I've shot at the enemy. I've been to war. Tell me this is different."

"I'm going," Moran said. "I've got to get out of here."

He was at the door, pushing it open when Nolen said, "George, tell me something else and be honest."

Moran looked around. "What?"

"Tell me you don't want to see the man dead." When Moran didn't speak Nolen said, "See? It's why I can tell you about it and expect best wishes. I know where your heart is, buddy. I'll tell you something else too and put money on it. Here . . ." He dug into his shirt pocket and laid a folded bill on the counter. "Here's ten bucks says if you go to that man's house you're gonna get shot in the head way before I ever do . . . Come on, put up."

For another few moments Moran stared at Nolen hunched over the counter, the morning drinker with his bloodshot gleam and his slick-combed hair. He said, "Nolen, you don't have one chance of making it."

18

THREE LOUIS VUITTON full-size suitcases—brown fabric bags that bore the LV crests like a wallpaper design—stood in the upstairs hall, at the head of the stairway.

As Mary came out of her bedroom Altagracia was mounting the suspended stairway, ascending out of the forest of plants and small trees that filled the front hall, the maid frowning now as she saw the luggage.

"Señora, you going on a trip?"

"I hope so," Mary said.

"I take these down."

"No." She snapped the word and had to pause to regain her composure. "It's all right, I have to call a cab first, a taxi." She didn't want the luggage standing in the downstairs foyer, waiting. "But if you'll do me a favor—watch in front. The moment the taxi comes would you let me know?"

The maid nodded solemnly, "Yes, Señora," and

said then, hesitant, "That man call and I lie to him again that you not here."

"It's all right," Mary said, "I understand."

"I didn't want to, you been very kind to me. You go to trouble to make my work easy and then I lie against you." Altagracia looked at her with sorrowful eyes.

"I understand," Mary said, both touched and surprised. It was the first time Altagracia had confided, revealed a personal feeling.

"Does your face hurt?"

"No, it's fine." Surprised even more.

"Your mouth look a little swollen is all. I'm very sorry it happen. If you go I hope you come back."

My God, she sympathized. Mary could see genuine concern in the woman's dark eyes. She said, "I appreciate your saying that. Thank you."

"If I can do something for you . . ."

Mary was already thinking. "Do you know where Mr. de Boya is?"

"Yes, Señora, in his study. A man came to see him. The one, the fat one, his shirt comes out."

"Mr. Scully."

"Yes, I think is his name. He just come."

Mary hesitated a moment. "Maybe it would be all right if you took the bags down now. But not to the front hall, all right? I think—why don't you take them the back way to the garage? Then when the taxi comes I'll have the driver pick them up

there, it'll be easier for him." Offhand about it.
"All right?"

"Whatever pleases you, Señora."

For several moments Mary watched Altagracia,
a suitcase in each hand, descend the stairway that
seemed to hang in space above treetops—moving
so slowly—Mary wanting to hurry her, half-
expecting Andres to appear in the hall below. She
went into her bedroom, dialed Moran's number
and asked for him.

A voice she has never heard before said, "He's
gone . . ."

"Do you know where I can reach him?"

". . . probably never to return."

"Please," Mary said, "it's important."

The voice changed, brightening. "Oh, is this
Mary? . . . Mary, Nolen Tyner. How you doing?
We never met, have we?"

"Nolen, can you tell me where he is?"

"Yeah, he's on his way to your place."

"He can't come *here*."

"Almost my exact words," Nolen said, "but you
know George, that quiet type. You get him riled
he's a hard charger. Listen—"

"I have to go," Mary said.

"Okay, but when we have some free time let's all
get together. How's that sound to you?"

* * *

Moran jumped lanes, cutting in and out of the freeway traffic poking along in the rain, took 95 all the
way to the end, followed the curve into South Dixie
and didn't stop till he got to Le Jeune, where he
turned into a service station. The attendant was sitting at his desk inside.

"Fill it with regular, okay?"

The guy was adding or entering credit-card re-
ceipts, taking his time.

"No, make it ten bucks," and added, to get the
guy moving, "I'm in an awful hurry."

The attendant, an older guy in greasy coveralls,
said, "Everybody's in a hurry. Slow down, you'll
live longer."

Moran said, "If I had time I'd explain to you it's
just the other way around." It amazed him that he
was fairly calm. *Doing.* The guy gave him a strange
look as he went out. Moran stood at the pay phone.
He knew the number by heart, 442-2300. Then
wondered if he should call 911 instead, the emergency number. Which one would an anonymous
caller dial? Moran wasn't sure. The idea had come
to him on the freeway—suddenly there in his head
without any hard thinking—and it was a zinger: a
way to spring Mary without a confrontation with
Andres and a way to blow Nolen's plan at the same
time. Christ, and now he wasn't sure which number
to call. He said to himself, *Just do it.* And dialed
442-2300.

The male voice said, "Coral Gables Police," and a name that sounded like "Sergeant Roscoe speaking."

Moran said, "Sergeant, I want to report a bomb that's gonna go off."

"Who is this speaking, please?"

"It's an anonymous call, you dink. The bomb's at Seven-hundred Arvida Parkway; I think you better get over there."

"Sir, may I have your name and number, please?"

"Where the dock blew, asshole. The house's going next."

There was a pause at Coral Gables Police Headquarters.

"This bomb," Sergeant Roscoe or whatever his name was said, "can you tell me what type it is and where it's located?"

"Jesus Christ, the fucking house is going up, people're in it and you're asking me where the bomb is! Get over there and find it, for Christ sake!" Then added, for a touch of local color, "*Viva libertad! Muerte a de Boya!* You got it?" And hung up.

Jiggs Scully got a kick out of these guys that displayed pictures of themselves taken with politicians, celebrities, dignitaries—showing you the class of people they hung out with. Jimmy Cap did the same thing. The only difference, his pictures were taken with stand-up comics in golf outfits, horse breeders and a couple famous jockeys, five-eight Jimmy Cap with his arm around the little guys' shoulders. Jiggs noticed that Latin-American military gave themselves height by wearing those peaked caps that swooped way up in front, even higher than the ones the Nazis had worn; which showed you even your most hardassed rightwingers had some showboat in them.

He said to de Boya, "I was you, General, you have a sentimental attachment for your pictures there, I'd pack 'em away till we clean this business up."

"I don't see how anyone can get inside," de Boya said, sitting behind his big desk, all dressed up in a gray business suit.

"They don't have to get *in*," Jiggs said. "That's why I want to take a look around, see how many wires you got leading to the house and where they go. The word on the street, the house's next."

"I question that," de Boya said.

"I know you do, but what if that repair guy wasn't Southern Bell? It don't mean anything he showed a card, you get those printed ten bucks a hundred. No, the vibes—you know what vibes are, General? Like an itch, a feeling you get. The vibes tell me we're sitting on a ticklish situation here without much in the way of protection. I send you a couple of pros and—I don't mean to sound critical, general, you're the man in charge, but they aren't doing us much good in Pompano Beach."

The general looked like he had a bad stomach, bothered by gas, and the present situation wasn't going to relieve it any. A very emotional people. He saw de Boya look up: somebody all of a sudden rattling off the Spanish. Jiggs looked around to see Corky, mouth going a mile a minute, telling de Boya something that pulled him right out of his chair.

Altagracia appeared in the bedroom doorway, timid, not certain if she was announcing good news or bad. She said, "Señora, he's here," and now was startled and had to get out of the way.

Mary was moving as the maid spoke, out the door past her into Andres's bedroom, past the two suitcases she hadn't used, still lying on the floor, to the front window.

Moran's old-model white Mercedes was in the drive, behind a red and white Cadillac and Andres's Rolls. Mary pressed closer to the window, the glass streaked with rain, blurred, and saw Moran out of the car, Corky moving out from the house toward him. Mary left the window; she dodged past Altagracia again in the hallway and stopped.

"My bag, the small one."

"I get it," the maid said.

It gave Mary the moment she needed to take a breath, collect herself. She would be forthright about this final exit, walk out with style in beige linen and if Andres said anything she might give him a look but no more than that. Altagracia came out of the bedroom with her white canvas tote. Mary slipped the strap over her shoulder.

She heard Altagracia say, "Go with God."

Damn right. With her head up, a little haughty if she had to be. Then hesitated.

Andres appeared in the hall below, moving with purpose toward the front entrance. She saw his back and now Jiggs Scully shuffling to catch up, recognizing the man's shapeless seersucker coat.

They were outside by the time Mary reached the foyer, on the front stoop that was a wide plank deck, low, only a step above the gravel drive. She saw Moran in a dark sweater in the fine mist of rain, Corky raising both hands to push him or hold him off. *Now*, Mary thought. And walked out the door past Scully, bumping him with the tote hanging from her shoulder, not looking at him or at Andres as she stepped past them to the gravel drive. Corky turned, hearing or sensing her. But she was looking at Moran now less than ten feet away, his eyes calm, drops of moisture glistening in his beard. She wanted to run to him and see his arms open.

Andres said, "Stop there."

But he was much too late. Mary walked up to Moran and said, "Boy, am I glad to see you," in a tone so natural it amazed her.

His gaze flicked past her and back, still composed. "You ready?"

"My bags are in the garage. The door that's raised."

He looked over at the garage wing, an extension of the house, three of the doors in place, one raised open to reveal gleams of chrome and body metal in the dim interior. Moran took his time, listening, hoping to hear sirens coming for him twice in the same day—his first success giving him faith to try it again—aching now to hear squad cars screaming down Cutler Road toward Arvida; Mary looking at him like he was crazy. What was he standing there for?

"Mary." It came as a de Boya command. He stood with hands shoved deep in his coat pockets. "Come inside."

Moran said, "Stay where you are," touching her arm. He moved past her a step and said to Jiggs, "You tell him yet?"

It caught de Boya's attention. Jiggs didn't say anything; perhaps the first time in his life.

"I'll tell him if you won't," Moran said. "Hey, Andres?"

Jiggs said, "George, you got a problem?"

There it was in the distance, that sorrowful wail

not yet related to them here, but it was coming fast and Moran hoped he had enough time to say what he had to say and get out.

"Andres, this guy's out to take you."

Maybe it was already too late. Jiggs was looking at him, de Boya staring off, frowning. Was it the wind in the rain, a police siren, what? Jiggs heard it without letting on. He said, "George, you been drinking?"

Now a yelp-type siren chasing the wails, coming from beyond the mass of Florida trees bunched along the road.

Moran said, "Andres?"

He got a glance, still with the frown.

"Jiggs Scully'll kill you if he gets the chance."

De Boya's glance came again, like Moran was the distraction and not the shrill sounds piercing the rain.

"I don't know why I'm telling you, but if he asks you to go anywhere with him, tell him no."

There. For what it was worth. He'd lost the attention of Jiggs and de Boya now, both listening, heads raised to the cool mist as the sirens wailed closer. Moran turned to Mary, saw her eyes. "You have to get in my car. Right now."

She moved without pause, not even a questioning look and he could have taken the moment and kissed her.

Squad cars were coming up both ends of the

drive now, gumballs flashing, electronic sirens on high, some wailing, some yelping, giving the scene the full emergency treatment. As quickly as they arrived doors winged open and the police were on the scene, approaching the house.

Andres seemed bewildered.

But Jiggs was staring at Moran.

And Moran had to stare back at him, letting him know without saying a word who'd brought all this down on him.

A uniformed lieutenant was saying to Andres, with that impersonal deadweight of authority, "Sir, I'm gonna ask you to evacuate these premises. I want everybody out of that house."

Jiggs still hadn't moved, staring at Moran.

Moran smiled in his beard. Maybe Jiggs caught it, maybe not; it was time to go.

Mary was behind the wheel. She revved as he jumped in and pulled smoothly around Jiggs's car and the white Rolls. Squad cars coming with headlights on had to swerve out of the way as she pointed toward the garage and braked the old Mercedes to a skid-stop in the gravel. "My bags," Mary said.

The three matched pieces stood at the edge of the dim interior. Moran was out again, collecting the luggage, shoving it into the back seat. He took time to look toward the front of the house, the entrance-way.

De Boya was holding the police back with his iron will, resisting, objecting, pointing a finger in the lieutenant's face. No one was entering his house without his permission and he obviously wasn't granting it. Except to Corky now. De Boya said something to him that sent Corky running inside.

"Moran, will you come on!"

He turned to look at Mary. "Drive out to the street before you get boxed in. I'll meet you out there in a minute . . . Go on!"

She gave him a look with her jaw clenched and took off, horn blaring now, swinging out on the grass to get around the squad cars stacking up in the yard. There were cops with dogs now heading for the garage.

Moran moved to the off side of a squad car, its lights flashing, radio crackling in a dry female voice on and off. He watched de Boya head to head with Jiggs now. They looked like they were arguing. De Boya at first standing firm, but Jiggs beginning to get through to him. De Boya, impatient now, gestured toward the garage. When de Boya turned and hurried into the house, Jiggs stood watching. Though not for long. Jiggs was moving now, running with a surprisingly easy grace toward the garage. He went in through the opening and Moran's gaze returned to the front entrance, the cops milling around, servants coming out now with umbrellas. When he glanced toward the garage again there was Jiggs framed in the dim opening.

Jiggs holding a telephone, its long extension cord trailing into the garage, talking into the phone with some urgency as he watched the police in front of the house. Jiggs stepped back into the garage and reappeared without the phone, pushing his glasses up on his flat nose. He took the glasses off now, standing in the rain, pulled out part of his shirttail and began wiping the lenses. When he put the glasses on again, still intently watching the scene, the shirttail remained out, forgotten.

The slob. But look at him, Moran thought, fascinated. The guy was improvising, trying to put his act back together. He could hear Jiggs saying to him in the Mutiny Bar, "Gimme some credit, George," with that street-hip familiarity, his disarming natural style. He was fun to watch—as long as you didn't get too close.

Moran wanted to see de Boya again, but knew it was time to go: Mary waiting for him, anxious, Mary dying to get out of here. He moved down the line of squad cars looking back past Fireball flashers revolving slowly, the scene on hold for the time being. At the point where the drive curved into the trees he looked back one last time, hoping, deciding then to stretch it, give himself another minute, and saw de Boya coming out of the house:

De Boya hurrying to his Rolls followed by Corky and one of the maids, Altagracia. De Boya with a briefcase waving now at Corky who was carrying two suitcases to hurry up. Jiggs there now saying something to de Boya and de Boya shaking his head, Jiggs still trying, de Boya turning away as the maid came with a cardboard box in her arms, framed pictures—they looked like—sticking out of the open top, the maid waiting now to hand the box to Corky as he put the suitcases that were exactly like Mary's into the trunk of the Rolls.

Where was Jiggs?

Moran saw him then, getting in his Cadillac.

De Boya and Corky were in the Rolls now, the car starting up, coming this way across the lawn and Moran stepped into the trees.

19

"I TOLD HIM, I said don't go with him," Moran said. He wanted to believe he had warned de Boya and wondered if he would have to repeat this to himself from time to time.

"You don't *tell* him anything," Mary said, creeping the car toward a police officer in a rain slicker waving them to come on, come on, move it out. They turned off Arvida Parkway onto Cutler Road and the feeling of being released came over both of them at the same time, brought smiles and inside the old Mercedes was a good place to be with the windshield wipers beating and the tires humming on wet pavement. The weather was fine. They passed the fairways of Leucadendra and tennis courts standing empty, left the country club behind with a feeling of starting fresh, on a new adventure. Though Moran's thoughts would turn and he would see de Boya coming out of the house— "Spook him and make him run," he'd said to Jiggs in the Mutiny and it was happening.

He said, "If he lets Jiggs follow him or take him somewhere he's crazy. I told him. You heard me, you were standing right there." He had to stop thinking about Andres. But then asked, "Where do you think he'll go?"

"Well, he owns property all over. Apartment buildings, even farms, land he'll develop someday. He could go down in the Keys, anywhere." Mary glanced at Moran. "If you're worried about him, don't be. Andres takes care of number one, the son of a bitch. And if Corky has to give his life Andres will let him."

Right, it wasn't something new to these guys. Moran looked at her staring straight ahead at the windshield wipers sweeping, clearing the glass every other moment. He loved her profile. He could see her as a little girl.

"You're a good driver."

"Thank you."

"How's your mouth? Is it sore?"

"Not bad."

"The way your lower lip sticks out, it's kinda sexy."

"You want to bite it?"

"I believe I might. Did you hit him back?"

"I hit him first. It only made him madder."

"There you are," Moran said. "The first rule of street fighting, never throw a punch unless you can finish it."

Mary said, "What are you, Moran, my trainer or my lover?" She felt wonderful and wanted to say corny things about being free at last and tell him something that would bring amazement and he'd say "I don't believe it" in that way he said it. But that could wait.

De Boya sat half-turned in the front seat holding his briefcase on his lap. He would look back through the mist the Rolls raised in its wake and see Jiggs Scully's car holding the pace, less than a hundred meters behind. They were on the freeway northbound, passing the Fort Lauderdale airport off to the right, a jumbo jet descending out of the gray mass almost directly in front of them.

Corky said to the rearview mirror, "I can put my foot into it and leave him."

"No, we bring him along," de Boya said. "He knows something." They spoke in Spanish.

"You're sure of it?"

"We'll find out. He wanted to take me to Boca Raton. He tells me a very safe place. I'm supposed to say yes, of course, and put myself in his care."

"He has little respect."

"That's the least of it." De Boya watched the green freeway sign gradually appear. "Eighty-four, that's it, to the New River Canal Road."

Corky followed the exit ramp, his eyes on the mirror. "He's coming."

"I hope so," de Boya said.

They drove west for several minutes past fenced land that was desolate and seemed remote, resembling an African plain. There were no houses in sight until they got off on a dirt road turning to muddy pools, passed through a stand of pine and tangled brush to arrive in the yard of a cement-block ranch painted white, flaking, lifeless in its dismal setting. De Boya had bought the house furnished, as is, surrounded by ninety acres of scrub; the house would serve as a jump-off if needed, close to the Lauderdale airport; the property could always be developed someday, turned into a retirement village.

"He's coming," Corky said, steering toward the garage that was part of the house.

De Boya looked back to see the red and white Cadillac creeping into the yard. The car stopped and Jiggs got out to stand looking around, hands on his hips. The rain didn't seem to bother him.

"Stay with me," de Boya said.

He got out of the Rolls with his briefcase and approached Jiggs who was moving to the back of his car now, looking at his keys as though to open the trunk, then glancing at de Boya.

"This is it, huh? General, I got to tell you you'd be a lot more comfortable this place in Boca. Belongs to Jimmy Cap. Got a sauna, everything." He was bending over the trunk now.

"What do you have in there?" de Boya asked.

Jiggs straightened. "I got a forty-four Mag and I got a twelve-gauge pump gun, a Browning. I got flares and a five-gallon can of gas. What else you need?"

De Boya motioned to him. "Let's go inside."

"I thought you'd want some protection."

"Get it later," de Boya said.

As they started for the house Jiggs said, "You want me to help with your bags?"

"No, we'll get those later, too."

Jiggs said, "I was gonna say, General, I don't think you needed to pack those grips. Bomb squad'll take the day—we shouldn't be gone more'n one night. We can call 'em now you got a phone, see what they found."

"Yes, we'll do that," de Boya said.

"I wondered, the cops say who called 'em?"

"They don't know," de Boya said. "What I don't understand is what Moran was doing there. What was it he said? That you want to *take* me?"

Corky moved ahead of them to unlock the door.

"That's what it sounded like," Jiggs said. "Only thing I can figure out, he was trying to confuse you, General, get your head turned around so he could run off with your wife. You want me to I'll go pay him a visit."

"That would be all right with Jimmy Cap?"

"Jimmy said help you out anyway I can."

"But I learn he's out of town, uh? Has been gone for a week or so."

Corky held the aluminum screen door for both of them, de Boya first, Jiggs saying, "General, I hope you're not doubting my word," his tone offering a strong measure of injured pride as he gave the place a quick look: a living room that had the flavor of a hunting cabin, knotty pine walls, maple furniture, a poker table, Indian blankets. Jiggs pulled his shirttail out to wipe off his glasses. "I'll give you a number you can reach Jimmy Cap or they'll tell you exactly where he is. You don't mind, I'd like you to talk to him and get this straightened out." Very serious about it.

"Yes, I would too," de Boya said. "Let me have the number." He handed Corky his briefcase.

Jiggs put his glasses back on. His hands went to his breasts in the loose seersucker jacket and gave them a pat, then touched his right hip. "Yeah, I got it. In my wallet. General, let me go the can and take a leak first, I can almost taste it." He moved off toward the hall where he saw the bathroom door open, green tile inside.

De Boya watched until the door closed, then extended a hand toward Corky and snapped his fingers, twice.

Corky was opening the briefcase on the poker

table. He brought out a Walther P.38 automatic and handed it to de Boya. Now he took off his suit coat. From a shoulder holster snug beneath his left arm Corky drew a revolver, a Colt .38 with a stubby snout, and followed de Boya to the hallway. There was a bedroom at each end, doors open to empty rooms, neat twin beds with chenille spreads. The bathroom stood in between, its door closed.

They waited to hear the toilet flush, raised their pistols and began firing point-blank into the center of the door, the reports earsplitting in the confined area. Then silence. Corky turned the knob carefully, opened the door a crack, stepped back and used the sole of his foot to bang the door completely open.

Jiggs came out of the shower stall arms extended, holding a blue-steel automatic in both hands, ignoring Corky to level it straight at de Boya's face. He saw those ice-water eyes wide open for the first time.

"Something I learned a long time ago, General, never take your joint out with guys you don't trust. Specially you hot-blooded fellas like a lot of noise, shoot the place up. Come in here. Come on," Jiggs said, stepping back on broken glass and bits of porcelain to let them come in past him. "Drop the guns in the toilet . . . That's the way. You too, Corko. What's this a truss?" He snapped the elastic strap of Corky's shoulder holster. "You got a hernia? That's it, in the toilet. Now I want you to take your clothes off. That's what you do, right, General? Strip 'em down bare-ass."

As he began to undress de Boya said, "I pay for my life, uh? How much I have to pay you?"

"Gonna make it easy," Jiggs said, edging past them to sit down on the toilet. "Only take your suitcases. Corky, gimme the car keys. I'll get 'em after."

"I begin to think it's what you want," de Boya said, "but I don't see how you know about it." He paused unbuttoning his shirt, occupied with his thoughts. "Unless it was my wife?"

"You told me yourself," Jiggs said, "talking to Jimmy Cap, that day out at Calder. All the rest of the bullshit is just bullshit, way to get you here." He said to Corky, "What're you looking at? Come on, get your clothes off." He raised the automatic in Corky's face. "Can't figure out what this is, can you? Looks like your standard nine-millimeter Smith Parabellum except for that hickey sticking out." Jiggs dug into his side coat pocket, brought out a five-inch gunmetal tube and screwed it onto the threaded stub, the "hickey" that extended from the muzzle of the automatic. "Factory-modified. They call it a Hush-Puppy. Come on, General, take it off. Take it all off—like the broad says with the shaving cream. You too, Corko, drop the Jockeys, but keep an eye on the general there he don't try and cop your joint . . . Shoes, everything."

He seemed proud of his gun and showed them the profile with the silencer attached.

"Got a slide lock here on the side. You fire once it doesn't eject, so you don't hear the slide click open. You don't even hear that *poumpf* you get with a silencer. You know why? I use a subsonic round, very low muzzle velocity. Take the lock off you hear the slide jack open and close as you fire, but that's all, just that *click-click* . . . You guys ready? Leave your clothes on the floor there."

De Boya said, "You're going to take our clothes?" He stood straight, shoulders back and seemed to be in good shape, heavyset but not too much flab.

"I'll see they don't get wrinkled," Jiggs said. "Now get'n the shower. Go on, move."

"Both of us?" de Boya asked.

"Both of you the same time." Jiggs stood up now and motioned them into the stall. "Corky, watch yourself. Don't drop the soap." Corky was skinnier than he looked in clothes; chewing on that pussy mustache like he was going to cry. "Okay, turn the water on. Get it how you like it."

De Boya said, "What is the need of this?"

Jiggs said, "Just turn the water on, will you, please?"

He shot de Boya high through the rib cage with his arms raised to adjust the shower head, lung-shot him and shot him again in near silence as de Boya flattened against the wall and began to slide, smearing the tile. Corky was screaming now, hunching, holding his hands out protectively. He shot Corky twice in the chest through one of his hands, Corky's body folding to fall across de Boya curled up like he was trying to keep warm. He watched their heads jump with a final twitch as he shot them each again, watched the stream of water cleanse them, then pulled the shower curtain closed. He'd let the water run while he went out to get the suitcases.

20

THE BAR JIGGS HAD PICKED OUT for Nolen was on the corner of Atlantic and SW Sixth Avenue on the west side of Pompano, about thirty seconds from the freeway.

Nolen was wearing sunglasses and an old raincoat, creased with wrinkles, his cowboy boots hooked in the rung of the barstool that was as close to the phone booth as he could get: sipping scotch with a twist, fooling with the swizzle stick that was like a little blue sword. Four swords on the bar plus the one he was playing with. The bartender had tried to take them and Nolen told him no, he needed the swords to keep score. He was allowing himself six, no more than that. Just enough to keep his motor responses lubricated, idling. He didn't count the pitcher of sours; that was breakfast. It seemed a long time ago—still there in Moran's house sipping when he got the emergency call from Jiggs, Jiggs saying he was in de Boya's garage and the starting time had been moved up to right *now*,

he'd call him at the bar when they got to Boca; only
it might not be Boca, the general wasn't being very
cooperative. All that at once while Nolen was trying to ask him what he was doing in the garage, for
Christ sake, and what were all the sirens.

The place was dark and had a nice smell of beer,
the bartender down talking to the one other cus-
tomer that looked like a retiree with his golf cap.

They both looked up as the phone rang in the
booth and watched the weird-looking guy in the
raincoat and sunglasses almost kill himself getting
off his stool, the seat of the stool next to him spin-
ning, throwing him as he leaned on it to get up. The
bartender said, "I sure hope that's your call."

Nolen waved at him, went in the booth and
closed the door. As soon as he heard Jiggs's voice he
said, "The hell's going on?"

Jiggs's voice sounded calm. Nolen listened, holding back on all his questions as Jiggs told him
where to come, not Boca, but a place west of Lauderdale and not too far.

"Just tell me how it went?"

Jiggs's voice said it went fine, no problem.

"You got it?"

Jiggs's voice said he was going to get it out of the
car right now.

"Where's de Boya?"

Jiggs's voice said he was in the bathroom. The
voice stopped Nolen then. It said, "Nolen, you

want to talk on the phone, shoot the shit, or you want to get over here and help me count?"

Moran said to Jerry, "Mary's gonna be staying with us maybe a few days. Oceanfront Number One."

Jerry took a moment to adjust before coming on full of cordiality. "Why sure, that's the one with the view. Except today. But the paper says it's gonna clear up by tomorrow." He got the key and said to Mary, "You like to register now? Or you can do it later if you want."

Mary held back. Moran said, "Jerry, she's not here. Okay?" He took the key and handed it to Mary. "If anybody asks."

"I never saw this young lady before in my life," Jerry said.

"I mean even if it's the police. All right?"

Jerry sobered. He adjusted his golf cap, resetting it in the same position, cocked slightly to one side. "Yeah, well I don't see any problem."

"We won't take any guests for a few days. Not that they're breaking down the door."

"Turn the No Vacancy on?"

"No, let's not tell anybody a thing. I appreciate it, Jerry."

"I know you do," Jerry said. He gave Mary a wink, getting the feel of his new role.

Moran opened the door to the courtyard and

closed it against the rain coming in. "Jerry, how about Nolen? Is he around?"

"Got a phone call about an hour ago and left right after. Smashed as usual. I hope he don't get in a car wreck."

Moran went out with the bags.

Mary said to Jerry, "Nice seeing you again." Amazed at this natural response, her voice not giving her away. Outside, hurrying to keep up with Moran moving fast with the three bags, she said, "I don't believe it." Her voice raised in the wind. She said, "Remember how you kept saying that? When I called your room in Santo Domingo—'I don't believe it.' Remember?" Talking out of a compulsion to hear herself and know she was in control. " 'Come on, I don't believe it.' You said it about five times."

Moran said over his shoulder, "I believe it now," not stopping till they got to the end apartment off the beach, Moran hunching his shoulders against the rain coming in sheets off the ocean, Mary trying to hold her tote out of the way and get the door open.

They were soaked by the time they got inside and Moran let the bags drop. Mary closed the door and came to him, pressed her wet face against his wet shoulder, felt the familiar comfort of his arms come around her. It seemed late, so dark for afternoon. She pressed against him, hearing the wind moan out of the gray mass of ocean and felt an excitement that was hard to keep down. She said, "I've done something else you're not gonna believe," raising her face to his.

Moran saw her expression, the grin she was trying to hold back. He looked at her with the innocence of a straight man waiting for it and said, "Are you serious?"

She said, "Wait till I show you," and saw his expression change, starting to grin but not sure he wanted to.

Nolen found 84 and turned off the freeway at the peak of his whiskey rush, the glow carrying him along with a feeling of effortless control, gliding in the high excitement of a rainstorm, clouds hanging close enough to touch. (He had come out of the bar with his sunglasses on and thought it was midnight.) Now it was that colorless nothing kind of time, the eye of the storm. He found the New River Canal Road, not another car in sight and kept pressing, riding the wind, the black overcast his cover, until he saw the stand of pines off to the north. He touched the right-hand pocket of his raincoat and felt the hard bulk of the .45. Here we go . . . turned in and rode the Porsche through pools formed in the ruts, hearing the wake washing aside, saw the house and two cars in the yard now, the

wipers giving him quick glimpses. He rolled to a stop
on the off side of the Cadillac and now considered—
in spite of the charm he felt—the tricky part. Walking from the car to the house. He felt his mouth dry
and wondered why he hadn't brought a bottle with
him.

Well fuck it, he'd gone into houses on the east
bank of the Ozama with cotton in his mouth and
automatic weapon fire popping away and one place
had found beer inside, not cold, but beer all the
same and he hadn't gotten even a scratch in anger
during that war and was subject to serious gunfire
nearly every day and you know why?, because his
life was being spared for something big if not fame
that would come to him with more money than he
could count on a rainy afternoon in Florida. You're
goddamn right. He got out of the car and walked
up to that house . . . saw the door open a crack . . .
hesitated the moment he needed to clear the .45
and kicked the door in with a cowboy boot.

Jiggs sat in an easy chair that faced away from
the front windows and the door, so that Nolen
came in almost behind him. He saw Jiggs look him
up and down, Jiggs just sitting there. Nolen looked
past him at the two suitcases lying closed on a
round card table. He turned and looked toward the
hallway.

"Where's the general?"

"In the bathroom."

"Still?" Nolen looked at the suitcases again. "How come you haven't opened 'em?"

"They're open."

"Well, why don't you say something, for Christ sake?"

"I want to hear you," Jiggs said.

Nolen went over to the card table. He reached up to switch on the hanging fixture that was like an oil lamp with a glass chimney. He saw the suitcases were unfastened, unzipped, and looked at Jiggs again.

"Go ahead," Jiggs said.

Nolen lifted the flap of a suitcase and let it fall open. He saw newspapers. He saw the front page of the *Miami Herald* telling him Haitians had drowned in the surf at Hillsboro. He felt down under the papers. He threw back the flap of the other suitcase and saw more newspapers and felt through them all the way to the bottom. He looked at Jiggs, squinting at him.

"The general see us coming?"

"Nah, it wasn't the general."

"Well, did you have a talk with him? Christ!" Nolen whipped around, cocked his weapon as he stomped toward the hallway.

"I said it wasn't him," Jiggs said.

He waited, a clear picture of a rainy afternoon in his mind: Moran throwing the same kind of luggage into the back seat of a beat-up Mercedes, girl-

friend who was way ahead of everybody behind the
wheel of the getaway car. He heard Nolen scream:

"Jesus Christ!"

And waited for him to appear: barely moving in
his shroud raincoat, gunhand hanging limp, like
he'd been hit over the head and was now about to
fall.

"It was your buddy," Jiggs said. "Son of a gun
beat us to it."

"My settlement," Mary said, on the floor next to
the open suitcase. "Now do you love me?" She had
taken off her wet clothes, chilled, and held a cotton
bedspread around her like an Indian blanket; a
young girl at a pajama party eager to have fun. She
said, "What's the matter, can't you say anything?
You're looking at it, but you still can't believe it,
huh?"

"I believe it," Moran said without emotion.

He sat in his shirt and Jockeys on the edge of the
sofa, hunched over in lamplight to look at the
stacks of currency, packets of brand-new hundred-
dollar bills, rows of them filling the suitcase, remembering Scully telling him about the Igloo
coolers and a hundred thousand stacking up to less
than a foot high. He felt vulnerable and wished he
had run across to his house to change first. He'd

brought Mary here because of the three suitcases, because he thought she'd need more room for clothes than his house could offer.

He said, "All three are full of money?"

"No, two," Mary said. "I brought a few things, but I didn't want to load myself down."

"How much's in there?"

"I don't know exactly. It looks like a million one hundred thousand in each bag. But anything over two million Andres gets back. I only want what I have coming."

"You didn't count it?"

"George, this's the first time I've even seen it. I made the switch while Andres was downstairs in his den."

"The switch—you sound like a pro."

"No, it's my first job. I was gonna call a cab and then I found out you were on the way. My hero." She looked at him curiously, smile fading to a slight frown. "Does money make you nervous? What's the matter?"

He was looking at the scene on Arvida, flashing lights reflecting in the rain. "Andres and Corky came out with two suitcases, just like these."

"He has at least a dozen Louis Vuitton," Mary said. "I think he must have stock in the company. He kept two bags packed with his traveling money, always ready."

"Where'd he hide them?"

"You guessed it the other day and thought you were kidding. Under the bed."

"Come on—just sitting there? Not locked up?"

"Under two hundred and fifty gallons of water and inside a marble safe that looks like the pedestal of his bed. There's a tiny hole at the foot you can barely see. You slide in a magnetic key that's like a long needle and part of the marble slides open."

Moran said, "He trusted you?" and sounded surprised, thinking of her with Andres now rather than in the beginning.

"Why not?" Mary said, thinking of herself with Andres in that time before. "Something to impress the bride, a fortune under the marriage bed. Vanity, George. And if he hasn't trusted me lately, well, a cheater isn't necessarily a thief. He tends to sell women short."

"But what's in the bags Andres took? They weren't empty, were they?"

"No, I pulled out the suitcases with the money and then I thought, What if he gets suspicious when he sees me leave and runs upstairs to check? So I packed two other suitcases with old newspapers and shoved them under the bed. The worst part was carrying an armload of papers upstairs. I thought sure he'd see me and I couldn't think of a good story."

"You planned this? How come you didn't tell me?"

"I didn't plan it, I just did it."

Moran finally smiled; he couldn't help it. And for a few moments felt better about the whole thing.

"I was mad. My mouth hurt." Mary raised a hand to touch her face and the bedspread slipped from one shoulder. "Now, I can't believe I did it . . . Do you see a problem?"

Moran said, "Do I see a *problem*?" He reached over as if reminded and turned off the lamp. He could still see the neat stacks of currency. "Mary, I don't think *problem's* the word."

He was up now, moving to the window next to the door, parting the draperies to look out at the courtyard in a pale glow, a solemn stillness after the storm. It would be dark soon, dull light to dark without the color of sunset this evening.

She stared at his bare legs, shirttails hanging to cover the Jockey briefs. She thought about making a grab at him, get his attention.

"George, if Andres wants to fight about it, okay, we'll go to court. I'll bring the original prenuptial agreement—I hate that word—and the amendment he forced me to sign. It doesn't even look like my signature."

Moran didn't seem to be listening.

He said, "We've got to get out of here. I'm gonna run over and get some clothes on." He was still watching through the opening in the draperies. "We could hide the money . . . No, we'd better just go, quick." He glanced at her now. "Get dressed. And bring the wet things, don't leave 'em."

She said, "George, if Andres comes it's because he knows the money's here. We won't let him have it, that's all. I'll tell him to see me in court."

Moran turned from the window now. "And if Jiggs Scully comes, what do you tell him?" He picked up his jeans from a chair, wet and stiff, and pulled them on as Mary watched, eyes staring wide now, holding the bedspread around her. He said, "I'll be right back," and went out the door.

It gave her time to think, to relive the act, the awful anxiety of carrying an armload of newspapers up that open stairway, finding the key in the medicine cabinet of Andres's bathroom, down on the floor with her heart pounding pulling the suitcases out then retracing, replacing the key, taking the suitcases to her room, trying to compose herself, finally walking out past Andres . . . going through all that so she could give two million two hundred thousand dollars to Jiggs Scully? She thought, I've never even spoken to him.

It gave her a strange feeling because she could not think of a compelling reason to be afraid of

Jiggs Scully, except that Moran was and Moran knew him.

She dressed in sweater and slacks and waited, sitting on the arm of a chair to look out through the draperies at the empty courtyard in the beginning of nighttime darkness, watching his house, waiting for some sign of him. Gone longer now than she'd expected. The door opened and she jumped.

Then let her breath out in relief. "God, you scared me. Where'd you come from?" He moved to the window without answering, parted the draperies to look out and she said, "We're too late, aren't we?"

"They're out in front," Moran said.

For several minutes they watched the courtyard in silence, until a figure in a long coat appeared out of shadow, walking toward the beach. He seemed uncertain, almost as though he were lost.

"It's Nolen," Moran said, but didn't move from the window.

21

NOLEN REACHED THE SIDEWALK facing the beach-front, looked around disoriented, hearing the ocean but no other sounds, missing something. That amber glow at the door to each of the units. No lights showed, not in Moran's house, the office, anywhere; it gave him a spooky feeling, like the place was closed, out of business. He walked over to Moran's bungalow, opened the screen and banged on the door three times, so he could say he did. Then walked around to a side window to look in the house. There was nothing to see. An empty pitcher and two glasses on the counter, in faint light from the kitchen window. It seemed a week ago, drinking sours with Moran. He felt useless, in need of a lift. In need of a guide, he thought, stumbling through the lounge chairs now to make his way around the pool. A beer would hit the spot. Christ, even a Coke. But he walked past the machine in the alcove, went out toward streetlight reflections on empty cars and wet pavement.

Jiggs stood on the sidewalk by the Coconut Palms office.

"They're not there," Nolen said. "Nobody home."

"That's funny, isn't it," Jiggs said, "with his car sitting there."

Nolen wondered if Jiggs was going to bust the door in. But Jiggs turned to look in through the dark office, through the windows on the other side, to study the courtyard in moonlight and he seemed calm. Never any different, Nolen reminded himself. Never upset, never excited about anything.

"How many units in there?"

"I think twelve," Nolen said.

"How many're occupied?"

"None of 'em. There's nobody here."

"They could be in any one of those rooms."

"I think they're gone," Nolen said.

Jiggs turned from the office window. "He picked her up, he was getting her outta there, that's all. They were going on a trip they'd be up around Orlando by now, or the car'd be at Miami International. They're around here somewhere."

"Maybe they went to get something to eat."

"Stroll down the corner," Jiggs said. "That's what I'd do I thought somebody was coming after me."

Nolen said, "Yeah, but wait now, get in their head. They wouldn't know it's us coming anymore'n we know for *sure* his wife had the money when she left home. Maybe it's still in de Boya's house."

Jiggs was patient. He said, "De Boya thought he had it. If he didn't, who does that leave? You listening or you still smashed? Look, what I want you to do, Nolen, go in there in your room and keep your eyes open. Moran comes out, you been in a bar all day, you don't know anything what he's talking about. Stay awake till I get somebody to come over and take a look around. I'll try and get Speedy, but you got to stay awake till he comes."

"Who's Speedy?"

"For Christ sake you spent the night with him out cruising the bay. The guy Santos, with the Donzi. I want somebody check the place out isn't gonna fall over the furniture. I want to keep things as is for now so you can hit the sack and I can go up the corner, the Howard Johnson's and get my eight hours. Then in the morning, we need a couple more guys I'll get 'em. But you'll be awake, have your shower and shave by then, right?"

Nolen began to nod, concentrating, trying to get his mind working.

"No booze tomorrow, nothing," Jiggs said. He studied Nolen a moment. "You don't know what I'm talking about, do you?"

"I don't see where you need a lot of guys . . . or

you have to hurt anybody," Nolen said. "Just take it, get out."

"Jesus Christ," Jiggs said, "you think I want to bring some guys in, *now*, we know it where it is? I'm talking about a little surveillance, that's all. I want to know Moran and the broad're here and what room the suitcases're in. The sun comes out, looks like a pretty nice day—I want 'em to think, well, maybe we're okay, nothing to worry about, no reason to run or call the cops. It's not like hitting a bank, a liquor store; I don't do that. I want to come in here tomorrow have a quiet talk with 'em. Show 'em where we stand, say thank you and leave. I don't want a lot of confusion, somebody calls the cops, some old blue-haired broad up there in her condo. It's too hard to talk you know the cops're on the way. No, I want everybody to be re-laxed, their heads clear, their hands away from the buzzer."

"Just talk to 'em," Nolen said.

"I think that's the way to handle it," Jiggs said, "don't you?"

Watching at the window reminded him of times in Santo Domingo during his war: a motel yard or a narrow empty street at night were much the same, waiting for the unexpected, trying to sense or anticipate a sign of movement. Not wanting to see that muzzle flash. The vital difference was he didn't have an M-14 in his hands. It would be an M-16 today or he would settle for Nolen's .45 with its stopping power at close range and feel much better about the shadows along the edge of the beachfront wall and over back of his house and along the motel units fronting on the street. Nolen had appeared and left. A figure—it became Nolen without his raincoat—appeared again in moonlight reflecting on the office windows and disappeared into shadow. It was nearly two hours later he saw the door to Number Five open and a light go on, Nolen again, a glimpse of him before the door closed. Nolen had finally ceased his wandering and was home. After that was only the sound of the ocean.

Mary said, "You saw Jiggs; you're certain that's who it was."

"I saw Nolen's car pull in," Moran said. "I was going to the office to leave Jerry a note, tell him I'd be gone a few days. I saw Nolen get out of his car as Jiggs pulled up in that red and white Cadillac, you can't miss it. They had to have seen my car. Then after that Nolen wanders around, probably checked the bar up on the corner—where am I? I've got to be here somewhere. But that doesn't mean they think you're here too."

"I left the house with you. Jiggs saw us."

"I could've dropped you off, taken you to the airport."

"He knows better than that," Mary said. "And if he thinks we have the money, well, the only way would be if he's found out Andres doesn't have it."

Moran said, "He might think Andres faked him out and the money's still at home."

She said, "Do you believe that?"

"It's possible."

"You wouldn't bet on it though," Mary said. "You don't want to come out and say it because if Jiggs opened Andres's suitcases the chances are Andres is dead. Isn't that right?"

In the dark of the room he didn't have to answer immediately. He assumed Andres was dead and realized, now, Mary accepted the possibility.

She said, "If I find out he is, I doubt if I'll feel much grief, and I'm sure not gonna pretend to. But I'll tell you something, Moran," her voice gaining a quiet force, an unmistakable edge. "I don't know Jiggs Scully, I've never even spoken to him. But I'll be goddamned if I'm gonna give him my money. It absolutely infuriates me, that he thinks he can walk in and I'll simply hand it over. I've been sitting here wondering, is Andres dead? I have a feeling he is. Then do I call the police? What do I tell them? 'I think somebody killed my husband, at least it's possible, and now he's after my boyfriend, my lover

and me.' Do you like it so far? 'He's after us because we've got over two million dollars, *cash*, in a
couple of suitcases . . . ' And you know the first
thing they'll ask?"

"Where'd you get the money," Moran said.

"Exactly. Then try to explain, beginning with
Trujillo's assassination, why Andres kept two million dollars under the bed."

"First they check you out," Moran said, "see if
you've ever been arrested for narcotics."

"Yeah, find out if I was using the dock that blew
up to bring in cocaine and grass. 'No, I'm just a
housewife—I mean a homemaker, officer. I play
tennis and meet my lover at motels.' And after we
get through with all that, maybe, just maybe they'll
go after Jiggs and arrest him."

"For what?" Moran said. "He hasn't done anything we know of."

"That's right, we have to wait till he comes in
and takes it."

There was a silence. Moran said, "I'll talk to
Nolen. See what he knows."

"Now?"

"Tomorrow when he's hung over, in pain. Act
like I don't know anything and find out what's going on. I'll call your house, see if Andres came
back . . . You stay here, out of sight and maybe it'll
work. Jiggs'll sniff around and go away."

"I don't think I can do that," Mary said. "I know damn well if I see him I'll want to walk up to him and kick him right in the balls."

"You get mad, don't you?" Moran said. "You don't hold back."

"Why should I hide? I haven't done anything. How long do I stay in here? A couple of days? A week?"

Her tone was great; little jabs of anger that poked at Moran and stirred him, made him feel restless.

"You've got a point."

"Are you gonna bring me food every day? Wait till it's dark and sneak it in? While the police wait for Jiggs to do something, break a law? What is this, Moran? I've never hidden from anything in my life and it makes me pretty goddamn mad to realize that's what I'm doing."

"You're right," Moran said. Boy, she was good for him. "The hell're we doing sitting here?"

He moved away from the window, found the two suitcases in the dark and picked them up.

"Let's go over to my house and get a drink and something to eat. Christ, I'm starving."

"Now you're talking," Mary said.

22

IT SEEMED LIKE SEVEN YEARS AGO, in another life, coming out to bright sunlight to see Nolen in a lounge with a beer can resting on his chest, sandals and black socks V-ed as though he was sighting on that tanker bound for Port Everglades.

Moran said, "Well, here we are."

Nolen said, squinting through his sunglasses, "You want me to go first? All right. I waited in the bar out by Ninety-five all afternoon and Jiggs never called, so I came home. That's my story and I'm sticking to it. What's yours?"

"I was wondering," Moran said, "if you had any lemons."

Nolen waited for that to make sense to him and decided it didn't matter. "Yeah, I got some lemons."

"And I've got a blender," Moran said. "You didn't know that, did you? I'll get 'em when I pick up your trash. But I'm not gonna make your bed." He walked off toward the office saying, "I don't do beds."

Jerry was behind the counter looking through the mail delivery. Moran came around and pulled a black plastic trash bag from a Hefty box, Jerry saying, "Well, look at this." He handed Moran a letter. "Notice the postmark. Sosua, Rep. Dom. Is that anybody we know?"

Moran put the folded trash bag under his arm and opened the letter with a strange feeling, knowing it was from Luci Palma, the girl who used to run across rooftops . . . one page of ruled paper neatly handwritten, though each line rose on a slight angle, up and away and he thought, She hasn't changed. He read it standing there and put the letter in his shirt pocket when he finished. The letter made him feel good and at another time he would have read it to Jerry. But not now. He said to Jerry, "You call de Boya's again?"

"He still isn't back. Maid says they haven't seen him since yesterday. I called the Coral Gables Police, but they wouldn't tell me anything. Kept asking who I was, so I hung up."

"They get a lot of calls like that," Moran said. "How about that Trans-Am?"

"Still parked down the street."

"Jerry, you don't have to stay around . . ."

He said, "If I thought coming here was work, George, I wouldn't be doing it. I'm your police contact, aren't I?"

"You sure are. You got the number handy?"

"I know it by heart."

" 'Cause I might only say 'Jerry' but that's what it'll mean. Call 'em quick."

"They know my voice," Jerry said. As Moran went out he said, "Take her easy now. Don't do nothing dumb."

Moran said, "I keep trying not to."

Nolen took a sip of beer, turned his head enough to see Moran come out of the office unfolding a trash bag and go into Number Five with the passkey. Nolen yelled over, "In the fridge! Hey, and bring a beer!"

Moran came out within a couple minutes, the trash bag hanging weighted now with beer cans and whatnot, the sack of lemons and a cold one he handed Nolen. Nolen took it and popped it open to hold the two cans now on his chest, soothing the erratic action of his heart.

He said, "The last time I saw you, George, you stormed out of here, determination flashing in your eyes. I guess you didn't get shot, did you?"

Moran said, "No, but I bet somebody did. De Boya never came home. Hasn't been seen since he drove off in his Rolls."

Nolen took a drink of beer. "With police swarming all over the place."

"I thought you didn't talk to Jiggs."

"George, if I'm inconsistent, what's the difference? We're just gonna lie to each other anyway." He raised his head and took a long sip from the other can.

"You drink two at once? You been putting it away lately," Moran said, "haven't you?"

"Jesus, you sound like my wife."

"Is that right? I didn't know you were married."

"Three times. You sound like any one of 'em," Nolen said. "I got to win soon, man, get the fuck outta here. You make me nervous, feel like I'm being watched."

"Well, there could be truth to that," Moran said. "You know that Cuban you say wears sunglasses at night and drives a Donzi?"

Nolen squinted in the sunlight, adjusting his own glasses. "What about him?"

"Does he also drive a Trans-Am, black one with the hood flamed red and gold? He's parked in front of the Nautilus, next door, and if he isn't watching you then he's watching me." Moran half-turned to look toward the beach. "There's another one out there on an army blanket getting a Cuban suntan with all his clothes on. Your pal Jiggs doesn't care for 'em, but he sure uses 'em, doesn't he? Like the Mendozas, Rafi. He seems to use everybody he can."

"Don't," Nolen said. "You played that one to death."

Moran said, "Remember the day you came here?

We started talking about the D.R. and how some trooper across the Ozama almost killed me with a one-oh-six?"

"It was the next day," Nolen said. "We didn't talk much the first day. I registered and asked you where all your palm trees were. You wouldn't give me a deal on a room."

"But I did right after. You were trailing Anita de Boya and the piano player."

"I wonder if she's getting much these days."

"You were making a halfway honest living."

"Not bad. But living by your wits gets tiresome."

"Then you met Jiggs Scully. He still as funny as you thought he was?"

Nolen stared for several moments. He said, "George, the last thing I want is to see you get hurt. Will you do me a favor?"

"Let's talk about it in the house," Moran said, "while I whip up some sours. What do you say?" He started to go and looked at Nolen again, taking the letter from his pocket. "Guess who I heard from? Here, read it." Moran walked toward his house with the lemons and the trash bags.

Nolen puts his beers down and opened the letter.

Dear George Moran (Cat Chaser!!!):

Was that really you who was in Santo Domingo looking for me? At first I thought it was a lot of far fetch to think you would come here but then I think no it is something the Cat Chaser would do. (I got your address from the hotel) I am married now and have five big childrens going to school. I bet you dont know who I married. He is the one you shot and became wounded on the roof of the building that time. His name is Alejo Valera. He is a salesman of insurance and is also the manager of the Sosua baseball team. After that war he went to the training camp of the Cincinnati Reds but came home to play baseball here. He is very good. He say to tell you he is glad you did not kill him or we would not be married together and have our family. Well I must close this letter. I wish I had seen you but maybe some other time when you come. I tell people I know you and how brave you were in the war. You did not sit behind the barricades. You came to find us. I am very glad I did not shoot you. Do you still like the Rolling Stones? I like the Moody Blues now very much. Please come to see us.

Affectionately,
Luci Palma de Valera

Nolen straddled a stool at the counter, contemplating the foamy pitcher of whiskey sours, wiping froth from his mouth with the back of his hand. "Much better in the blender. All the difference in the world," he said and slid his glass toward Moran behind the counter for a refill.

"Tangy, isn't it?"

"Perfect," Nolen said, "for getting that morning goatshit taste outta your mouth. How many eggs you put in?"

"One to a blender," Moran said.

"Yeah, four makes it too heavy. I overdid it. Which is nothing new, I guess. I figure I've got about two years before I land in the weeds and have to join AA. You get to that point your choice is lead a clean life or die."

"Why wait," Moran said, "if you know it's coming?"

"I'm trying to get in all the fun I can."

"Yeah, I've noticed what a good time you been having."

"Well, shit, I try." Nolen thought of something as he took a drink and said, "Hey, that was a nice letter. Luci sounds like a winner. That part, she thought it was a lot of far fetch." Nolen grinning, nodding, being a regular guy. "That was a long time ago, wasn't it? Down there in the D.R. Not knowing shit what was going on. But I had a pretty good time, you know it? Even though I only got laid once and had to take penicillin for it. Come back with a dose and my trusty Forty-five. I used to fire it from up on that grain elevator. For fun, not hit anything."

Moran said, "How about if I buy it off you?"

"George"—Nolen took off his sunglasses to look squarely at Moran—"now we get down to it. I started to say to you outside, do me a favor. Use your head before it's too late. You have de Boya's money? Leave it over there in oceanfront Number One where you got your lady hiding and take off. Get far away from here."

Moran said, "How'd you know she's there?"

"The guy in the Trans-Am, Santos, was into B and E at one time. He snuck around here last night listening at doors. It's my guess if he heard anything it was in Number One and I'm right, that's where you got her, isn't it?" Nolen seemed proud of himself.

"Jiggs's coming for sure, uh?"

"You bet he is."

"How much you want for the gun?"

"It's not for sale. I'm telling you—you know all about how to take it and run; well, this time you gotta leave it and run."

Moran opened a drawer on his side of the counter. He brought out a packet of hundred-dollar bills secured with a money strap, a narrow paper band, and placed it in front of Nolen.

Nolen said, "Jesus Christ," and seemed afraid to touch it. "How much is that?"

"Ten thousand," Moran said.

Nolen's gaze came up, a solemn expression, mouth partly open. "You did it, didn't you? Jesus, you really did it."

"If that isn't enough . . ."

Moran reached into the drawer again, brought out another packet of inch-thick hundreds and laid it on top of the first one.

"How's that?"

"You're crazy."

Moran reached to take back the money.

"I'll go get the piece," Nolen said.

"I already have," Moran said. "When I picked up the trash. It's loaded, isn't it? Full clip?"

"Yeah but . . . George, don't try and be a hero, okay? You wouldn't have a chance. That man's a pro, it's what he *does*."

"It gives me a little more confidence," Moran said, "that's all. I don't feel so helpless."

Nolen was looking at the money again, almost in a daze. He said, "You really did it, huh?" A wistful tone, subdued. "Will you tell me something?"

"Maybe," Moran said.

"How much you get? Both suitcases."

"No, I'm not gonna tell you that," Moran said. "It isn't any of your business. It isn't any of mine either, when you get right down to it."

"Your lady walked out of the house with it, didn't she?" Nolen said, watery eyes showing the pleasure of it. "Where can I get me one like her?

Walked right out past her husband, Jiggs, everybody. Of course with you there to help."

"I didn't do much," Moran said. "But I'm looking after her best interest now. You understand I'm not gonna see anything happen to her." He watched Nolen touch the packets, finally pick them up and feel them, fingers gracefully playing along the edges, riffling the stiff new bills. "Nolen?"

"What?"

"When's Jiggs coming?"

"He said around noon. He said he'd set things up then get his eight hours and have a late breakfast. Then he'll stop by. That's how he said it, like it's a business call."

"What're you supposed to do?"

"Act dumb. Tell you I don't know anything, where Jiggs is or what he's doing," Nolen said. "But if you look like you're getting ready to leave I'm supposed to tell you he phoned and wants to see you for a minute, have a quiet talk."

"What do you do when he comes?"

"Exit. He's on then."

"Nolen?"

"What?"

"Where's de Boya?"

Nolen took a sip of whiskey sour and said without looking at Moran, "He's dead. So's Corky." Nolen's gaze came up slowly now. "Jiggs made them take their clothes off and get in the shower, both at once. Then he shot them."

"Because they didn't have the money?"

"He didn't even know it till after. He was so sure."

"Were you there?"

"When he did it? No, I came later."

"Where're they now?"

"Still in the shower. Place west of Lauderdale, out in the country."

"You don't suppose he's looking to make a deal," Moran said, "when he says he wants to talk."

"No, that's not Jiggs," Nolen said. "But he does have to talk to you, find out for sure you have the money and where it is. After that he'll kill you. That's why I'm saying leave it, forget the whole thing. You run with the money—it wouldn't work, I'm telling you." Nolen was emphatic now. "A woman like Mary de Boya, where's she gonna hide? The cops, once they find her husband, they'll be looking for her anyway. You see what I mean? It doesn't matter where she goes Jiggs'll be hanging around, threaten her till she pays up. So get it over with now, leave it." Nolen looked at his watch. "We've got less'n an hour."

Moran said, "You on our side now?"

Nolen said, "George, come on. You know where

I am. Nowhere. The idea, score off a guy like de Boya, it sounded great, worth the risk. But I saw him in that shower, man . . . I got sick and you know what Jiggs did? He patted my back while I threw up on two guns down in the toilet, telling me he'd take care of me. I wanted, today, I wanted to *look* like I was helping him but tell you to get out and then disappear, go to L.A. and get lost among the weirdos and hope to Christ I never make a name for myself. You said it the other day, George, I'm in a no-win deal."

Moran said, "What if we call the cops?"

"And what?" Nolen said. "He sees cops he waits. The only way, you'd have to have 'em hiding in the closet when he takes his gun out and then pray they're quick."

Moran thought about it, picturing Jiggs standing in the living room. "He sure likes to talk, doesn't he? Goes on and on."

"He puts you half-asleep," Nolen said, "telling you stories. Like a fucking spell he puts over you."

"No, he never rushes into it," Moran said, "he gives you time to think."

"This's the first time in my life," Nolen said, "I'm gonna suggest we leave what's in the blender and get the hell out."

Moran said, "Stay there," walked around the counter and said, "Mary?"

She came out of the bedroom, her expression

composed, eyes moving to Nolen to see him getting off the stool, surprised. She said, "Can you tell me exactly where Andres is?"

Nolen said, "I thought you were over in Number One. You've been right here all the time?"

"I wanted you to feel free to talk, be yourself," Moran said. "You said the place was west of Lauderdale."

"Yeah, like a farmhouse. Off Eighty-four."

Mary nodded, almost to herself. "I think I know where it is. Near the airport."

Moran said, "Let's wait a little while before we tell the police."

"But if you can't deal with him," Mary said, showing concern now as she looked at Nolen. "Isn't that right?"

Nolen shook his head. "I wouldn't even think about it."

"I just want to ask him something," Moran said. "Alone."

23

JIGGS STOPPED at the flamed Trans-Am and stuck his head in the passenger side. Hunched over like that his seersucker coat parted at the vent to show the seat of his pants hanging slack, as though he had no buttocks and all his weight was in front. When he straightened, pushing his glasses up, the Trans-Am came to life, rumbled and moved off. Jiggs came on to the Coconut Palms straightening his blue-striped tie, smoothing the front of his shirt. Entering the office he said to Jerry, "Hey, how you doing? My pal George around?" He looked at one of the inside windows and said, "Yeah, there he is. Nice seeing you again," and left Jerry adjusting his golf cap, staring after him as he went out to the swimming pool.

Jiggs saw Nolen in a lounge. He saw Mary in an expensive-looking T-shirt and white sailor pants also in a lounge, both of them up by the oceanfront walk in the sun, and a silent alarm went off in his mind. *Setup*.

He couldn't believe it; Moran didn't seem that dumb. Unless the cops were here and had coached him. *Make it look natural. Like nothing out of the ordinary is going on.* Fucking cops. Like they knew what they were doing. He saw Moran coming across from the front of his house, white T-shirt and old work jeans, barefoot. Maybe—it surprised Jiggs—Nolen was better at this than he gave him credit. Maybe these folks were in for a surprise and he'd tell in about half a second—now—all of them looking this way now and, yeah, they did seem to clutch up and were motionless as he approached them.

Jiggs said, "Beautiful day, huh? You get one of those hard rains it's always nice the next day. You notice that? Mrs. de Boya, how you doing? . . . George? Nolen there, he looks a little hung over. You okay, Nolen? Have a beer you'll feel better. I just had a pot of coffee. I wondered"—looking around—"George, you got a toilet I can use?"

"In the house," Moran said.

Yeah, something was up: Mary trying to act natural as she looked at Moran, Christ, gripping the arms of the chair. You'd have to pry her hands off. Moran walked over to the house with him and held the door open. Very polite this morning.

"It's through the bedroom."

"Thank you, George, I appreciate it. Be only a minute."

Moran walked around to the kitchen side of the counter. He moved the blender and the sack of lemons aside. Squared the telephone around on the end of the counter. He got a bottle of scotch from the cupboard. Brought a bowl of ice out of the refrigerator. Found two clean glasses. He poured about an ounce and a half of scotch into one and drank it down. He heard the toilet flush. He put ice in the glasses and was pouring scotch when Jiggs came out pushing his glasses up, buttoning his seersucker jacket and then unbuttoning it to leave it open.

"There he is," Jiggs said. "I had to take a leak, George, but I also hoped we'd get a chance to talk, just the two of us if that was possible. You understand, not get emotional about anything, right? Why do that? What I thought, let's lay it out, look over what we have here."

Jiggs stepped back from the counter and glanced around the room.

"You don't have a tape going, any of that kinda stuff, do you, George? I wouldn't think so, but somebody might've talked you into it." He was looking at the hi-fi system now.

"I can put a record on," Moran said. "You like J. Geils?"

Coming back to the counter Jiggs said, "George, I don't know J. Geils from jaywalking, which is about the only thing I never was arrested for. That's an exaggeration, of course, but the point I want to make—" He picked up the drink Moran set before him. "Thank you, I believe I will. Little pick-me-up. The point I want to make, I've been arrested, well, quite a few times, suspicion of this and that, I think on account of the people I been associating with the past few years. But I never in my life been convicted of anything. I'm cherry, George, as far as doing any time and I'm sure you can understand why. Because I'm careful. Because I don't go walking in someplace I don't know what's on the other side of the door. Entrapment don't ever work with me, George; because I don't partake of controlled substances, I don't fuck lady cops dressed up like hookers and I don't deal with people I don't know. So there you are. If you think you got me to walk into something here and you're gonna pull the rope and the fucking net drops on me, don't do it. Okay? Let's just talk quietly and make sure we understand each other."

"Fine," Moran said. "What do you want?"

"I want the two suitcases and everything was in 'em. You can tell me something first," Jiggs said, "cause the suspense is killing me. How much we talking about?"

"Two million two hundred thousand," Moran said.

"I'll tell you something. I enjoy talking to you, George, you got a nice easy style. I told you that once before. All right, how 'bout this? You keep the two hunner K, that's yours, for your trouble. You and the widow're gonna have more dough'n you'll ever be able to spend anyway. And you give me the rest. How's that sound?"

"What if we don't give it to you?"

"Then you got a problem. I put a lot of time in this, George. See, I don't have a pension plan, profit-sharing, anything like that. This's gonna be my retirement and if it doesn't come through I can't complain to some insurance company, can I? No, I got to take my beef to you and Mary and you know what I mean by that. See, I'd rather part friends, George. Maybe stop around and see you sometime in the future—how're things going? Shoot the shit about old times—by the way, something else I got to know. Where'd he keep it? The money."

"Under his bed," Moran said.

"Come on, you're kidding me. Guys like that"— Jiggs shook his head—"they're simpleminded, you know it? Under the fucking bed . . . Now where is it, under yours? I'd believe it. Jesus, I'd believe anything now. Whatta you say, George?"

"Mary says no," Moran said. "You don't get it."

"Yeah, but what do *you* say?"

"It's her money."

"I bet you can talk her into it, George. Lemme show you something." Jiggs got off the stool again and looked around the room. "What's that down there, top of the bookcase? Looks like a vase."

"It's a vase," Moran said.

"You buy that thing, George?"

"It was here when I moved in."

"Keep looking at it," Jiggs said. "Don't look at me, look at the vase. I'm gonna show you a magic trick I do." Jiggs moved back toward the front door so Moran would have to turn to face him, see what he was doing. "You looking at it?"

"I'm looking at it," Moran said, staring at the vase that was about twelve or fourteen inches high and glazed with the portrait of an old-fashioned girl holding a bouquet of flowers.

"You ready?" Jiggs said.

"I'm ready," Moran said.

The vase came apart, fragments of china flying outward with only the sound of it breaking, pieces hitting the floor.

Moran turned to Jiggs who was holding an automatic with a silencer attached that looked bigger than the gun.

"That's my magic act," Jiggs said. "Not a sound, not even that little BB-gun pop you usually get with a suppressor. Could be in a movie, out the track, you're walking up Collins Avenue, anywhere. You fall over. Person right next to you'd never hear a thing. What's this, a heart attack? . . . You understand what I'm saying? Could happen anytime, anywhere." Jiggs came back to the counter un-screwing the silencer. He dropped it into his coat pocket as he got up on the stool. "Or, you give me the suitcases, we part friends, wish each other luck."

Moran said, "Is that the one you used on de Boya?"

"George, you don't gimme any credit at all, do you? You think I'm gonna walk around with a piece they can do a ballistics on? I got I think four of these left now. Regular model Thirty-nine Smith only modified. Designed originally for the Seals in Vietnam. Guys'd slip ashore in the Mekong, take out some slopes and their buddies never hear a thing. You fire a subsonic nine-millimeter round. Notice the sights're raised so you can aim over the suppressor. Got a nice foam-rubber grip." He held the pistol up for Moran to look at closely.

"Pretty nice."

Jiggs slipped it into his right-hand coat pocket and picked up his drink to take a sip. "Have I made my point?"

"I believe you," Moran said.

"See, I was to demonstrate this in front of Mrs. de Boya," Jiggs said, "she'd be liable to come apart on me."

"I doubt it," Moran said.

"Well, playing it safe, I know I can talk to you, George. You got a nice even temper'ment." He laid his arms on the edge of the counter and took another sip of his drink. "Tastes pretty good. I don't usually drink during the day except special occasions. Last time I had a drink in fact we were at the Mutiny. Here we got another special occasion. So what do you say?"

"I just want to ask you something," Moran said and then paused. "Well, you've probably answered it."

"Go ahead, George, don't be bashful."

"Well, you wouldn't want to just walk away, forget the whole thing?"

"Oh my," Jiggs said, "I thought you were listening. What were you doing there, George, having dirty thoughts while I'm telling you my story?"

"I want to be sure I have it straight," Moran said. "You're saying if we don't give you the money you're gonna kill both of us. It's that simple, right? It might not be right now—"

"Probably wouldn't be," Jiggs said.

"But it could be anytime."

"I'm patient up to a point."

"Okay, that's all I wanted to know," Moran said. He reached over and picked up the phone.

Jiggs watched him.

Moran said, "Jerry, call the cops." He hung up.

Jiggs said, "George, am I hearing things? What're you gonna tell 'em. Some bullshit about I threatened you? I say I didn't, it's my word against

yours, George, you know that." Jiggs seemed tired
and a little upset. "There's nothing you can give the
cops they can put on me."

Moran took his time. He said, "I didn't call them
for you."

There was a pause. He saw Jiggs on the edge,
motionless, between knowing and not believing.

Moran brought Nolen's .45 out of the drawer
close in front of him and had time to rest the butt
on the counter, the barrel pointed at Jiggs's striped
tie. He saw Jiggs's right hand come up, clearing the
edge of the counter with Smith and couldn't wait
any longer than that. He pressed and pulled the
trigger and saw Jiggs blown from the stool, saw his
expression in that moment, mouth opening, and
the next moment saw him lying on the vinyl floor,
head pressed against the base of the sofa. He saw
the seersucker turning red, saw the hand holding
the gun move and shot him again, the first explosions still ringing in his ears. Within moments he
heard the door bang open, Nolen and Mary in the
room and saw their eyes, a glimpse of the look in
their eyes; but his attention was on Jiggs as he came
around from behind the counter with the .45 lev-
eled, pointed at a down angle, a thought coming
into his mind that he might or might not tell Mary
about someday: thinking as he saw the blood he
was glad he had not had the tile floor carpeted.

He went to one knee, picked up Jiggs's glasses

from the floor and carefully placed them on him, pushing the bridge up on his nose, looking at Jiggs's eyes staring at him, not yet sightless but lost beyond bewilderment. His mouth moving soundless.

What was there to say? Moran stood up.

He heard a voice say "Jesus" that sounded like Nolen and heard Mary close to him say "Moran?" Not sure now when she used his first name and when she used it last, if it depended on her mood or if it mattered. He felt . . . well, he felt all right. He felt much better than he did after shooting Luci's future husband on the roof in Santo Domingo in 1965. Was that why he went back—the real reason— because he had shot someone he didn't know? He wondered. The more he became aware of what he was feeling the more certain he was that he felt pretty good. Close to Mary, looking at those eyes full of warm awareness . . .

He said, "I don't have a lawyer. You think I'm gonna need one?"

Mary was smiling now, trying to. She said, "I don't know, George, you do pretty well on your own."

Finally there was that high-low wail in the distance, listening for it like he was always waiting to hear sirens. Boy, what next?

Coming Up . . .

A sneak preview of

TISHOMINGO BLUES

by ELMORE LEONARD

"America's greatest living crime writer."
The New York Times

Available now at a bookseller near you

DENNIS LENAHAN THE HIGH DIVER would tell people that if you put a fifty-cent piece on the floor and looked down at it, that's what the tank looked like from the top of that eighty-foot steel ladder. The tank itself was twenty-two feet across and the water in it never more than nine feet deep. Dennis said from that high up you want to come out of your dive to enter the water feet first, your hands at the last moment protecting your privates and your butt squeezed tight, or it was like getting a 40,000-gallon enema.

When he told this to girls who hung out at amusement parks they'd put a cute look of pain on their faces and say what he did was awesome. But wasn't it like really dangerous? Dennis would tell them you could break your back if you didn't kill yourself, but the rush you got was worth it. These summertime girls loved daredevils, even ones twice their age. It kept Dennis going off that perch eighty feet in the air and going out for beers after to tell stories. Once in a while he'd fall in love for the summer, or part of it.

The past few years Dennis had been putting on one-man shows during the week. Then for Saturday and Sunday he'd bring in a couple of young divers when he could to join him in a repertoire of comedy dives they called "dillies," the three of them acting nutty as they went off from different levels and hit the water at the same time. It meant dirt-cheap motel rooms during the summer and sleeping in the setup truck between gigs, a way of life Dennis the high diver had to accept if he wanted to perform. What he couldn't take anymore, finally, were the amusement parks, the tiresome pizzazz, the smells, the colored lights, rides going round and round to that calliope sound forever.

What he did as a plan of escape was call resort hotels in South Florida and tell whoever would listen he was Dennis Lenahan, a professional exhibition diver who had performed in major diving shows all over the world, including the cliffs of Acapulco. What he proposed was that he'd dive into their swimming pool from the top of the hotel or off his eighty-foot ladder twice a day as a special attraction.

They'd say, "Leave your number" and never call back.

They'd say, "Yeah, right" and hang up.

One of them told him, "The pool's only five feet

deep," and Dennis said, no problem, he knew a guy in New Orleans went off from twenty-nine feet into twelve inches of water. A pool five feet deep? Dennis was sure they could work something out.

No, they couldn't.

He happened to see a brochure that advertised Tunica, Mississippi, as "The Casino Capital of the South" with photos of the hotels located along the Mississippi River. One of them caught his eye, the Tishomingo Lodge & Casino. Dennis recognized the manager's name, Billy Darwin, and made the call.

"Mr. Darwin, this is Dennis Lenahan, world champion high diver. We met one time in Atlantic City."

Billy Darwin said, "We did?"

"I remember I thought at first you were Robert Redford, only you're a lot younger. You were running the sports book at Spade's." Dennis waited. When there was no response he said, "How high is your hotel?"

This Billy Darwin was quick. He said, "You want to dive off the roof?"

"Into your swimming pool," Dennis said, "twice a day as a special attraction."

"We go up seven floors."

"That sounds just right."

"But the pool's about a hundred feet away. You'd have to take a good running start, wouldn't you?"

Right there, Dennis knew he could work something out with this Billy Darwin. "I could set my tank right next to the hotel, dive from the roof into nine feet of water. Do a matinee performance and one at night with spotlights on me, seven days a week."

"How much you want?"

Dennis spoke right up, talking to a man who dealt with high rollers. "Five hundred a day."

"How long a run?"

"The rest of the season. Say eight weeks."

"You're worth twenty-eight grand?"

That quick, off the top of his head.

"I have setup expenses—hire a rigger and put in a system to filter the water in the tank. It stands more than a few days it gets scummy."

"You don't perform all year?"

"If I can work six months I'm doing good."

"Then what?"

"I've been a ski instructor, a bartender . . ."

Billy Darwin's quiet voice asked him, "Where are you?"

In a room at the Fiesta Motel, Panama City, Florida, Dennis told him, performing every evening at the Miracle Strip amusement park. "My contract'll keep me here till the end of the month," Dennis said, "but that's it. I've reached the point . . . Actually I don't think I can do another amusement park all summer."

There was a silence on the line, Billy Darwin maybe wondering why but not curious enough to ask.

"Mr. Darwin?"

He said, "Can you get away before you finish up there?"

"If I can get back the same night, before show-time."

Something the man would like to hear.

He said, "Fly into Memphis. Take Sixty-one due south and in thirty minutes you're in Tunica, Mississippi."

Dennis said, "Is it a nice town?"

But got no answer. The man had hung up.

This trip Dennis never did see Tunica or even the Mighty Mississippi. He came south through farm-land until he began to spot hotels in the distance rising out of fields of soybeans. He came to signs at crossroads pointing off to Harrah's, Bally's, Sam's Town, the Isle of Capri. A serious-looking Indian on a billboard aimed his bow and arrow down a road that took Dennis to the Tishomingo Lodge & Casino. It featured a tepee-like structure rising a good three stories above the entrance, a precast, concrete tepee with neon tubes running up and around it. Or was it a wigwam?

The place wasn't open yet. They were still land-

scaping the grounds, putting in shrubs, laying sod
on both sides of a stream that ran to a mound of
boulders and became a waterfall. Dennis parked
his rental among trucks loaded with plants and
young trees, got out, and spotted Billy Darwin
right away talking to a contractor. Dennis recognized the Robert Redford hair that made him appear younger than his forty or so years, about the
same age as Dennis, the same slight build, tan and
trim, a couple of cool guys in their sunglasses.
One difference, Dennis's hair was dark and
longer, almost to his shoulders. Darwin was turning, starting his way as Dennis said, "Mr. Darwin?"

He paused, but only a moment. "You're the
diver."

"Yes sir, Dennis Lenahan."

Darwin said, "You've been at it a while, uh?"
with sort of a smile, Dennis wasn't sure.

"I turned pro in '79," Dennis said. "The next
year I won the world cliff-diving championship in
Switzerland, a place called Ticino. You go off from
eighty-five feet into the river."

The man didn't seem impressed or in any hurry.

"You ever get hurt?"

"You can crash, enter the water just a speck out
of line, it can hurt like hell. The audience thinks it
was a rip, perfect."

"You carry insurance?"

"I sign a release. I break my neck it won't cost you anything. I've only been injured, I mean where I needed attention, was my first time at Acapulco. I broke my nose."

Dennis felt Billy Darwin studying him, showing just a faint smile as he said, "You like to live on the edge, uh?"

"Some of the teams I've performed with I was always the edge guy," Dennis said, feeling he could talk to this man. "I've got eighty dives from different heights and most of 'em I can do hung-over, like a flying reverse somersault, your stan-dard high dive. But I don't know what I'm gonna do till I'm up there. It depends on the crowd, how the show's going. But I'll tell you something, you stand on the perch looking down eighty feet to the water, you know you're alive."

Darwin was nodding. "The girls watching you . . ."

"That's part of it. The crowd holding its breath."

"Come out of the water with your hair slicked back . . ."

Where was he going with this?

"I can see why you do it. But for how long? What will you do after to show off?"

Billy Darwin the man here, confident, saying anything he wanted.

Dennis said, "You think I worry about it?"

"You're not desperate," Darwin said, "but I'll bet you're looking around." He turned saying, "Come on."

Dennis followed him into the hotel, through the lobby where they were laying carpet, and into the casino, gaming tables on one side of the main aisle, a couple of thousand slot machines on the other, like every casino Dennis had ever been in. He said to Darwin's back, "I went to dealer's school in Atlantic City. Got a job at Spade's the same time you were there." It didn't draw a comment. "I didn't like how I had to dress," Dennis said, "so I quit."

Darwin paused, turning enough to look at Dennis.

"But you like to gamble."

"Now and then."

"There's a fella works here as a host," Darwin said. "Charlie Hoke. Chickasaw Charlie, he claims to be part Indian. Spent eighteen years in organized baseball, pitched for Detroit in the '84 World Series. I told Charlie about your call and he said, 'Sign him up.' He said a man that likes high risk is gonna leave his paycheck on one of these tables."

Dennis said, "Chickasaw Charlie, huh? Never heard of him."

They came out back of the hotel to the patio bar and swimming pool landscaped to look like a pond sitting there among big leafy plants and boulders. Dennis looked up at the hotel, balconies on every floor to the top, saying as his gaze came to the sky, "You're right, I'd have to get shot out of a cannon." He looked at the pool again. "It's not deep enough anyway. What I can do, place the tank fairly close to the building and dive straight down."

Now Darwin looked up at the hotel. "You'd want to miss the balconies."

"I'd go off there at the corner."

"What's the tank look like?"

"The Fourth of July, it's white with red and blue stars. What I could do," Dennis said, deadpan, "paint the tank to look like birchbark and hang animal skins around the rim."

Darwin gave him a look and swung his gaze out across the sweep of lawn that reached to the Mississippi, the river out of sight beyond a low rise. He didn't say anything staring out there, so Dennis prompted him.

"That's the spot for an eighty-foot ladder. Plenty of room for the guy wires. You rig four to every ten-foot section of ladder. It still sways a little when you're up there." He waited for Darwin.

"Thirty-two wires?"

"Nobody's looking at the wires. They're a twelve-gauge soft wire. You barely notice them."

"You bring everything yourself, the tank, the ladder?"

"Everything. I got a Chevy truck with a big van

body and a hundred and twenty thousand miles
on it."

"How long's it take you to set up?"

"Three days or so, if I can find a rigger."

Dennis told him how you put the tank together
first, steel rods connecting the sections, Dennis
said, the way you hang a door. Once the tank's put
together you wrap a cable around it, tight. Next
you spread ten or so bales of hay on the ground inside for a soft floor, then tape your plastic liner to
the walls and add water. The water holds the liner
in place. Dennis said he'd pump it out of the river.
"May as well, it's right there."

Darwin asked him where he was from.

"New Orleans, originally. Some family and my
ex-wife's still there. Virginia. We got married too
young and I was away most of the time." It was
how he always told it. "We're still friends
though . . . sorta."

Dennis waited. No more questions, so he continued explaining how you set up. How you put
up your ladder, fit the ten-foot sections on to one
another and tie each one off with the guy wires as
you go up. You use what's called a gin pole you
hook on, it's rigged with a pulley and that's how
you haul up the sections one after another. Fit
them on to each other and tie off with the guy
wires before you do the next one.

"What do you call what you dive off from?"

"You mean the perch."

"It's at the top of the highest ladder?"

"It hooks on the fifth rung of the ladder, so you have something to hang on to."

"Then you're actually going off from seventy-five feet," Darwin said, "not eighty."

"But when you're standing on the perch," Dennis said, "your head's above eighty feet, and that's where you are, believe me, in your head. You're no longer thinking about the girl in the thong bikini you were talking to, you're thinking of nothing but the dive. You want to see it in your head before you go off, so you don't have to think and make adjustments when you're dropping thirty-two feet a second."

A breeze came up and Darwin turned to face it, running his hand through his thick hair. Dennis let his blow.

"Do you hit the bottom?"

"Your entry," Dennis said, "is the critical point of the dive. You want your body in the correct attitude, what we call a scoop position, like you're sitting down with your legs extended and it levels you off. Do it clean, that's a rip entry." Dennis was going to add color but saw Darwin about to speak.

"I'll give you two hundred a day for two weeks guaranteed and we'll see how it goes. I'll pay your rigger and the cost of setting up. How's that sound?"

Dennis dug into the pocket of his jeans for the Kennedy half-dollar he kept there and dropped it on the polished brick surface of the patio. Darwin looked down at it and Dennis said, "That's what the tank looks like from the top of an eighty-foot ladder." He told the rest of it, up to what you did to avoid the 40,000-gallon enema, and said, "How about three hundred a day for the two weeks' trial?"

Billy Darwin, finally raising his gaze from the half-dollar shining in the sun, gave Dennis a nod and said, "Why not."

Nearly two months went by before Dennis got back and had his show set up.

He had to finish the gig in Florida. He had to take the ladder and tank apart, load all the equipment just right to fit in the truck. He had to stop off in Birmingham, Alabama, to pick up another 1,800 feet of soft wire. And when the goddamn truck broke down as he was getting on the Interstate, Dennis had to wait there over a week while they sent for parts and finally did the job. He said to Billy Darwin the last time he called him from the road, "You know it's major work when they have to pull the head off the engine."

Darwin didn't ask what was wrong with it. All

he said was "So the life of a daredevil isn't all cute girls and getting laid."

Sounding like a nice guy while putting you in your place, looking down at what you did for a living.

Dennis had never said anything about getting laid. What he should do was ask Billy Darwin if he'd like to climb the ladder. See if he had the nerve to look down from up there.